Kalorama Road

Kalorama Road

E. Denise Billups

Books by E. Denise Billups

For those I cherish

Contents

* * *

I'm not afraid to die. I've always believed I would die young. But not this soon, not here, not tonight, and not by those hands. Surrounded by tattered, aromatic petals, a dark silhouette watches my naked, bleeding flesh. I tilt my head, an eternally engraved image, a tormenting ghost—an inescapable, haunting memory. Sweet, soft, rose petals, a lifelong obsession. How Ironic. Maybe what we cherish is near at death, some sign of mortality, some hint of what we become. A cold breeze scented with roses, an invisible trail across dark soil, awaiting discovery. Finally, he's here...

Part One
Forgotten

Prologue

IT'S COMING. I know it is. Restless and awaiting the hour, I watch seconds tick ... Fifty-sevepn ... Fifty-eight ... Fifty-nine ... Midnight. Like clockwork, my cell phone chimes, announcing an email that arrives every month for the last two years. A reminder from an anonymous sender, posing an unanswerable question that won't let me forget one memory-less night. It's torture. A night I wish never happened haunts dreamlike, vaporous, appearing and receding with crushing anxiety, preventing me from seeing clearly. I should have listened to my instincts and never gone to that off-campus party. But as Grandma Blu always said, *"What's done is done."*

Often, I've pondered what-if scenarios and wished I could rewind time. Especially when I revisit the hesitant moment in my dormitory vestibule, debating whether to stay or go to the off-campus party. I took the latter choice and bolted from the dorm into the chilly autumn night toward the waiting Jaguar's tinted windows. Grandma Blu's warning, "Never get into stranger's cars," roared loud. But the person behind the wheel wasn't a total stranger, although we'd never spoken before she invited me to the party. For an entire semester, we sat two rows apart and barely acknowledged each other's existence until she appeared one day after class.

Lively and wielding a smile, she'd approached with curious eyes, sized me up like a tailor, and invited me to a party. Her odd approach left me more than hesitant. *Why after three months the sudden interest?*

She'd introduced herself as Belle, a sweet and innocent name unsuitable for someone so brazen. But she was beguiling, upbeat, and fun. I couldn't resist and accepted her invitation. In retrospect, I should have said no. *But you didn't, Allie.*

The closer I'd grown to the car, the louder Grandma Blu's warning screamed in my mind. *"Never get into a stranger's car unless you're one-hundred percent sure."* I lacked one percent assurance of the blond from Literature 301. Cautiously, *I'd approached* the Jaguar, and searched tinted windows for the obscured driver. The car door flew open, and Belle leaned toward the passenger side. Her lips curled a smile as she'd said, *"Girl, it's freezing. Get in."* I did in awe of her stunning transformation. She was no longer the fresh-faced nineteen-year-old student in jeans and T-shirt but dressed in a black dress with heavy charcoal eyeshadow that framed thick, false eyelashes. Her hair, blown silken blond, had transformed Belle into a sexy siren.

As we drove past Emsworth University, Bell grew silent. The farther we traveled from campus, the more anxious I'd become. Most off-campus parties were within walking distance, but this I hadn't expected. Past Kalorama Square, I'd wanted her to turn the car around. My instincts in overdrive reared me conscious of landmarks in case I found myself without a ride back to the dorm. As a girl, I'd often imagined what I'd do if kidnapped by dangerous stranger's grandma had alluded to. I devised a plan to memorize surroundings, street signs, and landmarks, but I never conceived a foolproof escape. When I think about it now, the imagined getaway was incredibly comical. But the farther we traveled from campus, the sharper my alarm. I'd revisited childish musings and studied the route past Kalorama Square.

The car slowed at an impressive home, swiveled into the driveway and through retracting garage doors. At the time, I believed it was Belle's family's home given access inside. When the car halted, and the garage door closed, I began to worry. We entered a space more grandiose than its exterior and much too extravagant for a student party. I'd expected a home swarming with college students, not silent halls, and thought we were the first to arrive until voices emanated from remote spaces.

Belle led me into a billiard room through sparse guest, delivering me to a wide-eyed teenage girl seated at an open bar. *"Allison,"* Belle had said in a sweet, apologetic voice, *"I have to take care of an urgent matter."* She motioned to the puckered-browed girl, *"She'll take care of you until I get back."* She leaned into her ear and whispered quickly. The girl shook her head; I'd assumed a yes to whatever was said. Belle smiled. *"I'll be back in a jiffy."* She vanished, leaving me in a room of mismated young women and older men, which looked like a secret society. And from their stares, I'd sensed I was the evening's main course.

Belle never returned, and the young woman abandoned me at the bar. A fiftyish looking man slid into the empty stool beside me and introduced himself as Pennington. His eyes consumed every inch of me, and I grew anxious. Pennington placed a drink in my hand. A delicate flute with a cobalt rim contained a mixture much too sweet—sugared I'd assumed to conceal alcoholic potency. When I finished, he refreshed my glass with more intoxicating liquid.

Soon, strangely disoriented, figures blurred, my body, a distant island, appeared detached from my head. An urgent need to flee swept over me. Then Pennington refreshed my drink again. His fingers stroked my arm as if sampling a delicate fabric. I smiled and glanced away, sensing his eyes on my body. He'd whispered, *"Don't be afraid, everyone's here to have fun. Just relax."* Then I felt his hand on my thigh. Incensed, I pushed him away and staggered from the room in search of Belle.

Stumbling through the home, I wandered upstairs on invisible legs, floating with a giddy high, arriving at the landing. When I approached a small, moonlit alcove, a concerned man had asked, *"Sweetheart, are you okay?"* His words sounded miles away. My lips parted, but words wouldn't come. On wobbly legs, I continued down the hall in search of Belle and followed echoing voices to the first door. With fading hands, I twisted the knob, and the door squeaked open. Several images blurred into view, shadows I couldn't distinguish. Like a camera lens, my mind snapped shut and opened the next morning. The previous night was a blank canvas. Several months later, fuzzy images would appear and recede quickly.

I've never determined the number of people in that room. However, I've pondered inebriated double vision. Though never certain, I suspect something evil happened in that house, and the resultant amnesia acts as a shield, protecting me from wicked horrors. With a deep sigh, I drag my mobile from the nightstand, and as I'd expected, my anonymous sender's address appears with a single, bold, small-capped question.

Do you remember what happened at 1414 Kalorama Road?

1

We Meet Again

THE LAST TIME I saw Allison was two years ago. She sat alone on Emsworth University's campus quad steps talking on her mobile, oblivious to autumn's first snow dusting the campus white as she gazed at her Ugg clad feet. A black ski parka hugged snug around her slender figure. A beige wool ski cap framed worried brown eyes. Her bee-stung lips puckered and curved with hushed words. Despite obvious distress, I thought she looked more beautiful than I'd ever seen.

Hesitantly, I'd approached and sat across from her with concern. She glanced up for a minute, and in that instant, I'd wanted her to recognize me, but when she didn't, I figured it best she hadn't. Intently listening, her low voice rose and fell an octave with alarm as she spoke about the off-campus party three days prior. Worried something horrible happened; her pitch intensified a fearful trill. Allison's anguish had wrenched my heart and conscience, prompting a consoling need to reveal Kalorama Road's treachery, but I couldn't. Self-conscious, her eyes flitted about the quad and met and held my gaze an eternal second. And as I'd suspected, she'd forgotten everything, including me.

Now, here I am, two years later, about to see Allison again and worry her memory has returned. Ahead, a slanted building and large, red number nine graces the sidewalk like artwork, proclaiming my arrival at 9 West 57th Street. Distracted by memories of Allison, I enter her office building's revolving door, unaware I've circled past the exit twice. On the third rotation, I jump through the egress into a glassy lobby, and just in time, rescue my coattail from swift-moving flaps. More alert, I approach the security desk.

"I have an appointment with Allison Bertrand at McClelland."

"May I see your identification?" The security guard asked.

"I'm thirty minutes early," I said, pulling my driver's license from my wallet.

He shakes his head. "It's okay as long as someone's there," he said, checking the computer and calling upstairs to confirm my appointment. "Mr. McThursten is here to see Ms. Bertrand … Okay," he said, hanging up with a smile. Returning my driver's license with a guest pass, he points toward the left. "Thirtieth floor, elevator bank two."

"Thanks," I said, following his directions, arriving at a talking elevator.

Unknowingly, my father has thrust Allison back in my life. If he hadn't sent my manuscript to McClelland Publishing, I wouldn't be here. I had no intention of publishing the book. When I heard Allison's voice on the phone, I didn't know who she was until she revealed her name on the second call. I couldn't believe the fawned-eyed student from Emsworth University who'd entered my life one harrowing night had my manuscript. What are the odds of that? I couldn't resist seeing her, so here I am, ten floors from her office, wondering if her memory has returned. If so, will she remember me? The elevator opens in front of two large glass doors, and in that instant, I consider not entering, but the elevator doors close, squeezing and forcing me out. A gray-haired receptionist looks up and buzzes me in.

"Mr. McThursten, you're early. Allison will be here soon. You can hang your coat over there," she said, pointing to a closet by the door.

I proceed to hang my trench, and when I turn around, the gray-haired receptionist is standing behind me.

"Allison just called. She's minutes away. Meanwhile, you can wait in the conference room until she arrives," she said, leading me toward a room near the windows. "Can I get you coffee or tea?"

"No thank you. I'm fine."

"She won't be too long. Help yourself to magazines," she said, pointing at the side table and closing the door with a smile.

Too tense to sit, I approach the window and stare at Central Park's rectangular green, running through a city of cement skyscrapers thirty stories below. But Allison's fawn eyes and the stolen kiss takes precedence over city views. A kiss I can't forget. Will she remember? If she does, I'll have no choice but to tell her the truth. I glance at McClelland's clock. In twenty minutes, I'll find out.

2

Have We Met?

GOD, I CAN'T BELIEVE I OVERSLEPT.

Bypassing Fifth Avenue's congestion, the taxi winds across Central Park toward 57th street, through cherry blossom-covered trees, gripping me with spring fever, but the anonymous email still sits foremost in my mind. I dismiss the mysterious message with thoughts of Ryan McThursten, the reluctant author I'd hounded for months until finally, he'd agreed to meet and discuss a contract with McClelland Publishing. With my luck, Ryan will change his mind and decline McClelland's offer again.

Nonetheless, I seldom have high expectations of others. Since my parent's divorce and the troubling, off-campus party, I always expect the worse, believing any moment, an unforeseen, life-altering event will upend my world. For me, at least, happiness is a fleeting fantasy, a pendulum that swings cold, warm, and occasionally hot. I prefer a tepid medium between content and discontent, knowing at any moment life can swerve without warning. But for now, I welcome spring's temporary bliss, knowing over twenty-four hours emotions will sour.

I dial the office and tell the receptionist I'm in a taxi five blocks away. I'm surprised but thrilled when she says Mr. McThursten has arrived. Of all days to oversleep. The cab exits the park, speeds past the first traffic light, and I pray it's nonstop the entire way. The taxi races through the second yellow light with a sharp left turn, arriving at the building's side entrance. I exit the cab and hurry upstairs breathlessly.

Joy evaporates the moment I enter McClelland. The receptionist's worried expression and the office's ominous hush feels like a bombshell ready to explode. Although for weeks, employees have been aware of McClelland Publishing's merger with SNC Media; I sense another disaster waiting to happen. Softly, I walk toward the temp who's replaced our regular receptionist. A retiree, I'd learned, who returned to work when she lost her savings in the previous recession. It's bothersome seeing her support everyone. She should be enjoying her retirement.

She looks up with a pleasant smile and states, "Mr. McThursten's in Conference Room A."

"Thank you," I said, staring at my wristwatch. Ryan is early. But he's here, and God knows it was a struggle getting him to the office. If he waits too long in the conference room, he might change his mind again. "Send him down in five minutes," I said, hurrying to my office. I'm eager to meet the talented author whose novel I discovered in the slush file. But most of all, I'm anxious to see the reluctant man who rudely hung up on me.

Two months ago, I was bewildered why McClelland rejected the captivating novel. Surely it was a mistake. Soon after I found the manuscript, I'd called the author to part good news, expecting an elated response. But when I'd stated enthusiastically, "This is McClelland Publishing..." he'd interrupted before I could finish my sentence. "I'm not interested in publishing my book, but thanks for the call." And then he hung up. His indifference hadn't fazed me. It seems every way I turn, something blocks my attempt at fulfillment, but I persisted. His disinterest explained why the manuscript was in the slush file, but his attitude left me more perplexed.

Despite the nippy dismissal, I was glad whoever resigned the manuscript hadn't deleted it. I couldn't imagine this story unpublished and relentlessly pursued the author with gentle supplications via voice mail. After several appeals, he finally answered my call, apologized for his initial response, and agreed to a meeting.

In my office, I throw my bag under the desk and quickly open the manuscript, but before I can check my face and hair, I hear my name.

"Allison?"

"Yes?" In the doorway, my wide-eyed coworker beams at the attractive man by her side. I confess, I'd taken a siesta from men, but my heart woke with an instant and unexpected attraction. He could be a cover model for McClelland's romance novels. I'm pleasantly surprised by his age and appealing six-foot frame. I hadn't expected him to be so attractive. Every fiber of him exudes sex. Washboard abdomens, hugged by a bright white T-shirt, appear beneath a gunmetal blazer. Dark-washed denim exposes a slight bow in his long legs. From his writing, I'd expected someone older, not a twentyish looking hunk. Immediately, I ponder the flaws beneath his gorgeous skin.

"This is Ryan McThursten."

Before I can respond, a curious breeze stirs the manuscript, sending pages flying across the room. Ryan rushes in, retrieving and piling the disheveled papers atop my desk. The strange breeze abates, and the office quietens.

"That was strange," I said, unable to take my eyes off Ryan.

He looks toward the door where Catrina stares with an amused smirk. "It was probably air pressure when the door opened."

I twist my lips dubiously. "That door opens and closes throughout the day and has never caused a stir like that." But I don't overthink it.

Ryan extends his hand and grins—I'm sure at my awed expression. Embarrassed, I return his firm grip and assume a professional demeanor. "Please, take a seat," I said, examining his wrist swathed in bracelets. No wristwatch, perhaps why he arrived early. Amusingly, I catch Catrina still beaming at the entrance. "Thanks, Catrina." Wide-eyed, open-mouthed, and with rapid fist thumps against her chest, she slowly closes the door. I stifle a laugh and settle my eyes on Ryan.

"Can I get you something to drink, coffee or tea?"

"No, thank you, I'm fine," he said.

His voice stirs something familiar. Have I met him before? I open my mouth, ready to inquire, but banish the question quickly. Impossible, I would remember him. A sweet fragrance fills the room, much too floral for a man's cologne. Maybe it's Catrina's perfume.

"Are you okay?" Ryan asked.

The scent engulfs the area. "Do you smell that?"

"Yes, I thought it was your perfume."

"No, I'm not wearing any."

"Smells like flowers," he said, looking around the office.

"Maybe someone in the hall sprayed air freshener," I said, but the smell surrounds the desk as if it emanates inside the room, not outside. I dismiss the aura with a smile at Ryan. "I hope you weren't waiting too long."

"That's my fault. I usually arrive thirty minutes ahead of time for appointments. I guess its impatience," Ryan said with a grin.

"That's a good practice. I'm just glad you didn't change your mind this time Mr. McThursten—Ryan."

"Ryan is fine," he replied as if he'd read my mind.

"I hope our accommodations from Washington to New York went well?"

He adjusts his body in the seat and props his elbow on the chair with an alluring self-assurance. "I drove. I prefer driving over flying. But the hotel is perfect." He pauses, resting his brown eyes on mine. His mouth parts to say something then closes. All the while, his eyes never leave my face.

Silence leaves me acutely aware of my appearance. I fidget with the tacit pause, waiting for him to speak. His expression changes swiftly with whatever he was about to say and didn't, so I break the silence. "Excellent, yes, Le Parker Meridien Hotel has great service." Averting my eyes from his unflinching gaze toward his disheveled manuscript, I start rearranging skewed pages nervously. "Well, as you know, I was captivated by your writing, and McClelland wants to publish your story," I said, finding his eyes again.

He smiles. "This was a tough decision, and I've hesitated too long. As I mentioned on the phone, my father sent the manuscript. It wasn't meant to be read by others." He pauses mid-sentence as he clarifies the novel had been curative, but of what he didn't say, but from his reserved manner, I assume there's more to his story.

"Ryan, this is a big step. It's hard publishing personal information for the world to see, but you're a talented writer."

"Allison ... is it okay if I call you Allison."

"Of course." My name on his tongue elicits sudden warmth and sends my mind scrambling to distant places, trying to recall the familiarity. The instant déjà vu and attraction have me confused and wondering if I've met him before. No, I would never forget his attractive face. The room grows colder, and I can't explain the sudden chill. "Are you cold," I asked, rubbing my arms briskly.

"It's a little chilly, but I can handle it."

"You sure you don't want coffee to warm you?" I asked, rising from my chair and moving toward the small coffeemaker purchased when I grew tired of running upstairs to the office cafeteria. I notice Catrina, who shares the room, has already brewed a pot. "It's already made," I said, hoping to change his mind.

"Well, in that case, I'll take a cup."

"Cream and sugar..."

"No, I prefer dark," he said.

I pour two cups, one dark, one with cream, and return to the desk, placing Ryan's cup in his hand. Suddenly, the room is quiet, chilly, and fragrant. I know Ryan senses it too because he turns his head and sniffs softly. The scent has settled in the corner around the small sofa. I'm tempted to investigate, but that would look strange. Ignoring the fragrance, I give Ryan my full attention.

We both take a sip of coffee. Ryan's eyes lock with mine, and I lower my eyes into the cup, wondering when I've ever been a blushing idiot. At the same time, we place our cups on the desk. Ryan leans back with a smile.

"After our last conversation I was worried you wouldn't show up," I said.

His angular jaw softens with a one-sided grin. "I've done much deliberation since your call. You don't need to convince me any further," he said reassuringly.

"I'm so relieved and happy you're going through with the publishing. You've made a good decision," I said with a smile.

"Well," he said, looking down at his wrist and twisting a colorful beaded bracelet around a triple-helix silver cuff, "I'm not doing this to be a renowned published author. I could care less. But I feel ... Well, let's put it this way, it's for my brother."

* * *

That was the first, and possibly the last time I'll ever see Ryan McThursten. Three hours later, and without any warning, management pulls my division into the conference room. Another impromptu sales meeting, I assume. But the bombshell I'd been fearfully sensing and traipsing around suddenly explodes in all our faces. No one saw it coming. Months before the merger, we were given assurances. After all, McClelland has a policy of no layoffs. Why would anyone worry? We're confident McClelland has our backs, but management's rigid conduct says otherwise. Wide-eyed, I listen as McClelland discards employees like last year's model.

"We regret to tell you we're closing several divisions..."

A collective shock of disbelief sends a horrified gasp across the conference room. The announcement, like a boulder tumbling onto my path, hurls me precipitously over the edge. Momentarily dazed, I sit listening but not comprehending my life has changed in an instant. All I can think about is my schedule, the number of manuscripts I've been working on, and the meeting with the editing team about Ryan McThursten's contract. How I make it back to my office is a wonder.

I sit at my desk, appalled at management's callous dismissal. A surge of anger swells, and then infests my mind with outrage. After four summer internships and two years of hard work and dedication as an

Acquisitions Editor, all I receive in turn is three month's severance. Angrily, I screech, "WHAT THE FUCK!" I deserve better.

My stomach bubbles venom. Anger swells vengefully. Swiftly, I send valuable contacts to my personal email and log onto a blog I'd created months ago with hopes of writing but quickly abandoned. I vent to wordless exhaustion—a much-needed tantrum publishing a rebuking post about McClelland's merciless layoff.

I exhale long and slow, then grab the phone and call the one person who can console me, the one person who's been my anchor for years. A prerecorded message spills robotic through the phone, "This number is no longer in service." My mind clicks. How could I forget Grandma Blu passed away two months ago? Then I dial the only other person who can assuage my anger. Voicemail mirrors my sister's voice. I want to scream, NIK, CALL ME BACK IMMEDIATELY! But I don't want to appear the needy little sister losing her shit, unable to cope with problems. So, I continue packing my belongings and leave the office without a goodbye to anyone, not even Catrina, one of my dearest friends.

How comical, I think, as I exit onto Avenue of the Americas, merely six hours ago I'd entered the building joyful with hopes of a new contract. But like every good thing in my life, time at McClelland has expired. I refuse to look back at a building where I've built a career soon after college, a place akin to a second home. Brimming with anger and aware of strangers' furtive glances, I avoid the subway and opt for a taxi's backseat privacy. Dazed, I barely hear the driver asks, "Where to?" A subdued voice answers, "1630 York Avenue." I sit numb and oblivious to the city landscape past the window. Temporarily, I stuff anger inside an abyss, a detrimental place suffused with painful memories. Tears will come later.

3

Three Faces of Grief

STRAINING UNDER SUMMER HEAT the air-conditioner hiccups, shudders, and thumps. I roll my head toward the noisy corner where the AC resumes a peaceful hum. With apathy, I gaze at the ceiling. *Numb.* Softly, I rest my hands on my chest. *It still beats* regardless. I wish to place my heart in a jar, protect and shield it till sorrow's done. Grief ... I've never suffered five stages—denial, anger, bargaining, depression, and acceptance—just three. How can you deny reality? And bargaining is useless when circumstances are beyond one's control. You can only mourn the loss. Three faces of grief have visited in my twenty-four years. The first time was during my parent's divorce, second, Grandma Blu's death, and third, McClelland's layoff. Each visit, though different, was painful all the same.

When my parents announced their divorce, the life I knew ended. Unlike my sister's grief, a riotous monster spewing paroxysm of anger, I was paralyzed with sadness and suffered pain in silence. But for both of us, sorrow carved slow-healing wounds and left identical scars of constant insecurities. The second face of grief, death, came three months ago with Grandma Blu's loss—my anchor and source of comfort throughout my parent's crazy separation. That pain, still fresh, hasn't healed. I suspect with time, it too will subside, but will always be tangible. The third red-hot grief was McClelland's layoff. Another death of sorts I've filed under miscellaneous. Though different from the previous, it's still a loss I mourn deeply. A loss of worth, a loss of lifestyle, a daunting change, and yet again, forging a new reality.

The layoff is still an open wound. Every emotion and thought that spring day, is indelibly etched like ink across my memory, as vivid as cherry blossoms viewed from the taxi window. I fume, thinking of McClelland's dishonesty. Management never had our backs. Now, retrospectively, I realize the lay-off was a godsend, deflating complacency I'd never allow, but did, putting trust in a profit-seeking company unconcerned about people. The unexpected blow left me confused and searching for a new normal.

Although the lay-off was a month ago, I frequently reflect on my loss but grow tired of drowning in grief. For days, I wake numb with anguish, lying sleepless, staring at misshapen shadows roving the ceiling—a devil's pitchfork aimed to sling me from inertia. Though grief is fading, the loss of Ryan McThursten's contract is infuriating. After the daunting effort to gain his trust, I should be his editor. *This is so unfair ...* Well, I reason, the layoff was for the best—a necessary kick to jumpstart my writing. I sigh with a despairing glance at the laptop, but exerting mental energy is unfathomable.

Outside the window, a garbage truck thunders through a pothole and triggers a blaring car alarm, but indifference holds me unmoving. Headlights flood the window, casting shadows across the dark bedroom. Finally, tired of lying on my back, I sit up, yawn, stretch, and grab the laptop from the nightstand. Opening my blog to a post I'd written the previous night, I notice the blogger named *Undaunted*, a blogger who'd become a follower soon after the rebuking post about McClelland, has left comments again.

I cringe, remembering bloody poetry and disturbing words, which left no wish to explore her blog. I've considered blocking her, but that would be rude. The sudden desire to write dwindles restless, so instead, I check my email, finding more of the same junk mail, car note payment alert, and a myriad of other bills. Just as I'm about to close the laptop, a familiar email address catches my attention. Three bold words torment fearfully.

"Do you remember?"

The untimely arrival strums an eerie chord, registering greater fear. I sit straight, wondering why the email is so early. The question, now truncated from nine to three urgent words, heightens alarm. Is my tormentor growing desperate for an answer? I can't keep ignoring this. They're not going away. After two years, I've hoped the harasser would stop. The first time the email arrived, I was paranoid, now, I'm downright frightened.

Quickly, I close the laptop, slide off the bed, and walk toward the window, hoping the lavender sunrise sprawling the East River will distract fearful thoughts. Ahead, on the FDR Drive, diametric white lights wend toward a routine destination. A view that inspires calm most mornings has no effect today. Fearful someone who saw me and knows what happened that night is watching, unseen but there, impatiently awaiting an answer. I fear they won't let up until I give them what they want. I look twenty stories below at Manhattan's empty sidewalks. *Who are you?*

Down the hall, a closet door screech—Nikki's daily dash to dress for work. Grabbing my laptop, I head to the door, hoping breakfast will distract anxious thoughts.

4
Lil'sis

TRUDGING FROM THE BEDROOM, I stop at the sight of a suit-clad man sneaking down the hall. I adjust my long pajama top falling mid-thigh and hope he doesn't glance back at my disheveled appearance. On tiptoes, I follow and watch him creep downstairs and exit the duplex's front door. Nikki's new boyfriend, the one she hasn't introduced yet, I assume. I can't keep up with her men, her interest wanes so fast. Her constant change of boyfriends forever a mystery. I've always believed the men end the affair, discouraged by her domineering personality and career.

I continued down the stairs into the open-concept kitchen and glance around the space, the duplex Nikki, and I inherited from mom when she moved back to Louisiana to take care of Grandma Blu. With Blu's death, mom decided to stay in a home she'd been raised. The duplex, Nik and I redecorated is modern and chic but lacks the warmth of a home. Every item appears new, unused because Nikki and I are seldom here. Spending most of our time at work; the duplex became just a place to shower and sleep.

Finding the remote, I turn on the TV across the room, catching the tail end of California wildfires. A humorous weatherman announces, "Another sweltering day, 92 degrees, but feels like 102 with the humidity."

"Great, it's only June," I muttered, grabbing a carton of orange juice and eggs from the refrigerator. I decide toast, scrambled eggs, and Nik's dark-bold-Chilean coffee is enough, given the wasted pancakes prepared several days in a row. I don't know why I bother. Lately, neither Nikki nor I care for breakfast. But breakfast always evokes happy childhood memories of Nik standing at the stove over food sizzling, and breakfast redolent air. For a moment, I allow myself to visit that happy place in mom's kitchen as Nik and I shared a meal around the kitchen table, laughing and talking, as utensils clatter melodiously on ceramic bowls. Then I exhale a calmer breath.

As children, breakfast and dinner were synonymous with security, permanence, the emotional safety Nik, and I lacked as children. Meals were our anchor, refuge in our parent's unstable world. Products of a broken home, we alternated between households of two career-obsessed individuals too busy to parent properly. They thrust their parental duties on prepubescent Nikki. I became her charge. With an eight-year age difference and motherly responsibilities, Nik appeared much older in her teenage years. She's never forgiven our parents' neglect and often retaliates with angry words. "*Some people aren't meant to be parents.*" Although names were unspoken, the intended target was implied.

Now, here I am at twenty-four, cooking Nik breakfast and subconsciously conjuring childhood before our security was ripped apart. I can't complain after all the years she took care of me. Since the layoff, I've tried to appear useful and resilient around my workaholic sister. I retrieve two plates from the cabinet, place them on the counter, and then pause at a familiar name on the television. Franklin Emsworth, a name I haven't heard since college. The news reports a new museum to be constructed in the District of Columbia by Emsworth's Real Estate Development Corporation. A Real Estate Developer and great-grandson of Emsworth University's founder gave a sendoff speech at my graduation.

Instantly, a frosty breeze sweeps my bare calves and thighs. Shivering, I rush toward the window and turn off the AC, but oddly, the chill grows icier, engulfing the space. An ensuing pressure clamps my chest. My heart races and the room begin to swirl. Light-headed, I inhale and exhale deep, averting a full-fledged anxiety attack. I haven't felt one this strong since college and wonder what brought it on.

"Good morning, sis," Nikki said, striding into the kitchen straighter than an African princess toting a basket atop her head, chest leading first.

Her wheatish brown skin is glowing, a complexion Nikki and I inherited from French-Creole ancestors of Louisiana. "It's a good morning for one of us," I said banishing unease with humor. Nikki stands half-dressed in bra and pants; a cream blouse dangles in her hand. Sandy brown waves, flat-ironed bone-straight, fall softly against her bare shoulders. She looks so much better with her natural waves, but she'll disagree strongly. Feigning annoying lil' sis outgrown years ago, I say "Someone's glowing this morning. Who was the black suit sneaking out?" I jab naughtily.

"You saw him?"

"Uh-huh," I said with skewed lips. Knowing my expression will irk Nik as it always does when I stumbled on her secrets. "I saw his backside before he snuck out the door—"

"He wasn't sneaking out, Allie. He overslept and was in a rush."

"Who is he?"

"Shane," she said with an irrepressible fish-eyed expression that swims across her face whenever she's made some blunder.

"Are you kidding me? Shane? Annoying, boisterous Shane from your office ... I thought you couldn't stand him. And what happened to your no-dating-men-from-work policy?"

"We're not dating," escaped abruptly, trailing emphatic. "Last night, well, you know ... It just sorta happened," she said, turning her head in dismissal. "Have you seen my briefcase?"

"There, on the console," I said, itching to tease her about Shane. "Hmmm ... I'd love to be a fly on your office wall today with all that sexual tension floating around—"

"Allie, stop it! Besides…" she murmured, burying her head in the briefcase, "…we're professional enough to handle it."

I expected this sensible response from Nicole Rachel Bertrand, Esquire. But with all her sensibility what happened, why'd she let her guard down for one night? It's just not like her. "Okay, if you say so sis," I replied with a playful zip of my lips.

Nibbling on toast, I study Nik scanning her daily planner as she does most mornings. *We're so different.* My overly protective sister, all brains and no-nonsense attitude, she's daddy's spitting image, softened by feminine attributes, round face, kind brown eyes, and full-determined lips. Where she's been blessed with his temperament and intelligence, I've inherited mom's good looks and romantic ideals. Even our sense of fashion is different. Nik veers conservative; hiding curvaceous assets under traditional garb and wears her hair in conventional styles. Unlike her, I'm bohemian with artistic taste, wearing my French-Creole heritage wavy beneath my shoulders. My clothing is free-spirited, gauzy, layered, flowing, and accessorized with Boho jewelry. But most days I prefer straight-leg jeans and T-shirts.

Nik slouches over the counter, head buried in her mobile, and my eyes widen at her breast overflowing the tan lace push-up bra. Until this moment, I hadn't realized how big they are. "Nik, those things are humongous," I screeched.

Nik's face stiffens with surprise. "It's the Bertrand curse," she states, tugging consciously at the bra.

"Curse? I doubt it." I know full-well Bertrand women praise their ample breast and narrow hips. I remember Grandma and the women on dad's side of the family. They were all big-breasted. Somehow, I'd inherited attributes from grandfather's family, perky boobs, not small or large.

"Allie, you've seen my breast before, why the sudden surprise?"

"They just look bigger today." And they do as if she's grown a bra size or two.

"It's the bra, it's too tight," Nik said, quickly dismissing the topic. "What you got planned today?" She asked a notch mellower.

There's that tone which says, I'm not prying, her supportive, non-judgemental attempt to give me space. I appreciate her efforts, but her patience makes me feel like crap, a failure as she tramps around content and successful. I know I shouldn't feel like a failure, after all, I've worked hard two years with zilch to show for it. We've never been competitive or jealous siblings. And she'd never lord her success over me. Our likes and dislikes have converged and diverged over the years. But we've always been supportive of each other. Best friends.

"Oh, you know..." I groused, turning my face toward the TV "...just more mind-numbing job search," I lied, pursing my lips to still my face. Somehow, Nik always senses when I'm lying. Maybe a small twitch appears when I speak untruths. But it's only a partial lie. I had all intentions of looking for work. After two weeks of searching a tight job market, frustration ensued. Discouraged, I stopped looking. The desire to devote talents to a publishing firm extinct, nil. Only the need to finish that elusive novel remains. "How's your day looking?" I asked with no general interest in the cases, and legal jargon that goes over my head, only wanting to deflect attention away from me.

"More of the same ... angry husbands and wives fighting over this and that," she said, staring at her wristwatch. "At nine, I'm in court with a client whose wife's suing for divorce."

Nik's finally that lawyer she aspired to become at sixteen-years-old. I remember her loud decree of defiance to our parents like it was yesterday. *"I'm going to be a lawyer, or maybe a family counselor, so other kids aren't tossed about like Allie and me,"* she'd huffed and strutted out the room. That came on the heels of their nasty divorce settlement. I suspect the courtroom experience as our parents fought for custody made a profound impact along with her crush on mom's attorney. Now at thirty-two, an accomplished lawyer, she hardly has time for sisterly talk, except the new ritual of breakfast chatter.

"I don't know how you do it. All that heartache day in and day out, I'd be so discouraged with marriage."

"Uh-huh, well, mom and dad already ruined it for me."

"Is that why you chose to become a divorce attorney?" We both know the answer to that question, but I asked anyway.

"Well, yeah ... Wasn't it obvious," Nik said with a guffaw. "The nasty, drawn-out divorce they dragged us through would have affected anyone."

I suspect the divorce had other ramifications, such as her inability to sustain a relationship. Maybe it did for both of us. But I try to forget that pain. It's a part of me I seldom visit, hidden but still there. "Nik," I murmured, "Do you think mom and dad had true love? I don't remember ever seeing signs of affection. Do you?"

"True love, like those romance novels you managed at McClelland?"

"Nik, you know that's not what I meant; real love, not some fictitious brand."

"I'm just messing with you Allie," she said with an impish grin. "Well, whatever it was, true love, lust, it didn't last. But, yeah, I do remember little flirtations before their relationship went stale like most marriages, although it was rare. Anyway, you wouldn't remember. You were barely walking or talking," she said, throwing me a curious glance. "Allie, you gotta get your head out of those romance novels. Life's seldom as romantic as those books. Have you ever read one where people are struggling to feed their kids and pay bills? I bet you haven't. And there's a reason for that. It's called escapism, people using those books to fill their empty, boring lives with passion. Sis, in my world, people have to get on with living, not loving. With all the love addiction, I'm surprised the divorce rate isn't higher than fifty percent."

God, Nik! I thought with pity. I'm no psychologist, but it's obvious she's a casualty of divorce, the wounded cynic, marred for life. Issues unresolved, held in abeyance until someone or something triggers scary emotions. "Thanks for the lengthy clarification, but I'm no delusional romantic."

"You're not? Wow! Allie, that's the biggest lie you've told yourself—"

"Nik stop it. I'm not that shallow teenager anymore," I said defensively knowing darn well Austen, Bronte, Wharton, and countless writers shaped my romantic ideals. But I swiftly learned real love is messier and seldom end happily ever after.

Nik's eyes squint. "You're talking to me, Sis. I know all your little secrets," she said with emphasis and a clever arch of her thumb and index finger into a little slit. "Besides, I've seen the guys you date. They're all attractive, intelligent professionals. The moment one burp, you lose interest. I know you, Allie. Probably better than you know yourself. Believe me, men with all your romantic requirements don't exist."

How annoying! She makes me so angry when she does that. She thinks she knows me, but she's talking about a younger me. I'm no longer that girl, looking for the perfect man. I know better than that. I wish she could see the mature me. The one who's been burned many times chasing perfect, only finding flawed men behind perfect facades. "Okay, Ms. Expert," I said, not wanting to travel this road. Especially with someone who can't keep a relationship. I revert to the original topic. "Nik, I'm just curious about mom and dad. There's so much I don't remember before the divorce. For instance, I don't remember ever hearing them say I love you to us or to each other."

Nik peers with discerning eyes. "Allie don't take it personally. It was their upbringing. I don't believe their parents ever showed them affection, and the apple doesn't fall far from the tree. They didn't know how to be doting parents. But they wouldn't have fought so hard for custody if they didn't love us."

"Hmmm, I guess..." I mumbled, pondering whether it was love or entitlement, like the deed to the house. I turn to the stove, fill two plates with eggs, and spread strawberry marmalade on toast. "It's just discouraging, two people afraid to demonstrate love," I said, turning and finding Nik glued to her mobile. I wish she wouldn't do that when we're talking. I roll my eyes with an exasperated breath and refuse to appear needy lil' sis.

Setting the plates noisily on the granite island, I hope she'll sit for a second. She doesn't. I'm annoyed but used to being ignored by Nik when her mind's somewhere else. *I'm lil' sis again.* I pour a cup of coffee, lean back on the counter, study Nik, and wonder what changed? "Nik, are you happy?"

"What?" she asked as if offended. I recognize that tone; it's one she assumes when anyone questions or reproaches her character or behavior. "That's a strange question. Why would you ask me that?"

"Well, you're always working, even on the weekends. What happened to fun Nik, the one who enjoyed clubbing, shopping, and traveling? Don't you want more out of life, a little fun? And what happened to that other guy you were dating last month?"

"Wow, what's with all the questions this morning?"

There's evasive Nik again, answering a question with another question. "I'm just making observations, sis." Slowly scooping strawberry marmalade with a deliberative lick from my finger, I surmise I've hit on some truth because she doesn't look me in the eye but stare away and fumble through her briefcase.

"You know what it's like to love your work. You were pretty devoted to McClelland," she said, crouching to adjust the strap on the sensible black kitty heels.

"Love ... I wouldn't exactly use that word with work."

With pinched brows, Nik rises from her crouch. Finally, her eyes meet mine. "Then what do you want? What do you love? What do you want to do, Allie?" she asked commandingly, just like dad, a tone that used to make me tense and self-conscious, but now makes me defiant.

"Honestly," I said with a straight face, "I'd love to drag you away from that office, take a cross-country trip by car as we planned years ago, and just cruise nonstop with no destination."

"Come on, Allie. Stop playing. What do you want to do?"

"You know the answer to that."

"Write? So, why aren't you?"

I shrug apathetically, feigning insouciance. But beneath the pretense, I'm annoyed Nik can't see my misery standing here in my PJ top, hair unwashed for days. God, I haven't worn makeup for weeks or tried to look presentable. I'm yearning to scream, isn't it obvious

I've lost my way! I'm too damn depressed to write. I don't know how to begin again, not just writing but life. But instead, I say, "I have a case of writer's block."

"You're just depressed over your job."

"You think…"

"Don't be sarcastic with me, lil' sis," she said with a playful smirk, breast jiggling as she placed hands on hips. "Okay, Allie, the only way over this funk is to dive into your passion. What about that blog you started? It's a good cure for writer's block. Plus, it's an excellent venue to showcase your work to potential employers. What about freelancing? You're so talented. You could start your own business, and I'm willing to help. Just tell me what you need to get started."

If it were as easy as that, I would have started days ago, I think with a sigh of annoyance. Annoyed because Nik always knows what I'm thinking. After years of making my own decisions without any input from her or the family, I don't want her opinions, not at the age of twenty-four. I exhale a hot breath. "I don't know Nik. I'm not sure I want to be an Editor anymore, and freelancing is tough." But she's right about the blog.

"You've got to do something. Just do it. Keep blogging, maybe it'll spark your writing." Cupping her mouth and drifting toward the powder room, Nikki closes the door swiftly. Water sprays, the toilet sounds, a muted cough, and gag ensue with another flush. Silence. Moments later, Nik exits the powder room and quickly heads upstairs.

"You okay?"

"Yep," she said, pinching her nose and continuing upstairs. Five minutes later, she reemerges with a matching gray gabardine blazer on her arm, and the scent of vanilla fills the room.

"Hey, you're leaving? Aren't you going to try my delicious eggs and toast I slaved over?" I asked with a mock pout.

"Sorry, early meeting today," she said, grabbing her purse, briefcase, car keys, and peeking at her face in the foyer mirror. "Start writing, Allie," she said, blowing a kiss. Her perfume wafts and lingers in the air as the door clicks behind her.

"I'll try," I replied forlornly to no one but the air and listen to the elevator on the other side of the door ring open and shut.

5

Nikki's Secret

DAMNIT! I FEEL HORRIBLE rushing out like that. Allie looked so desperate for me to eat her breakfast. If only I could. She's trying so hard to be useful. But if I'd stayed in that room a minute longer smelling those eggs, I would have thrown up again, and she would have known, seen the sickness on my face. And I'm not ready to reveal the pregnancy. But if I have one more morning like this, she's going to know something's wrong. I'm surprised she hasn't noticed yet. The last two weeks have been horrible. I can barely eat.

I can't believe I'm pregnant! I'm always so careful. The moment Shane said the condom slipped; I knew I was in trouble. Though he said it hadn't come off and hadn't slid very far, his silent pause and excessive reassurance revealed he was just as nervous as I was. After years of precautions, one mistake, and I'm knocked-up. I wish I hadn't stopped taking the pill, but I had to, it was making me sick. Well, the damage is done, there's nothing you can do. No amount of wishing will change the fact. *You're pregnant!*

But I can't have this baby. And I can't tell Allie. If she suspects I'm pregnant or even considering an abortion, she'll protest, and I don't need her religious beliefs right now. *Shane … God, I can't tell him either.* Although I've worked beside him for five years, and occasionally dated over the years, we've never established a real relationship. Regardless, with his staunch Catholic upbringing, he'll be swift to take responsibility and opt for the respectable solution. He'll want to run straight to the courthouse, set-up-house like the perfect couple—and that's not happening. No way will I make mom and dad's mistake, marrying because of pregnancy, not love. Their scorned bastard child—I can't believe they thought I wouldn't find out about my illegitimate birth. Thanks to Grandma Blu's slip, I discovered they'd rectified my bastard status and married six months after the pregnancy. I'm not going to bring another child into this world without a father, and I'm just not ready for matrimony, probably never will be.

* * *

I hadn't expected Pro-lifer's waving banners and blocking the clinic's entrance to accost my already fragile state, making a difficult decision more painful. This is just what they want to do. Force women to doubt their choices and run in the opposite direction. Fixing my eyes on the entrance, I push through the chanting crowd, and dodge incriminating faces and provoking placards without timidity. Before I enter the door, a woman runs up to me, shoving a pamphlet in my hand and slinging deliberate question to render doubt and shame. "Are you aware of the ramifications of taking a life? That child deserves to live." Ignoring her tirade, I rush inside straight to the elevator.

On the third floor, I waver in the hallway when I notice couples entering the clinic. Suddenly, uneasy and ashamed of being alone, I curse my intractable nature, and surprisingly, wish Shane was here to accompany me inside. After all, this is his child too, one he'll never know about. Just when I'm about to turn and leave, a thirtyish-looking man and a girl, no more than eighteen, push the door from behind me. The door releases to an overcrowded space like an emergency room. Immediately, faces peer up, eyes examining me as if I've stepped into the wrong room. *Is it my single status, entering unaccompanied by a partner?* I hadn't expected the clinic to be so crowded, especially not on a weekday. I notice casually dressed women and assume it's my business attire and briefcase warranting such attention. Perhaps they think I'm one of the Pro-Lifers ready to give a speech or some legal authority prepared to ban the clinic's operation. What was I thinking, dressing so conspicuously? Obviously, I wasn't thinking. I'd planned to go straight to work after the procedure and pretend this never happened. Wishful thinking, I suppose.

I pause with uncertainty, and for a brief second, consider leaving, but the unbearable morning sickness forces me toward the receptionist. *If anything, it will be a relief to be done with constant nausea.* Instantly, I retract that thought, ashamed I'd feel relief, not remorse for my actions. I give my name, fill out forms, and find myself lying when the receptionist asked, "Will there be someone to take you home after the procedure?" *Of course not! No one knows about this but me,* I retort mentally. I shake my head, and respond tersely, "Yes, he's waiting downstairs." I finish signing a release form, failing to read it thoroughly, only wanting to speed up time and be done with this day.

Taking a seat in the back of the room, I study rows of teenagers and young women watching the flat-screen television anchored to the wall. Some read magazines and talk sporadically to their partner with no sign of remorse or distress as if they're at a routine doctor's visit. Am I the only one torn about this decision? The only sign of disquiet is the nervous man beside me who intermittently glances at his partner. The woman's eyes never leave the front of the room, ignoring his imploring stares. I suspect the decision wasn't mutual and wonder whose choice it was to abort. I catch the man's worried eyes and smile awkwardly. Instantly recognizing his pain, I surmise abortion wasn't his decision but the decision of his steely partner.

Beyond his face, I notice a wall covered with information on birth control. *That's what got me here in the first place.* I scoff and fidget with the Pro-Life pamphlet shoved into my hand earlier. Pictures of aborted fetuses with the caption, "Murder" wrench my gut and tug at my heart. Swiftly, I close the leaflet and study young women in their teens and twenties, who'll undoubtedly conceive again. Not me. I've never wanted to be a mother. Over the years, I'd squashed any desire for motherhood, but I can't help wondering if it's because of my stunted childhood and years of taking care of Allie.

Regardless, I can't bring a child into my imperfect world. And I won't be another selfish parent like mom and dad. But abortion was never part of the equation. There was no doubt in my mind I'd ever get pregnant and never considered what I'd do if it happened. Now, unimaginably, I'm about to exterminate life. Will I regret this tomorrow or years later? Suddenly, I'm aware of my hand's uncomfortably, tight grip on my belly. I glance down and relax the squeeze, then press gently below my navel. I imagine the undetectable fetus growing inside, a part of Shane and me at rest in my womb, unaware its nascent life will soon be ripped away.

I can't do this!

Before I can reconsider my actions, a greater force impels me from the chair. I suspect my conscience won't let me end this life even if I reassess my options.

Outside the building, the persistent woman who'd crammed the pamphlet in my hand smiles, and states, "You're doing the right thing."

"How would you know sanctimonious twit?" I growled angrily. "Stop harassing innocent people and crawl back to your holier-than-thou existence!" Throwing the pamphlet at her feet, I race past the staunch mob; unaware the moment I sprung from the clinic chair, I'd made my final decision.

6

Coffee Dialogue

WHEN THE DOOR CLICKED behind Nik, I exhale, slump into the chair, and agonize about the mysterious email. I've never told Nikki about the off-campus party black-out because I'm too ashamed. The only person who knows is Lisa, my college roommate. Nikki would have blamed me for being gullible enough to attend a stranger's party. Mom and dad would have chastised me and worried unnecessarily. They didn't have a clue what was wrong when I came home for winter break and refused to return to school. I couldn't go back. Every time I thought about that party, I'd have an anxiety attack.

Mom dragged me to the doctor, but I didn't need a professional diagnosis to reveal I was having anxiety attacks related to memory loss. I pleaded with the doctor not to say anything to mom, explaining I wanted to tell her myself, but I never did. He prescribed medication and referred me to a therapist, but I tossed the prescription and never went to counseling. I returned to school and took up yoga classes and long hikes in Rock Creek Park. I refused to take medication for something I felt would ease with time. But I'll never be able to tell Nikki, not now, not after two years.

Restless, I stare into oblivion, until I notice speckles of breadcrumbs and strawberry marmalade littering the counter. Instantly, an image of my neat-freak sister's obsessive-compulsive behavior compelling her toward the object of annoyance, and scrubbing the mess clean, looms in my mind. If one dish remains dirty in the sink, Nik gets antsy. So, similarly, I scour the kitchen spotless.

Ten minutes later, aimlessly, I stare out the window at two figures crossing my view, a young woman guiding an elderly woman into Carl Schurz Park. The senior turns and tugs a small dog waddling behind her, while her young assistant surveys surroundings with caution. The woman's frailness prompts memories of Grandma Blu's slender frame months before she passed. Outfits she once filled round and healthy, swung loosely around her thin, frail frame. She resorted to wearing sensible, old-lady dresses, as Nik and I called them. Although her voluminous curls haloed thinly, the gray softened her face beautifully. But Grandma Blu never complained. She embraced her twilight years, as she called it, as gracefully as she had her youth. Regardless of her failing body, her beautiful, keen mind remained as sound as ever. At once, I miss her encouraging words and lasting caresses—hugs I'd curled into and never wanted to leave. I close my eyes and imagine her soothing voice. *You'll be all right, sunshine. You'll be all right ...* The comforting mantra suspends when a newscaster reports city crime on the rise.

I inhale and exhale anxiety stirring beneath, glance at the muted television, then quickly turn it off. I refuse to spend restless hours watching TV as I'd done the first week of unemployment, slumped miserably on the sofa, fiddling with dirty hair, and watching marathons of my favorite shows. That grew boring after a week. Words Grandma Blu plied resonate as if she were beside me. *The devil finds work for idle hands.* Even today, I heed her words and schlep to the shower.

Emerging from the bathroom, I retrieve the laptop, head to the dining table, and open my blog—Coffee Dialogue. The anonymous email dangles annoyingly on the edge of thought. I need to stop avoiding and start acknowledging my fear, but today I'm not ready. Swiftly, I wipe the email and tormenting night from thought, turning attention to my uninspiring blog design and envision a professional editor's blog. I sample several themes, hoping one will inspire my imagination. After an hour of crafting an artistic page befitting an editor, words still elude me. One word, one sentence, to ignite my imagination ... That thought elicits Ernest Hemingway's words in *A Movable Feast*, a maxim he used to get over his writer's block. *All you have to do is write one true sentence. Write the truest sentence that you know.* So, I write the truest sentence I can conceive:

My name is Allison Arielle Bertrand, and at the age of twenty-four, I'm struggling to write one freaking sentence.

Of course, I rewrite, delete, and revise several times until I devise my blog's tagline: *Your life is a novel; write your destiny.* Although writing eludes me, I've successfully created a blog providing information on the publishing world, and a venue to advertise my editing services. The site contains no trace of Allison Arielle Bertrand's identity except my contact information for potential clients. Coffee Dialogue will remain my online alias. *Complete anonymity.*

But then, I notice the tiny avatar, a professional photo used on Mc-Clelland's website. With haste, I delete all traces of me. The empty gray box that contained my picture, now void, needs an analogous avatar. *Coffee ... Dialogue ...* A laptop and coffee mug, although it depicts my blog's name, lacks creativity. Hmm, I need books. Rummaging through Nikki's eclectic coffee cup collection, I find a simple, white mug, fill it with the morning's leftover brew, rush to my bedroom, and grab four books from the bookshelf.

On the dark oak dining table, I arrange the coffee cup and books beside the laptop—coffee on one side, books stacked on the other. Uninspired, I find a pair of Nik's black-rimmed readers, a pen, and pad and place them in front of the computer. *It must look like the perfect writer's space.* Finding a small lamp in the bedroom, I angle it over the laptop. Something's missing. I imagine my desk at work, plastered with sticky notes. Finding a yellow sticky pad, I scribble the site's tagline: *Your life is a novel; write your destiny.* Placing the sticky note on the edge of the keyboard, I snap a photo with my cell phone camera. This will be my blog's avatar. After uploading the image, and admiring my work,

I still lack the inspiration to write. So, instead, I peruse photography, cooking, traveling, and poetry blogs until my cell phone jingles a familiar tune.

"Catrina!" I squealed deafeningly through the phone. After sharing an office together for two years, Cat became one of my closest friends. Since the layoff, I've missed our conversations, but mostly, I miss her wacky humor and ability to make me laugh with that quirky Scottish accent.

"Allie, I miss you so much! It's not the same here without you."

"What? I thought they let you go."

"They did," she hastened to explain. "McClelland called me last week and offered my old job back with another Editor, one of the new guys from the parent company. I'm so sorry. I couldn't turn it down. I need the money."

"God, no, Cat, don't apologize. I would have done the same in your position. How's it going so far?"

"It's okay. If it makes you feel any better, it sucks here. Everything's changed with the new group. Nothing compares to working with you. Allie, remember Ryan McThursten?"

"Of course, I do." After losing his contract, how can I forget? Besides, I can't stop thinking about our first meeting, and the odd feeling we'd met before.

"Well, when he found out you wouldn't be handling his novel, he backed out … changed his mind again."

"Really," I said with a big grin. Not many people would turn down a contract. Ryan's actions pique my interest more than that arousing moment in my office. I feel surprisingly venerated he'd rejected McClelland because of me.

"He wanted to know how he could get in touch with you. I hope you don't mind. I gave him your email address. I figured if you want to talk to him, you can give him your phone number yourself."

"It's okay. I don't mind."

"So, have you been looking for work, Allie?"

"No, but I'm thinking about freelancing."

"Well, you already have your first client?"

"Who?"

"Ryan. Not a bad catch for your first novelist. Girl, he insists on working with you. What did you do, cast one of those Creole spells on him?"

"Yea, right, even if I knew how I wouldn't." That comment coming from someone other than Catrina would have offended me. But after years of tongue-in-cheek remarks about each other's heritage—and God knows I've made many jokes about her Scottish ancestry—I've grown comfortable with our playful banter.

"Mr. McThursten is set on you, and I bet it's not just your skills—"

"Nah, it's all professional. Besides, he's way out of my league."

"Allie, no one is out of your league. Have you looked at yourself in the mirror? You always turn heads, everywhere you go. I don't think you're aware of the effect you have on men. Why are the beautiful ones so insecure? I don't get it. Anyway, I saw your reaction when Ryan walked into the office. I've never seen you look so infatuated. And Ryan looked like he just won a prize or something. I thought the moment I left the room you two would be rolling on the floor—"

"Cat, stop it—"

"No, I'm serious. I swear an invisible bolt of lightning struck you both," she said with a deep chortle.

Was it that obvious? It couldn't have been I was so calm and professional. I guess she knows me better than I thought and lying to Catrina is impossible.

"Maybe that's why the papers flew off your desk. By the way, that was strange. I couldn't believe what I saw. It looked like an invisible hand swept the papers off the desk."

"I thought it strange too. Ryan said it was from the door opening, but it's never happened before."

Catrina chuckles again. "See I was right. It was all that electricity sparkling between you two."

"I admit I was a little taken by his looks. But I'm sure any woman would have had the same reaction."

"Ay, lass, ye're reit aboot thae," Cat said playfully in a thick Scottish brogue followed by a quick snicker I've grown so fond of. "I almost lost my footing when I saw Mr. McThursten. Did you see that swagger on him? So confident that one—"

"Ha! I almost lost it with your mimicry," I interjected, remembering the difficulty I had stifling a laugh in front of Ryan.

"You can't turn him down. This could be the new start you were looking for. And if you need an assistant to handle all your clients, you can count on me."

"All my clients ... I'm glad you have such confidence in me. But if I'm as inundated as you believe, you'll be my first choice. But Catrina, I think you should give up the assistant gig and become an editor." I've often wondered why she settled for an assistant position. She's qualified to be an editor with a communications degree from NYU. Besides, she does my job better than I can.

"I don't know if that's the route I want to take yet. I'm just like you, I'd rather be writing than editing. And I know, you're going to say I can do both, but I just have to give it some more thought. Allie, I've got to go, but I'll give you a call later. Oh, check your email and be brave. I'm sure you're going to be just fine."

"I will. Thanks, Cat. Love Ya."

"Love you too, lass."

I end the call with a smile, realizing how easily I say those words my parents had difficulty expressing, perhaps because I seldom heard them as a child, or just refuse to be like my parents.

* * *

Although I've considered several times calling Ryan McThursten to see if McClelland is treating him well, I never thought I'd hear from him again or thought he'd want to work with me exclusively. The turn of events is surprising. Slight thrill colors doubt in my mind, but I thwart the tenuous emotion with a dose of realism. Happiness isn't an emotion I care to visit or can afford. Not now, besides, it never lasts. I'm sure some threat is waiting to dash this instant thrill apart.

However, I allow a pang of guilt to surface. After all, Ryan turned down a contract for me. *That's insane!* He deserves that publishing contract. But I deserve some recognition for changing his mind, getting him to accept the offer ... *Don't I?*

Opening my email, I check the inbox, and for sure, there it is, RMcT@gmail.com sent three days ago.

Allison,

Catrina was kind enough to give me your email address. I hope you don't mind. When I heard about the rash layoff at McClelland, I had a change of heart. I declined their offer. I couldn't possibly be affiliated with a publisher that carelessly discards its staff. Besides, it was your passion for my story that convinced me to publish the book. If anyone deserves to manage my manuscript, it's you. After meeting you and seeing your work, I know we will work well together. And I'm confident you can polish my manuscript to its finest. If the offer still stands, and you don't mind working long-distance by email or phone, I'd love for you to edit my novel. I look forward to speaking with you about your compensation and other details.

Ryan

Lingering over his email, I debate whether to call. With all my doubts, am I ready to forge an alliance, commit to Ryan? He has an opportunity with one of the most prominent publishing firms in the country. Will I be doing him a disservice if I accept his offer? It would be selfish not to have him reconsider his actions. Slowly, I begin to type my response.

Ryan,

I was surprised to hear you turned down McClelland again. It's becoming a habit with you. But, seriously, I regret your decision was because of me. You should reconsider. You need to think long and hard about this. I don't want to stand in the way of a lucrative contract. But if you're certain this is what you want to do, I'm honored to edit your novel. You must understand I'm not an agent. However, I do have many contacts in the industry and can get your manuscript to the right people for publishing. As far as compensation, we can agree on the terms later, as I am

*new to freelance work. My contact information is below. I look forward
to speaking with you soon.*

Allison

Suddenly lighter, I begin to believe Catrina is right. This is the path
to a new start ... Ryan McThursten. With renewed energy, I head
toward the shower, more optimistic than I've been in weeks, letting
warm water purge sadness I've marinated in since McClelland.

Stepping from the shower, I wipe condensation from the mirror.
Almond, hazel eyes, I've avoided for days, stare back. I examine my
face for the Allie I've misplaced. She's there somewhere, waiting for
the right moment to start again. Like Grandma Blu, I whisper those
comforting words, "You'll be all right sunshine."

Instead of the one-sided braid I've worn for several days, I let my
hair dry loose and free. I don't bother with makeup, there's no place to
go. And I'm not ready to venture out into the world feigning normalcy,
a fake demeanor of happiness. I stroll into the bedroom and search
through my closet, throw on an old pair of shorts, a vintage T-shirt,
and head back to the kitchen. With thoughts of Ryan, I finish off the
cold eggs and wonder why he seemed so familiar. I swear I've heard
his voice somewhere before.

7
Coffee Journal (CJ)

IN MY DREAM, someone's crying, but as sleep fades, they appear muffled moans from Nikki's room, sounds of passion, not tears. Grabbing the pillow, I cover my head for a moment until I can't breathe. Another whimper of pleasure and I blush, imagining Nik's horror, knowing I heard every cry of ecstasy. *I'll never tell.* Silence again, but I can't sleep.

Rolling sideways and peeking from beneath the pillow, the laptop winks from the nightstand. I yawn and acquiesce to wakefulness, grab the laptop, and curl into the headboard. For several minutes, I stare bleary-eyed at my blog, until feet thud against the floor—*Shane stepping from Nikki's bed.* At any moment, he'll make a secret exit from Nikki's bedroom.

They're so ridiculous!

I'm not fooled by Nik's pretense of a one-night stand … *Nope!* There's more happening than she lets on, I reason as I recline deeper into the king-sized pillows and position the laptop on my thighs. With no desire to cook breakfast, I open my inbox for the umpteenth time since last night and fret over Ryan McThursten's email. It's been two days since I replied to his message and still no call. *Did he receive my reply?* Of course, he did. The outbox shows the email was delivered 10:02 a.m.—two days ago.

Nik's bedroom door squeaks open and shut. Feet patter lightly toward the staircase. Shane's shoes squish down the stairs. And I imagine him flinching with every step. I'm itching to scream, I HEAR YOU! Or better yet, open the door and say, GOOD MORNING, SHANE! I snicker, imagining him tripping down the stairs, caught absconding like a coward. A lover kicked out before daybreak by a discreet paramour. *Poor Shane ... Or is there something else going on.* The front door closes with a perceptible click.

Why is Nik hiding the affair? It's impossible with our rooms sharing paper-thin walls. I can almost hear them breathe (well not literally). I shake my head in disbelief and wonder how long this will keep up. I hope she doesn't drop him the moment the affair becomes serious. Or will Shane end it, frustrated by her unwillingness to commit? I hope neither. Nik deserves a good man in her life. But I wish they'd drop the pretense. We're both grown woman with needs, and I'm not judging. I could care less they're having sex in the next room. But apparently, Nik's uncomfortable with my proximity. *Well, Allie ...* It's time to assure her lil' sis is okay with her guest.

I exhale, stare at the screen, and for the third time, reread Ryan McThursten's email.

Mr. McThursten, have you bailed on me again?

Elusive joy wanes uncertain. Had I misunderstood his intent? Thoroughly, I scan his message to the last word, then, inconceivably, at the end of the email is an attachment. That's a major oversight.

How'd I miss it?

Clicking download, the attachment opens to Ryan's manuscript. "Hmmm... " Did he expect me to start before we speak? *No,* his email clearly states he wants to talk. Perhaps he's waiting for me to call. Just as I'm about to compose another email, my blog site chimes a heavenly harp alert. A new comment from a blogger named Coffee Journal.

"Like your blog title, Coffee Dialogue."

Thanks, I respond cerebrally, *and who are you pray tell?*

Curiously, I click Coffee Journal's avatar—a green quill pen, and a white coffee cup. A bold three-dimensional, forest-green door with a brass lion head knob appears. *Wow, so real . . .* My impulse is to turn the cyber knob and peek inside the virtual world. With that thought, the doorknob spins. Words oscillate a large gold font:

Come In.

Placing the cursor over the knob, I click once. The door opens to a stained-vintage, purple background. Words vacillate.

WELCOME TO COFFEE JOURNAL (CJ)

The page is enchanting with a curling Edwardian Script font. Three-dimensional bay windows end at dark wooden floors, creating an illusion of being inside looking out onto a tree-lined street. In the middle of the virtual room, stacked books sprawl chocolate floors around two velvet wingback chairs anchoring an antique table, a cozy reading space. Remarkably, the chairs swivel, an invitation to take a seat, or in the virtual world, a request to click and read. *Wow . . .* The graphics are impressive, and I'm sure the artistry belongs to a professional web designer. My cursor blinks over the rose wingback chair. Words appear:

PLEASE SIT AND READ MY POETRY.

I click, and the chair swivels to another page, revealing poems, Haiku, and ballads. I try the other chair, the purple one, and again, words appear.

PLEASE SIT AND READ MY SHORT STORIES.

A page unfolds, chronicling Coffee Journal's—CJ's travels overseas and many short stories. I click back to the cozy reading space with wingback chairs flanking an antique table holding two white coffee mugs. Cream foam etched with latte Art in the shape of a quill pen, and heart adorns each cup. I click the quill pen. Foam disperses, and coffee dwindles in slow sinking motion—an illusion of being sipped. When the cup empties, the bottom drops to another page. CJ's bio appears with a single line:

POETRY AND COFFEE ARE THE ONLY CONSTANTS IN MY LIFE.

No name, no background, like me, he or she prefers anonymity. I click the foam heart. Just as the first cup, coffee dwindles, opening to photos of a coffee shop named Poet's Corner. The street outside the cafe appears like the scene from the virtual bay windows. Enthralled, I comment: "Love your web design, it's so beguiling. Makes me want to stay and read forever in the cozy space. Is there such a place?" I wait for a response, imagining fingers poised to respond, but nothing appears.

My blog beeps with comments from two bloggers: *The Storytelling Epicurean,* and again, *Undaunted.* Avoiding Undaunted, I click first on *The Storytelling Epicurean's* avatar (a white chef's hat). A page opens to glossy, life-sized photos of mouthwatering cuisine with recipes and lyrical narratives expressing the recipe's origin. I salivate over a decadent chocolate dessert oozing with cream, and pages of tasty-looking dishes until my stomach growls hungrily. *Hmmm*... I imagine preparing these recipes in our underutilized kitchen. *Maybe I will*... And I click subscribe, now a follower of *The Storytelling Epicurean.*

I hesitate on *Undaunted's* comment then bravely read: "Thanks for the information. I'm clueless about the publishing world, and I'm trying to publish my novel. Your blog is insightful."

Undaunted. I wonder what inspired that name? I can only imagine a result of her poetry. I click the avatar—a photoshopped picture of a rose transposed over a twentyish-looking blonde with green eyes. The altered photo gives her face ghostly transparency; only the eyes and hair are distinct. The page opens with a pure white design, laced with a reddish tint, which appears like blood oozing from the page's edge. The background is a faded almost invisible bed of white rumpled sheets and pillows. In the middle, lie a single red rose, its image, a lurid red in contrast to faint white sheets, creates intrigue.

Like an intruder spying through a peephole into someone's bedroom, I glimpse her world for the first time. Short stories expose tormenting relationships. Bitter, bloody, bruised poems infested and crusted with scabs seethe distrust and hatred, too painful to read.

Soiled and troubled by her words, I quickly skip to her bio but find only a picture of a single red rose. I don't know how to respond to her work. It's so personal and raw, I feel like an intruder. But I have to reply to her comment. So, I write, "Don't give up on your book. Keep trying," I remark simply. But my heart wants to say, I'm so sorry for your pain, and the asshole who brutally betrayed you. A triple knock on the door pulls me from *Undaunted's* world.

"Allie!" Nik inquired on the other side. She opens the door slowly and switches on the light.

Brightness stabs my eyes, and I flinch and squint with one eye open. "Are you okay?"

"Just on the computer," I murmured, rueful of my idleness. I'm by no means enjoying being unemployed. And getting up at the crack of dawn every morning to be useful, has grown stale. I sit straight and press my back into the headboard, blinking rapidly until Nik's worried glare clarifies.

"I'm leaving, but I thought I'd check on you before I left. I thought something might be wrong when I didn't hear you in the kitchen."

"Nope, just felt like blogging, besides, you barely eat my breakfast anyway."

"I'm sorry, Allie," she said, leaning into the door frame. "I don't have much of an appetite lately. But one of these mornings, I'll surprise you," she said, veering to another topic. "So, you're over the writer's block?"

"Nope, but I'm making progress on my blog."

"Oh, that's a good start," she said with raspy words and swallowing audibly.

Detecting subtle changes, I sit straight with concern and study Nik closely. Is she losing weight? Maybe she's just overworked, but her sallow skin and strained voice tell me she's coming down with something. That's unusual for Nik. She's always had a strong constitution and never gets sick. I'm the one forever catching some nasty bug. "Are you okay—"

"Allie, stop looking at me like that."

"Like what?"

"Like that! That probing, shrewd, suspicious glare mom gets when she suspects something's wrong. Next, you'll be feeling my forehead for a temperature. It freaks me out!"

I chuckle because she's right. Mom did have a second sense about her daughter's health. We couldn't put anything past her. Regardless, Nik's touchy this morning. If it weren't for her bark, I'd believe her. When she's this tetchy, it means she's hiding something. "Well! Excuse me for being concerned."

"There's nothing to be concerned about," she said, smiling wanly and glancing away from my probing eyes. "So, stop worrying. It's just a little scratchy throat."

That's a blatant lie? She's trying to conceal her illness, but why? Is the neck rub feigned to appease my concern? "You sure that's all? Maybe you should take a day off."

"Can't, busy calendar today."

Busy calendar? "Do you know how silly that sounds?" God, she's just like dad, so dedicated to his work he'd never take a day off even if he was dying. I guess I understand. There were days at McClelland when I worked through colds and other maladies, but I can't help worrying. I rarely see Nik sick.

"As I said, it's just my throat. I'll be fine. Well, I'm heading out. I guess I won't see you until tomorrow morning," Nik said, turning off the light. I suspect to hide the pallor of her complexion from my probing eyes. Just as Nik's about to close the door, my blog chimes with another comment from Coffee Journal (CJ).

"What's that?"

"Oh, it's just some blogger commenting on my site."

"Male or female?"

"I can't tell. They're using a pseudonym."

"Be careful, Allie. Don't put too much of your personal information on the web. Well, I'm leaving. I won't be home until late. I have to attend another boring business affair which will probably run late into the evening. You'll be asleep when I get home."

"I hope Shane's there to help you enjoy it." She doesn't reply but throws me a look that says he's not up for discussion. "Oh, tell Shane to stop sneaking out and have breakfast with us one morning," I said straightforward, fully aware she'll say no, but it's worth a try.

Nik lifts her brow and opens her mouth to snap back, but instead, she replies with aplomb. "I'll think about it when you write the first chapter of your novel." She pulls the door then turns with a grin and says, "Love ya, sis."

She's annoyed, so I press my lips suppressing a grin. "Love you, too." The door shuts behind Nik. I stare at the closed door, questioning why she's concealing her illness. I hope it's only a sore throat as she says and nothing serious. Maybe she's just overworked. But I suspect it's more than she's revealing. Slinking into the pillows, I return to CJ's comment.

"Do you like coffee?"

Hmmm, isn't it obvious with a blog named Coffee Dialogue? I think but reply kindly, "Yes, I drink a cup every morning."

"Dark, medium, or light?" CJ typed speedily.

"Medium with light cream, no sugar," I replied even quicker.

"I like mine dark, bold, no cream or sugar."

Okay, Mr. or Mrs. Bold-with-no-cream-or-sugar. Where's this conversation leading? I pause for a moment—a response fails me. Then a picture pops on the screen of a window overlooking a waterfront in the distance of a brilliant aurora exploding through trees. CJ's not a New Yorker. Wherever he or she lives, dawn is just arriving. "Beautiful view," I typed with skeptical pecks, wondering if the view is from CJ's home or a stock photo from the web.

"Right now, I'm watching dawn from my office window. It's so spectacular; I thought I'd share. Can you see the sunrise from where you are?"

Small talk with an online stranger. I'm reticent to engage but deem the innocuous chat fun and continue with caution. "Yes, I can, from my bedroom window," is all I reveal.

"Where do you live?"

Nikki's warning resonates in my mind, but there's no harm in revealing the state I reside. Besides, I deleted my biography. There's no other personal information. I pause, and then type each letter with slow fingers, stopping and pausing, twisting my mouth and squinting indecisively. I relent, and press send. "New York and you?"

"Alexandria."

"Virginia … I attended Emsworth University in the District of Columbia, not too far away." I'd often visited Alexandria while in school, admiring the quaint historic town. "I've never met anyone from Alexandria."

"Now you've met me," CJ responded with a smiling emoji.

Not really. You're just disembodied words in cyberspace. I pause and consider whether CJ's a man or woman. God, it would be embarrassing if it's a teenage prankster. Swiftly I type, "How old are you? I'm not talking to someone underage am I?"

"I'm twenty-five," CJ replied with a grinning emoji. "I assure you I'm old enough. How about you?"

"Twenty-four. You can't be sure these days with all the stuff happening over the Internet."

"I agree. You have to be wise, though it's difficult to tell the good guys from the bad online. But I assure you, I'm one of the good guys."

So, you say. Why would I trust a total stranger? That would be foolish. *Good guys.* "So, you're male?"

"Yes, and you?"

"Female." From his poetry, I'd already pictured a man. His choice of words appeared masculine. Or was it his preference for dark coffee? Unexpectedly, I'm curious about this coffee-loving poet. But this is probably a passing conversation that'll stagnate after today. Again, I'm lost for words as I watch the blinking cursor. Communicating with total strangers isn't exactly my cup of tea. I'd rather talk with a person I can see, hear, and touch, not just words.

In the dark, I stare at the cursor with horror stories of cyber offenders and psychopaths plotting words, crafting false personas to garner an unsuspecting victim's confidence, criminals gathering pieces of other's lives and feigning charming benevolence, all the while luring the gullible into his scheme, floods my mind. Suddenly, hesitant, my sensible half wants to end the conversation, ignore our brief words. But the inquisitive half is intrigued and wants the nascent cybernetic experience, wants to uncover intents lurking beneath CJ's typed words. His blog site is so compelling, his poetry superb, his photos reveal a lovely soul. I ignore my fear and type, "So, I see you like taking pictures."

A response doesn't come. I imagined the blinking cursor CJ's mind, deliberating his next words. After a long pause, I assume he's stepped away from the computer. Or as I had, grown suspicious and fled the conversation. Curiously, I feel slighted, wanting him to respond. Instantly, I'm embarrassed by my pathetic need. *Maybe this is how it starts, a gullible person* sucked into dangerous liaisons, looking for companionship in stranger's words.

But you're smarter than that Allie. Step away.

Throwing my legs over the bed and sliding to the edge, I head toward the kitchen with my laptop, place it on the counter, and start preparing coffee. All the while, my ears are apperceptive to every blog alert.

Behind me, the laptop chimes a heavenly invitation. I stir expectantly, wondering if it's CJ, but I don't want to appear eager, so I wait until the coffee's ready. Then I take a seat at the laptop and beam at CJ's response. Suddenly, I'm relieved like someone receiving a much-awaited call after the first date. The other party has confirmed his interest. But after knowing him all of twenty minutes, my interest is puzzling. I continue to read his reply.

"Sorry, I couldn't respond sooner. I had to take a phone call. To answer your question, yes, photography is another passion. These are pictures of my hometown. Now and then, I update my blog with photos from hikes in the countryside." Before I can respond, a photo of a big red mug filled with dark coffee appears. "I'm having my morning brew. Have you had yours yet?"

My curious mind lost in the photo, sleuths every item for a clue to his identity. The red coffee mug sits atop a well-organized oak desk. Only the room's border is visible with truncated edges of items: A windowsill overrun with leaves of potted plants, a dark oak bookcase in the distance with blurred book titles. I enlarge the photo to one hundred and thirty percent, trying to discern book titles. But the letters remain blurred. On mossy green walls, the bottom of a picture frame provides no clue of the photo it holds. To the right of the frame, a tan leather sofa arm is discernable. On the desk, a stainless-steel laptop lies beside a large MAC desktop. A mouse pad reads Poet's Corner. Boundaries of CJ's office hold only minuscule views of his life. There are no clues to the psychopath I've imagined. *But what would those clues look like?* I wouldn't know, but from what I see, his office appears normal.

I type with quick strokes, a response to his last question. "I'm drinking it now. It's not my usual brand, but my sister's strong Chilean blend."

"Take a sip with me."

His words resonate intimacy, and I imagine persuasive eyes and sultry intonations. The numbness holding me dispassionate melts a little. His prompt is too irresistible to ignore. Cautiously, as I've done with every urge to defy practicality, I hesitate, but something in me wants to deviate. Tired of doing the right thing, I defiantly mumble, "What the hell!" There's no one else to share my morning. Besides, it might be fun sipping coffee with a disembodied stranger from Alexandria. So, I reply, "Sure."

"Nice. Now on the count of three, sip with me."

I laugh nervously like someone on a first date. *What the heck, Allie?* I chuckle as CJ types the countdown.

"One…"

"Two…"

"Three … Sip."

Drolly, I take a sip and snicker with surprise at how good that felt. So, this is what my life has come down to, sharing coffee with a stranger over the Internet. It's just too ridiculous to believe.

"Thanks for sharing coffee with me. Maybe we can share coffee moments again sometimes," CJ typed.

What! I admit that was interesting in a bizarre way, but why would he want to share coffee with a stranger? *Is something wrong with him?* Is this his usual approach with women online? *Or is he just a lonely poet?* I'm wary but intrigued by CJ's blog and poetry. It can't hurt connecting with other bloggers with similar interest, *can it?* Like a reticent date playing hard to get, I type gingerly, "Perhaps."

8
Falling Vases

A LOUD SHATTER wakes me from sleep. I squint at light flooding the room and sit up in bed, believing I'd fallen asleep during the middle of the day. Then I remember working late on the computer and stumbling to bed around midnight. I glance at the clock. *Eight in the morning,* I've overslept. I must be tired, or I'm coming down with Nik's illness. Why didn't she wake me? Now that I think about it, I didn't hear her come in last night. If she had, it was past midnight. Did I dream or imagine glass breaking? Did Nikki drop a glass, but why is she home so late?

I exit the room, lean over the banister, and glance below and call, "Nikki? Is that you?" There's no response, but I sense someone in the kitchen. I hurry downstairs and turn the corner into the dining room much too fast. My flip-flops slip on something, sending my legs airborne.

I catch the dining table chair with one hand, the other breaks a hard fall with a smack on the floor and a sharp pain rips my palm. Broken glass and scattered roses surround me, while my blood reddens a pool of water. Scattered roses agitate my mind with an elusive, fuzzy figure approaching across cold, dark wooden floors in black loafers. The image recedes, obscured again. Pressure clamps my chest. When the room begins to spin, I close my eyes, hold the chair tight, breathe deeply, and wait for the spinning to stop. My mind settles, but the room grows frosty, downright freezing. The sweet scent of roses putrefies. A shadow moves across my eyelid, and I open my eyes quickly, staring up and around the room, then back at the anxiety-provoking scene on the floor. The putrid odor dwindles.

Gripping the chair, I rise, tiptoe around shimmering glass toward the faucet, and let the cold water rinse the blood from my palm. The narrow cut isn't as bad as it feels, just a lot of blood and a biting sting. I wrap my hand in paper towels, pull several more roles, and start cleaning the spill. Bending over the roses, I ponder the memory elicited of black loafers. I close my eyes, willing the image to reappear, but like thick yarn threading a needle, the image refuses to twine mind's eye. Over the last two years, the images have been fleeting, but never this vivid, and never that particular image. Is my memory coming back?

As I stoop to the floor to pick up glass shards, I wonder if Nikki brought the roses from her business dinner or perhaps they're a gift from Shane. I dump glass detritus into the garbage and retrieve more paper towels. When I turn from the counter, I freeze with my eyes on a single red rose, and rumpled sheets spread across the laptop screen. The blog looks more ominous than it had three days ago. Who turned on the computer? I turned it off last night, and I haven't visited Undaunted's blog since that first time. Did Nikki use my computer? No, she knows how sensitive I am about privacy. She wouldn't, but no one else could have. Agitated, I log off and close the laptop. Finding another vase, I fill it with water, twelve roses, and leave them near the sink.

I cast my eyes toward the stairs, wondering if Nikki is still home. It's unlike her to leave before saying goodbye. Recalling how pale she'd looked the previous morning and the scratchy throat; I hope she's not in bed sick. I rush to the second floor and knock twice. No answer. Hesitantly, I open the door a crack, fearing Nik and Shane's shocked faces peering back. But instead, Nik's neatly made bed comes into view. Did she come home last night? *She had to, the roses.* Wandering to my room, I find the mobile and dial Nik's number. On the other end, Nik's winded breath and rapid footsteps echo through the phone.

"Hey, Allie."

"Nik, you had me worried. Why didn't you wake me up?"

"I had to meet a client early and didn't want to disturb you. You always wake up so early. I thought you could use the sleep. Allie, can I call you later? I'm rushing to a meeting. We'll talk soon, love you," she said, disconnecting the call.

I'm relieved she's okay but irked by her quick dismissal. Motionless, I stand with the phone in my hand deliberating another uneventful day and wishing for some excitement. I suspect the daily tedium of sameness has triggered resentment toward Nik's busy life. A living purgatory comes to mind as I stomp downstairs, pausing on the bottom step with the drone of city noise through an open window. Oddly troubled life outside evolves while I remain the same, I close the window quickly. *The city continues without me.* I wish time would pause until I'm ready to start again. It's then, with the window closed and the room silent I realize the air conditioner is off, but why is the room so cold.

I gasp, startled by a loud crash. "Not again!" I rush to the kitchen, finding the vase in shards on the floor. *That's impossible.* I placed it toward the back next to the sink. *Didn't I?* "What's going on?" Again, I clean the floor, baffled, and recounting my actions. I recall a month ago when I washed a tumbler with hot water and placed it upside down on the cold counter, the steam collided with the cold and the glass slid and slipped from the edge. Maybe that's what just happened. *But I didn't use hot water.* The only explanation is the flowers were too close to the edge and fell. Searching for something plastic or unbreakable in the cabinet, I spy a tin storage canister and place the roses in the center of the dining table. "There you go, pesky flowers, safe from the edge."

Instantly, the room spins. I sway, bump the table, and catch the flowers tipping over the laptop. With the familiar pressure on my chest, I grip the table's edge, close my eyes, breathe deep, and soothe my way back from that anxious place with images of Grandma Blu's porch. A safe place Nik and I sat beside grandma Blu watching fireflies and stars light the summer night—a place of calm that always allays worries. The spinning stops. I haven't had two consecutive attacks this strong since college. Since the layoff, they've grown stronger. Maybe I need to eat. Yesterday, I barely touched a morsel of food, but right now, I need caffeine.

Discovering the coffee canister empty, I search the fridge and cabinets, realizing I haven't been to the grocers in two or maybe three weeks when I notice the wilted veggies and molded bread, which I discard quickly. Again, believing I've overlooked a hidden container of coffee, I scour the cabinets only finding Nik's recent addiction—ginger tea. She says it's for her throat, but I still think she's hiding something.

Well, it's time to get some fresh air anyway, Allie. If anything can motivate me to leave the duplex, it's coffee, although, I dread putting on a pretense of normalcy. For that reason, I've been reclusive, ignoring friend's request to socialize after the layoff, afraid they'll see how mirthless and lost I've become. And besides, I don't need their pity or want to inflict my sorrows on others. For now, socializing is pointless. Only the immediate need to figure out the rest of my life holds meaning. I recognize this emotional funk and know it will soon pass, but such knowledge doesn't make the present any easier.

Before I change my mind, I rush upstairs and bandage my palm. A sharp snap catches my wrist, and I hope it's not sprained from the hard fall. I sense it swelling and stiffening but hurry to dress, throwing a T-shirt over a gauzy white skirt, and pulling my hair, again, into a one-sided braid. Quickly, I wash my face, brush my teeth, and study my skin in the mirror, expecting telltale lines of grief, but the same face, a little thinner, stares back. I apply light lip gloss and bronzer and wonder when I've ever worried about my appearance so much. I've never cared about what people think or say. But why do I bother now? Another bout of anxiousness surfaces, but I thwart resistance and rush out the door.

9

She'll Show Herself Soon

THE ELEVATOR OPENS to a nervous teenage boy, reigning multicolored leashes of several large dogs. In the corner, a teenage girl glued to her mobile never looks up as I sidled next to a professional-looking couple holding hands. Before the elevator door closes, I've sized everyone up. Awkwardly shy, the teenage girl uses the cell phone to disengage from society. From the adolescent boy's nervous state, I'm sure dog walking is a newly acquired summer job. And the couple, although they're holding hands, appear stiff, almost strangers by each other's side—perhaps a one-night stand or new affair.

The moment the elevator door closes, my cell phone rings with a ringtone I'd assigned Ryan McThursten. After three days of waiting, I refuse to let his call go to voicemail and fumble quickly through my bag. Averse to broadcasting my conversation to the small group, I lower my head, turn toward the elevator wall, and whisper, "Hello."

"Allison, this is Ryan. Have I caught you at a bad time?"

"No, no, I'm just on the elevator, heading to the supermarket for a little shopping, but I can talk." *Did you have to tell him where you're going?* I disparage with a roll of my eyes.

"I'm sorry it's taken me so long to get back to you. I had some personal business that required traveling."

Expecting a reserved demeanor, I'm surprised by his engaging tone. "I hope nothing serious?" I hear my voice invade the silent space. Self-consciously, I throw a cursory glance around the elevator then back at my flip-flop-clad feet, wishing the elevator would hurry to the lobby so I can talk privately.

"No, nothing I couldn't handle."

"I'm glad you called. I thought you changed your mind." I listen intently and picture a contrite expression on his attractive face as he apologizes for his capricious behavior, explaining he'd given me the wrong impression of his character.

"I'm generally not this unreliable, but I had to attend an urgent family matter..."

I open my mouth to inquire, then pause; wary of intruding on his privacy. I know so little of his personal history. As a rule, when an author signs a contract, I try to gather information about their life. But with the sudden layoff, I hadn't had a chance to decipher Ryan's past. Is he married with children? Are his parents alive? Where did he go to school? What's his favorite pastime? These are aspects I would have discovered by now.

"...But, believe me; I'm ready to give you my full attention. I won't be changing course again. I'm eager to hear your suggestions," Ryan said through my thoughts.

"Well, there are a few minor changes I'd like to discuss with you later..." The elevator door opens, rousing deafening barks from excited dogs as they scramble on claws, pushing everyone aside, and jerking the teenage boy from the elevator. I hold back, waiting until the elevator empties, and then saunter behind the couple, and the teenage girl still lost in her mobile. "Ryan, sorry, got a little noisy there. So, I'll start today and by the end of the week, call you with feedback. Is that okay?" Loud barks render Ryan's voice inaudible, but I catch the tail end of his question as he asks how to pay for my time. Finally, I can say I'm ready for business after taking an essential step to self-employment. Cupping the phone, I respond, "I've just added PayPal to my website. I'll send you the link when I get home."

"Sounds good, by the way, I'm sorry about McClelland. But honestly, I think you're better off without an employer's limits. You can call the shots now."

I approach the sunny exit, pull sunglasses from my shoulder bag, and cover my eyes, not so much to block the light, but my watery eyes. Given my doubts, I thank Ryan for his support and end the call.

When I exit the air-conditioned lobby, a balmy breeze lifts my skirt and cloaks my bare legs with warmth. Although humidity is oppressive, my sun-deprived skin welcomes summer. I turn my head and catch the young woman from the elevator turning the corner. Even now, her eyes remain glued to the mobile. I raise my brows in disbelief, hoping she doesn't fall into a manhole or collide with a car. On the corner, the stiff couple part ways, she enters a taxi, he continues on foot in the opposite direction, occasionally peering back until the cab turns the corner. Hmm, I'm sure a one-night-stand goodbye, both wondering if they'll ever see each other again. Across the street, the tense dog walker struggles as he's pulled behind impatient dogs into Carl Schurz Park. I hope he makes it back intact.

Instead of the beeline to the grocery, I cross the street into the park, following a narrow path straight to the promenade overlooking the East River. I lean over the railing peering into the water, when behind me, a pleasant voice says, "You look lost." I turn and notice the elderly woman I'd seen a few days ago from the window. Up close, she appears in her late eighties, and the small dog by her side looks just as old as she.

"No, I live just a block away."

"No, dear, I didn't mean geographically lost," she said with a slight chuckle. "I meant spiritually. I've seen that expression before."

Am I that transparent? In only a few minutes, she'd seen the truth. Astonished and bothered simultaneously, I try to negate her assessment with a sunnier disposition, happy-go-lucky Allie. A role I've played many times, but I'm tired of performing and banish the pretense, unafraid to bare my true self in front of this woman. I've always felt comfortable around the elderly, maybe it's because time has rendered them vulnerable, exposed their truth, there's no reason to hide my own. I stroll toward the bench and sit beside her. "What gave me away?" I asked, wondering how she'd seen through my façade.

"Well, when you've lived as long as I have, many qualities about people become apparent. You remind me of someone I knew years ago. She had that same look and carriage when she was unhappy."

"Oh," is all I say because she's right. She'd seen through my pretense of normalcy. I look toward the railing at a bird she stares at intently.

"You know, we make life a lot harder than it should be. That pigeon there knows its purpose. Unfortunately, humans fill their days with unnecessary matters and doings. It's taken me a long time to realize what's important. I'd be happy with that bird's simple life," she said with a chuckle. Turning her face toward me for the first time since I sat beside her, she asked, "What's your worry, dear?"

Again, I'm surprised by her boldness. "Well, I recently lost my job, so I am, as you say, lost."

"Ah, I see. Well, that's easy to cure. You just find another job, but I assume that's not so easy these days." She pauses and with filmy eyes glazed wisdom's whitish-gray, looks past my face. Her eyes remind me of Grandma Blu's. "You're so young and should be enjoying yourself. Perhaps a little fun is called for?"

"I suppose," I said, catching her analytical expression. And as I've often done with the elderly, I ignore time-battered skin, imagining a youthful soul disguised beneath. I study her face, reconstruct time, and conjure a bright-eyed, young girl. The image fades with a thick-accented voice. A young woman with radiant, chocolate skin approaches with curious eyes.

"Mrs. Edelstein, it's time to leave," she said, addressing the woman beside me with a thick, Jamaican accent.

Mrs. Edelstein looks straight ahead, searches the side of the bench with her hand, and locates what I thought at first a walking cane, but it's a Hoover cane used by the blind. She holds out her elbow, and her aid slides her hand beneath, hoisting her from the bench.

She's blind, but how did she see me.

"I'm sorry; I didn't know—"

"That I'm blind," she interjected. "People usually don't until I use this thing," she said taping the Hoover Cane on the ground. Dear, I see better than most, elements sighted people seldom notice." She faces me with glazed eyes staring past my face. "Someone's with you."

I look around, believing she meant someone was behind me, but there's no one there. "I'm not with anyone," I said.

"She'll show herself soon," she said.

Puzzled by her statement, I stare dubiously and mumble, "She?"

"She's someone you knew once, someone who was in your life a short time. She's found her way back."

Someone I knew once. Found her way back, from where? I ponder with furrowed brows. She's senile and has me confused with someone else, I believe.

The Jamaican woman throws me a keen eye. "You should listen, she's usually right," she said, leading Mrs. Edelstein away.

"It was nice speaking with you," I said.

"You, as well, dear. You'll find your way soon," Mrs. Edelstein said, tugging at the sluggish dog's leash. The Yorkshire terrier waddles close as the aid leads them off the promenade onto a tree-covered path, their clothing patchworks green, pink, and blue through shrubbery then disappears from view.

She's usually right, rings in my ear. About what? I've heard the blind have keener senses than seeing people, but what ability would allow such perception. And who has found her way back? Okay, Allie, forget it. She's senile and confused, I think, stepping into the grocer, but Mrs. Edelstein's assistant is confident in her abilities.

Nonsense...

Desperate for caffeine, I head to the breakfast aisle, filling my basket with two glossy bags of expensive French Roast coffee. I didn't prepare a grocery list but bookmarked a recipe on my mobile. *The Storytelling Epicurean's* blog opens to a recipe I've craved for days—Polenta Lasagna with tomatoes and peppers. I peruse aisles filling my basket with ingredients and some of Nikki's favorite treats.

At the register, an aloof cashier rings up items quickly. I raise my shades on my head and pull the debit card from my purse. Bitterly, the cashier asks, "Debit or Credit?"

I smile, but she remains stoic. "Debit," I said, annoyed at her frosty customer service. If she's miserable she's young enough to change jobs, I think. I glance at a photo taped to the cash register. Two children, between the ages of nine and ten, recline on a carpeted floor, smiling up at the camera. She can't be their mother. She's much too young. I imagine a teenage pregnancy, a high school dropout with limited career choices. She catches my eyes, and I say, "Beautiful children."

Finally, a warm smile cracks her frozen countenance. She brushes the photo gently. Her eyes crescent; pinched lips soften. "My little ones; they're my world," she said.

The silver lining to her dreary job, I muse. "You're blessed." I don't know why I said that, perhaps, to provoke a smile.

10

Precursor To A Murder

BACK AT THE DUPLEX, I prepare coffee and ponder Mrs. Edelstein's comment. *"Someone's with you. She'll show herself soon."* If she's not senile, who did she mean? Perhaps she meant my college roommate Lisa, who I'd intended to call. A floral scent skims my nostrils. I peer at dark, wilting roses that were fresh and colorful an hour ago. Perhaps they're day's old flowers Nikki brought from the office.

My cell phone buzzes with an alert from CJ, but I don't respond right away. Comforted by rising steam from the hot cup, I head to my new workspace, the rarely used breakfast nook tucked in the kitchen's far corner, with an adjoining view of the park. Sliding atop the cushioned bench, I lose myself in intersecting pathways snaking through the park. Then I remember the elevator conversation with Ryan and my promise to email the PayPal link. With haste, I do as I promised.

My first client. My own business. A glimmer of joy escapes with the thought of self-employment and earning my first payment. It won't be easy. I understand it requires much work, but I have nothing but time, I think. I venture to my blog and stare wide-eyed at growing followers. In twenty-four hours I've gained seventy-five, increasing followership to three hundred, more than the paltry fifty a week ago. Twenty comments await my response. *Undaunted's* left a request with a telephone number, a (202) area code I recognize as the District of Columbia.

Undaunted: "Please call me. I'm interested in using your services. As I've stated, I've been trying to publish my book with no success. Maybe you can help."

Remembering the bloody poetry, I can only imagine the rawness of her story. Delving into torturous words is troubling, but I can't be selective, not at this stage of freelancing. I jot down her number and continue to read comments from authors looking for publishing information. My blog chimes another alert from CJ. Is it another coffee moment request? I doubt it at this hour.

CJ: "How's your morning going?"

I'm eager to respond but hold back, not wanting to appear overzealous. So, I ignore CJ's comment and inspect the new PayPal feature on my blog. Elation follows when I notice my first customer purchase, but I'm confused by the pending status. A Patrice Jensen of the District of Columbia forgot to submit a manuscript. *Hmmm, did PayPal alert her?* I scribble her telephone number next to Undaunted's. The digits appear similar. Am I experiencing a dyslexic moment? Plainly, the numbers are the same—Undaunted is Patrice Jensen. Maybe the pending purchase is why she asked me to call.

After ten minutes of avoiding CJ, I finally respond, "Good morning." His response is instant, eliciting an image of him glued to his computer. Or perhaps, he's installed the blog app on his cell phone as I had.

"Good morning, Coffee Dialogue. You're starting late today. I was admiring your blog's improvement. Looks like you're ready for business."

"Yes, the improvement is why I overslept," I respond with a frowning emoji. "I was up late installing new features."

"Have you had coffee yet? I'm on my second cup now, but I'd love to share a sip," CJ typed.

Gazing at the cup in front of me, I'm amazed how in only one day, reluctance has morphed to willingness. And I wonder why? Does this say something about my character, or am I just bored, filling an empty void? Letting go and having fun is so hard, my rational mind forever thwarts foolhardy impulses. *Allie, he's not asking for sex.* Besides, it's just words, words with someone I'll probably never meet. *"Step outside your comfort zone sometimes, and you'll discover there's nothing to fear,"* more of Grandma Blu's wisdom. But I'm certain she didn't mean dealing with a total stranger over the Internet. But it's all innocent, I think. "We can do that," I typed.

"What are you wearing, and where are you?" CJ typed.

Whoa! Alarm thwarts spontaneity with rationality. "Why do you ask?"

"That must have come off the wrong way. You probably think I'm some pervert. I assure you I'm not. But given we've only just met, there's no way to judge my character. I'm visual and just want to picture you as we sip coffee. Is that okay?"

He's right. There's no way to discern his character. Not yet, so I respond with a blushing emoji, "Next you'll be asking the color of my undies," I jest, impulsiveness defeating caution. But I genuinely want to see if he takes the bait and how far he's willing to go. If he goes further, his real character will unfold.

"Hmmm … I'm afraid to reply to that. I'll appear like one of those online perverts."

"It was my suggestion, not yours," I reply with a bashful emoji. I'm somewhat reassured, but still wary. Maybe Mrs. Edelstein is right. *"Maybe a little fun is called for?"* I continue the playful exchange, typing a detailed description of my surroundings. "I'm in the kitchen, sitting with my back against the breakfast nook—a mahogany pedestal table circled by a white-cushioned bench. It adjoins the window overlooking the park. Right now, the sun is streaming across the table, onto my light blue T-shirt and gauzy white skirt. My legs stretch to the opposite end where my bare feet rest on sunlit cushions. Now, can you picture me?"

"Perfectly! It sounds serene and inviting."

I remember snippets of CJ's office from the photo and imagine him sitting in front of the computer. "I bet you're at your desk, staring at a large screen. So, what are you wearing?"

"You would have been right an hour ago. But after the rush crowd has left, I take advantage of the quiet and write in my favorite spot near the window. I'm sitting in the velvet wingback chair you saw on my blog. My laptop is on the antique table, and occasionally, I glance at the surrounding scenery through bay windows. My outfit is simple, your basic black T-shirt and jeans."

I picture the cozy space with two velvet wingback chairs surrounded by books. At first, I'd believed the area was a library or in someone's home. "What business do you work for?"

"I own a coffee shop."

That explains his blog title and love for coffee. "Impressive, so, you're a coffee enthusiast, writer, and business owner. What's the name of your shop?"

"Poet's Corner."

That explains his avatar, the quill pen that scribbles Poet's Corner underneath a white coffee mug. "Great name, what inspired it?"

"Well, the shop serves as an artist's venue to showcase their work during the weekend. You know poets, writers, singers, and musicians. We also serve some tasty coffee creations named after famous poets to enhance the theme of the shop."

"What a wonderful idea! It must be a large space."

"It's a decent size for what we offer. Our patrons describe it as cozy comfy. There's a small stage that overlooks the main room or living room as regulars call it. That's exactly the ambiance I envisioned when I took over the shop. So, Ariel, I'm looking at my laptop, waiting for your coffee-sip countdown."

"Oh, it's my turn today."

"Yes, you control this session."

"Okay, well, then..." Wanting to be original, I type, "Raise your cup. Press it to your lips. Now sip." Slowly lifting the cup to my lip and taking a swig, I picture the red mug pressed to his lip and his throat rippling with coffee. Does he have a mustache, perhaps a beard? Or is he clean-shaven with a short, neat haircut? For a moment, I ponder whether he's attractive, average, or just plain unappealing?

"Aww! That tastes good. I like sharing with you." CJ typed.

My mind pokes at me again. I don't take CJ seriously but playfully respond. "Hmmm ... Do you do this with all the women on the Internet?"

"Nah, just you, I have to admit I've never done anything like this before."

Ha! I bet you have. I want to believe him, but it's unlikely he chose a random female to start sipping coffee with, and if he's not lying, why me? I type, "Why did you choose me?" Quickly, I delete the question and type a lighthearted response to conceal suspicions. "I bet it was my catchy avatar."

"You probably won't believe me, but I figured a blogger named Coffee Dialogue must be a coffee lover like me. And besides coffee, we both have a passion for writing."

How did he discern my passion for writing? Since the layoff, I've written a few short stories and tried my hand at mediocre poetry. Had he read the heated McClelland post? With a grimace, I type, "Yes, I can get keyed-up about writing."

"It's obvious, Coffee Dialogue, or should I call you CD?"

CD sounds so plain. I deliberate a better penname, but nothing comes to mind except Ariel my middle name, which I've always loved. But since he's using his site's initials, I should probably do the same. *Nah!* "You can call me Ariel. And what may I call you?" The cursor blinks ten times before I receive a reply.

"I like the way CJ sounds. Please continue using it. So, Ariel, what constitutes a "perfect" day for you?"

Hmm, I ponder. *No one's ever asked me that question.* But an image of me sitting at my laptop crafting an intriguing story, and by evening, unwinding with a glass of wine after a successful day of writing is all I can picture. I don't convey this because it's too simple. But for me, it would be a perfect day. Instead, I reply, "I've never thought about it."

"What was your first thought when I asked?"

Why am I embarrassed to share this? I don't know this person. My little fantasy is too simplistic, but what does it matter? I type, "Writing a novel in an inspiring place until nightfall and celebrating my creation with loved ones over dinner and a glass of wine," I embellished.

"Then that's your answer. You should strive for that."

Slowly, I type words that prick at my conscious. "I lack inspiration, besides in the real world one needs an income."

"Inspiration is everywhere. You'll find it soon. And I'm sure your talent as an editor will pay the bills."

Inspiration is everywhere, lingers in my mind. "I'm still waiting for a muse to show its face."

CJ replies with a winking emoji, "It will."

Before I can ask CJ what a perfect day looks like for him, another message appears. "Well, Ariel, business is calling. Don't forget our coffee moments tomorrow. Begin your perfect day!"

"You too," I typed sadly, not wanting the conversation to end. Who is this man whose words cause a yearning for more? *Allie, be careful.*

At the bottom of CJ's blog, I click his followers—a whopping ten thousand. How did he gain such a huge following? Did he use the same coffee moment technique? *Allie! You're starting to scare me. Don't let this man inside your head.* You don't need this in your life right now. But like the snooping girlfriend, I read CJ's conversations with his followers. Most are admirers of his poetry and photography. Some are coffee lovers, the majority, poets, and writers praising his blog, much as I had. I notice a few of his followers are now following me. Is that how blogging works, bloggers follow their follower's fans? Then I see Undaunted, and The Storytelling Epicurean are his followers as well. Did they find my blog through CJ?

I continue reading and find no evidence of coffee moments with other bloggers. But I'm horrified when I see every conversation I've had with CJ is visible. *No, no, no!* How embarrassing. Immediately, I want to delete our dialogue, but I can't. I don't want potential customers reading personal moments. I've got to be careful going forward with CJ.

I return to *Undaunted's* request, check the time—ten thirty-five. Apprehensively, I dial her number. The phone rings three times before a woman answer, "Hello," in a cheerful tone, not what I expected after reading her somber prose.

"Hi, may I speak with…" *Should I call her Undaunted or Patrice,* "…Patrice?"

"Yes, who is this?"

"You left a message on my blog, Coffee Dialogue."

"Oh, yes, Coffee Dialogue."

"Please call me Allison," I said with a chuckle.

"Allison, hold on one second," she said. Through the phone, heels clack and a door squeaks and clicks, then silence. "I'm glad you phoned. I wasn't sure you would. I've been looking for an editor for a while. I hired one a year ago but wasn't satisfied with the work. I'm hoping you can take a look and give me your professional opinion, and of course, edit where you see fit."

Her words sound rushed. I believe I've caught her at the wrong time. So, I speak just as fast. "Can you tell me a little about your novel, the genre or storyline?"

Her voice grows lower almost to a whisper and words speed as if she's reading. "It's a thriller novel. The protagonist is a college student who discovers her best friend is involved in unethical business revolving around high-profile, Washington, D.C., figures. The plots filled with blackmail, murder, etcetera, etcetera," she said in a flat voice.

"Sounds thrilling, I can't wait to read it. I noticed your purchase is pending—"

"Yes, I decided to wait for your call before purchasing your service. I didn't see your bio and wanted to hear more about your background first."

"That's smart." How thoughtless of me. Strict anonymity is impossible in the business arena. "Well, I can assure you with six years at

McClelland Publishing, and a communications degree from Emsworth University, I'm qualified. I guess I should put that on my site."

"It would be to your advantage. McClelland's a reputable firm. In fact, they turned down my manuscript, so this is a twist of fate getting the advice of an ex-employee."

"You did—"

In the background, footsteps approach. "Damn it, Poppy! What's taking so long?!" A male voice bellows.

"Oh, um ... I'll upload my manuscript today," Patrice whispered. "Let's talk later and thanks for calling," she said abruptly hanging up.

"That's odd." My overactive imagination conjures a man entering the room just as Patrice hides the phone behind her back, her face, a mask of secrecy. Suddenly, I realize it was desperation I heard in her tone; possibly she didn't want this man overhearing our conversation. *"What's going on with Patrice?"*

An hour later, I receive Patrice's manuscript: *PRECURSOR TO A MURDER.* Swiftly, I browse chapters formatted chronologically like a journal. Midway through the novel, the writing style changes as if written by another person. I halt at a haunting scene of a young naïve student's first encounter with an unctuous blond named Belle. A chill race down my spine.

No, it can't be!

I turn the manuscript over front and back, fan through pages, looking for a note or something that says this is a joke. There's nothing. Immediately, I want to trash the manuscript, delete every terrifying word. Belle, Darnall Hall, and the black Jaguar are elements only I know about, things that happen to me that crazy night. Undaunted knows, but how? I've never spoken a word of that night to anyone. But Undaunted's written the night of the off-campus party as if she were with me. Every word accurately captures that deceptive evening. How could she know unless she was there? I want to close the manuscript, but I continue fearfully to the final chapter, which concludes with a glaring question.

What happened to Belle?

Strangely, I feel the author is asking me directly as if I know the answer. At the bottom of the page, an ominous note reads:

If anything happens to me, please mail this manuscript to Detective Pennington at 1414 Kalorama RD NW, Washington, D.C. 20008 (202) 555-1212

The note jars memories of the large, bronze 1414 plaque above the beautiful Tudor home's door. A place I'd visited in nightmares, and amnesiac ponderings, and never wish to visit again. I'd often wondered who owns the home, and now I still wonder if it belongs to Detective Pennington. I linger over the note with growing apprehension. Who is Patrice Jensen? And how did she find me? Again, I open the manuscript and read chapter one. Engrossed in Belle's ghastly affair with a high-powered Senator, I continue reading until the room dims with afternoon shadows.

11
Drunken Dirge

IN A QUANDARY, my mind seesaws back and forth, trying to discern whether Patrice's cryptic note is a cry for help or merely fiction. Has she discovered information on Belle's mysterious disappearance? If so, why hasn't she gone to the police or this detective Pennington? Why me? The only conclusion I can draw is that she was at the off-campus party and saw me there.

Chewing on my bottom lip, I wrestle with this puzzle. Finally, I tear myself away from the manuscript and head to the wine cooler, all the while, pondering Patrice's true intentions. Filling the glass to the rim, I inhale a much-needed gulp, stare about the room and afternoon shadows heralding dusk. Soon the wine does its magic, suffusing my blood with dizzying warmth. The frenzy of thoughts subsides to a hush. Maybe this is what I've needed, alcohol-induced oblivion. Suddenly, I long for my drinking buddy, and dial her number. Then I realize she's commuting home from work, and just as I'm about to press end call, her voice sails through the phone with the whir of wind.

"Allie!" Catrina screeches through a wind tunnel. The window purrs to a close, silencing the breeze. "What's going on?"

"Cat, you're in the car, I'll call back later."

"Don't worry. I'm using hands-free. What's up?"

"Are you almost home?"

"Almost, I'm on the Sawmill Parkway, but I'm glad you called. You can keep me company. So, what's going on?"

"I'm not sure." I close my eyes and shake my head, annoyed I've allowed Undaunted to fill my brain with worry. I waver between revealing my quandary and saying nothing. But in the past, Cat's always had a knack for talking me through a dilemma and accurately seeing the truth in most matters.

"Allie, are you drinking? Is this *Allie-Alky* I'm speaking to?"

I chuckled at the nickname Cat uses whenever I drink. "I've had a few sips. I needed to relax, shut my brain off for a minute," I reveal. I must be talking fast, or my voice has assumed a high pitch which appears when I drink alcohol. Besides Nikki, Cat's the only other person who detects at a glance my alcoholic persona. I'm sure if I look in the mirror right now, a dreamy-eyed Allie will stare back.

"What's wrong?"

What isn't wrong? I think. A twist of fate or a sick prank has brought chaos into my life again, and I don't believe in pure chance. Patrice has come into my life for a reason, to turn it upside down until she finds Belle. Does she think I had something to do with her disappearance? *"She'll show herself soon."* Is Patrice the woman Mrs. Edelstein was referring to? "Cat, I'm hoping this is all just my overactive imagination, but I could use your brilliant mind as a sounding board."

"This sounds serious. What's going on?"

"I'm freaking out about a manuscript I received today—"

"You got another client? Allie that's great, congrats!"

"Don't congratulate me yet. I'm returning this one. Something's a little odd about the author. Frankly, I'm creeped out. The novel reads like a piece of evidence, not fiction."

"What do you mean evidence?"

Why is this so difficult? Cat's the most empathetic person I know. She won't judge my stupidity. "There's a cryptic note at the end of the manuscript, and I can't tell whether the author's trying to be creative or if it's a cry for help."

"Cry for help? Okay, I'm going to need more information. Slow down and tell me what happened."

I tell Catrina about *Undaunted's* bitter blog; how she became a client, the manuscript's detailed journaling and evidence of murder that will destroy a well-respected family. But I fail to mention the part about me. "I'm just trying to make sense of this. Maybe I'm jumping to the wrong conclusion, but I think the novel lacks an ending because she's anticipating a murder, or perhaps a murder already happened. And then, again, maybe it's my overactive mind. Maybe this is just her creative style of writing."

"What did the note say at the end?"

"It says if anything happens to her, to mail the manuscript to Detective Pennington.

"You're kidding?"

"No, I'm not … And there's more."

"Allie, what aren't you telling me?"

"Cat, I've never told anyone about this, not even Nikki. It happened during my junior year at Emsworth…" An image of Belle appears as clear as yesterday, sitting in the driver's seat wearing a provocative black dress, and aging, fake eyelashes and charcoal eyeshadow. I hardly recognized her. My intuition screamed danger the moment I slid into the passenger seat. I should have left the car immediately.

"Allie … Are you there?"

"Cat, honestly, I don't remember much about that night."

"Okay and…"

"Well, I remember arriving at the party and having a few drinks."

"Allie, you're killing me with suspense, come on just tell me what happened."

"There was this student named Belle, and she invited me to a party. I was hesitant to accept, but I did. You know what it's like being a student, always looking to make new friends. She picked me up at my dorm and drove me to an off-campus party. To make a long story short, I had two drinks, blacked out, and woke the next morning with no memory of what happened. Everything about that party is a fog."

After two years, I'm still too ashamed to tell her how I got back to the dorm.

"Are you sure you weren't drugged? That's happening a lot with that date-rape drug, what's it called?"

"Rohypnol."

"Did you see a doctor, you know, to make sure nothing else occurred that night?"

"If you mean rape, I wasn't. My virginity was still intact. And I felt fine the next day and saw no need to see a doctor. But, Cat the woman, Belle, who invited me to the party, disappeared that night. She went missing."

"Jeez, Allie … Did you go to the police?"

"No, I didn't, and don't judge me, but I was terrified. A day after the party, I received a mysterious letter telling me not to reveal my whereabouts that night to anyone, especially the police. The letter said dangerous people are involved, and my life was at risk. I never found out who the letter was from. So, I followed the letter's advice and never mentioned the party to anyone. But after reading the manuscript, I'm sure someone knows I was with Belle."

"So, what does this Patrice want from you?"

"I wish I knew … If this Pennington is a detective, maybe Patrice is in danger. Or maybe she's trying to warn me."

"Warn you? Allie, come on this is probably all fiction."

"That night happened Catrina, and if she weren't there, she wouldn't know."

"So why hasn't she gone to the police after two years? No, something's not clicking here. She's got another motive for sending you the manuscript. You said the novel lacked a conclusion which means she's still searching for evidence."

"There's nothing I remember that would explain Belle's disappearance. I barely recall leaving my dorm and arriving at the house. Everything else is a blank."

"Maybe the manuscript is an effort to resurrect forgotten memories; she's trying to help you remember."

"No, that's not possible. Only my roommate knew I lost my memory."

"Hmmm ... Maybe Patrice's tried everything, and you're her last option."

"I wish I'd never opened that manuscript or spoken to Patrice. The first time I saw her blog, my instincts screamed trouble. I had the same sensation when I spoke to her earlier."

"Why?"

"She sounded anxious and rushed me off the phone when a man called out. She started whispering, and before I could say anything, she hung up. I think she was afraid of the man who entered the room."

"That's revealing. I don't know Allie. Maybe you should do some snooping. This Detective, is it Pennington?"

"Uh-huh... why?"

"You should call the number on the manuscript and see if Detective Pennington is real."

I laugh. "And if he is?"

"Well, you'll confirm your suspicions. When you determine he exists, hang up and call Patrice back for more information. If she's not forthcoming, you might not have a choice but to speak with Pennington."

"Pennington might think it strange I'm calling and asking questions about Belle after two years. No, that's too risky."

"Just tell him you're researching for a novel."

"Research on what?"

"Hmmm ... How about runaway teenagers, or something along those lines, you're a writer, be creative. Keep the conversation brief and simple and don't reveal your suspicions until he tells you something that clarifies this mysterious manuscript."

"Yea, well, it's probably the only way to find out who Patrice is and why she's reappeared two years later."

"I'd love to check out Undaunted's blog."

"It's brutally honest stuff."

"Ooh, even better. I like brutally honest. Do you mind texting me the link? There might be hidden clues in her writing."

"I've warned you ... it's bloody harsh."

"Have you forgotten who you're speaking to? If I can handle the racy material we received at McClelland, I can handle this."

I laugh. How could I forget? Catrina has always been intrigued by raunchy novels and bloody murder mysteries. "Well, call me later, and tell me what you think. And Cat, thanks for listening to my worries."

"What are BFF's for? Call you later."

As soon as I hang up, I text Catrina *Undaunted's* blog address. Have I betrayed Patrice's confidence? No, the blog is public for anyone to read. I pour another glass of wine, head to the refrigerator with all intentions of preparing Storytelling Epicurean's recipe, but wine has quelled all desire to cook a complicated meal. Instead, I reach for a bag of prewash greens pour it in a bowl and prepare a simple dinner of pasta and salad. The Storytelling Epicurean's dish will have to wait another day.

After barely touching the meal, I pour another glass of wine and ponder detective Pennington's existence. On the laptop, I type his name and address into the browser. A Google Earth view of the homes and narrow, cobbled streets appear. I recognize the home, something out of a fairytale. When I returned to Emsworth my junior year, I drove past the house many times, parked and gazed at the door, hoping lost memories would resurface. They never did. Suddenly I wonder how Mr. Pennington can afford such an expensive home on a detective's salary.

Apprehensively, I dial the given number and press the mute button. The phone rings twice, and then a man answers, "Pennington." Quickly, I hang up.

He's real.

I jump when the phone rings in my hand. I can't believe he's calling back. I don't answer and wait for the ringing to stop. If it goes to voicemail, he'll know who I am. *Damn it!* That was stupid Allie. You should have picked up and explained that you dialed the wrong number. That would have ended it. Now, he has my name and number.

* * *

Two hours later, the phone rings. Noticing Catrina's number, I pick up swiftly. "Hi, Cat."

"Allie, Patrice deleted her blog."

"No, it can't be. Are you sure?"

"Yep."

"Maybe I gave you the wrong web address. Hold on one minute while I check." Typing Undaunted's blog address into the browser, a blank page opens with a note.

THE AUTHOR HAS DELETED THIS SITE.

In disbelief, I try again and receive the same message. "Why would Patrice delete her blog?" *Maybe she's updating the site.* I reflect on the lurid red rose and crumpled white sheets, now all gone, but I refuse to believe she'd simply erase her poetry. I check my follower's list and notice Undaunted's name is missing. "Could she have changed the blog's name?" I study the list of new followers, clicking on each avatar. "Maybe the site is down temporarily. When bloggers update their site, it could cause the site to go down for a moment."

"Allie, did you call Detective Pennington?"

"Oh my God, Cat, he's real. I did what you said and hung up when he answered, but he phoned me back immediately. I should have answered. Now he's got my name from my voicemail. This is all so bizarre."

"Well, don't you think it's time to call Patrice?"

"No, I'm too anxious. I need to relax and think this over. I'll call Patrice in the morning when I'm calmer."

"Allie, stop worrying. I'm sure when you speak to Patrice, she'll have an explanation for all of this."

After hanging up with Catrina, I can't silence my mind, even after four glasses of wine. I should be in a drunken stupor, but I'm not. So, I try to distract a frenzy of thoughts with something else. CJ ... Will he be on the computer this time of night? Imbued with alcoholic bravery, I type, "Hello, are you there?" He doesn't respond. Well, it was worth a try. Suddenly, I remember our conversations aren't private on his blog and quickly type, "Please do not respond on your site. I prefer to correspond by email or text if that's okay." Thoughtlessly, I leave my cell phone number.

Thoughts of Patrice's deleted blog persist doggedly. Over and again, I check the status of her site. Undaunted's bitter poetry is gone, vanished as if she never existed. When I type Patrice Jensen's name into the browser, several results appear. I click on each name until I've exhausted the list. But none of the search results resemble her photo. I add another search criterion, the District of Columbia, and the results show many Patrice Jensen's. Most are too old, too young, or of the wrong nationality. Recalling the name of the Senator in her manuscript, I search for Senator Greg Murphy of Washington, D.C.

The United States Senate official website opens in red, white, and blue. Strolling down the list of Class One, Two, and Three Senators, finally, Senator Murphy appears. I click the link to his web page. A man with salt-and-pepper hair, perhaps in his early sixties, stands with his arm circling two women, and his staff posed behind them. I enlarge the page and faces clarify. The caption beneath the photo reads Senator Greg Murphy, his wife, Sheila, and daughter, Penelope. I pause at eyes that appear sad, and carelessly, pour another glass of wine, and then a text buzzes from CJ.

12
Wretched And Doubtful

JUST AS I ENTER the duplex, the cell phone rings again for the third time in fifteen minutes. It's Shane, but I ignore him, unable to explain why I bailed on him after the meeting. For several days, I can't look him in the eyes without the urge to scream you've ruined my life! But it's not all his fault. I'm just as much to blame, but I need to shout at someone besides myself. Honestly, I can't be near him without the urge to tell him I'm pregnant. But I can't.

Taking off my shoes and placing my bag on the foyer console, sweat congeals to gooseflesh from the chilly room. Why does Allie have the air-conditioner so high? The fragrant scent of roses steeps the room, and I notice the roses Shane gave me the other night in a tin canister on the dining table. What happened to the beautiful vase? They were so bright, and red this morning, now, they're limp and dying. I rush to turn off the air conditioner, shocked to find it's not on. Allie must have shut it off recently. Right away, I notice an empty wine bottle and head toward the kitchen counter. Allie's been drinking, and alone? That's not like her. I look for a second wine glass, only finding one. *Did she drink the entire bottle?* Something's amiss. Or maybe she needed to unwind. God knows I could use a glass. But a whole bottle! She'll be painfully hungover in the morning.

At the breakfast nook, Allie's cell phone moves toward the edge, buzzing a muted vibration. Rushing, I catch it before it falls to the floor, wondering who's calling so late. Curious, I answer, "Hello."

"Yes, you called earlier but didn't leave a message. I got your number from my caller I.D."

"I'm sorry, who is this?"

"Detective Pennington..."

"This is my sister's phone. Can I take a number and have her call you in the morning?"

"She probably has the number already."

"I'll give her the message you called."

Detective Pennington. *Why did she call a detective? And why Washington, D.C.?* I questioned, staring at the phone. And she's left the laptop on. Leaning over to turn it off, I find the Internet open to Senator Greg Murphy's home page. It must be research for her novel. Just as I turn off the computer, Allie's cell phone buzzes with a text message from someone named CJ. She'll kill me if I read it. Then another text follows. I steal a glance uneasily.

"I hope you're okay. You have me worried. Text me in the morning. CJ"

Why is this CJ worried? Has something happened? Maybe that's why she drank an entire bottle of wine. *Allie, what's going on?* I think as I march upstairs. She's probably passed out from all the alcohol. Quietly, opening the door, I find her curled on top of the covers still fully dressed. *Yep, she's out.* She'll regret this in the morning. My cell phone rings a muted jingle, rousing irritation. "Give it a rest, Shane," I mumble, and grab my bag from the console.

I slog fatigued into the bedroom, and fling both my bag and body onto the bed, with an ensuing creak and thump as my tote hits the floor. Lazily, I gaze at contents scattering linear across the room. Three glowing faces stare back from pregnancy magazines I'd purchased reluctantly. *Marketing.* I'm sure not all women radiate perfect health during pregnancy. For a moment, I linger on *Pregnancy for Dummies,* splayed supine, and ponder the title's appropriateness given my stupidity this week. "Yep, that's me, a pregnant dummy," I murmured, and sweep the book from the floor. Inquisitively, I skim several pages, praying the second trimester is better than the first. "Thank goodness," I murmured, discovering nausea and drowsiness abate after the third month.

However, I grow concern people have already started to notice a change. I grimace with embarrassment at the narcoleptic episode at work. How could I fall asleep during a disposition? And with constant trips to the bathroom, coworkers are already suspicious. Pondering mood swings, pregnancy glow, and belly starting to grow, I realize my secret will soon be visible.

With heavy eyes, I place the book on the nightstand, but an alarming image of Allie, wide-eyed with discovery, causes me to retract it swiftly. Stuffing the paperback and magazines in the tote, I deliberate a hiding place—a place Allie rarely visits. With our distinct taste in clothing, she seldom visits my closet.

I place the bag on the top shelf and push it behind new clothes I'll probably never wear. Ribbons of earthy shades appear austere, and I puzzle sudden aversion to outfits I've always adored. Inexplicably, an urge to dress in Allie's light, feminine pastels assails me. Has pregnancy changed my preference for both fashion and food? Hormones are the only explanation for the sudden distaste.

I picture my pregnant body, and I'm disturbed at the idea of waddling back and forth to court with a swollen belly. A child wasn't part of my plan, but I can't stop this fetus from growing. I don't know how to be someone's mother. Children deserve someone who wants and plans for them. This is messed up, Nikki!

Without warning, my body grows too burdensome to hold upright. Finally depleted, and yearning for sleep's solace, I emerge from the closet too tired to shower, undress and curl into bed. But slumber doesn't come quickly. My mind whispers longings for grandma Blu's wisdom—the advice of a strong woman who never sugar-coated her words.

I imagine grandma would say having a child is the biggest challenge I'll ever face. She'd probably add a twist of sarcasm, alluding to my rebellious childhood. *This child will give you hell, just like you gave your momma, but it'll be the love of your life.* And always, she'd reassure, *"Sugar, you're strong enough to handle it."* Although a skeptic of her religion, I never disrespected her beliefs. Blu always believed God has a plan for everyone. I hear words she preached whenever I struggled with personal challenges. *"God's testing you again. Don't ignore his knock."* And of course, she'd give me the pros and cons but never placate with simple platitudes about the joys of motherhood. No, she wouldn't after raising five kids with a demanding teaching job. But I'm sure there were days she craved solitude, but we never heard any grievances. Some women, I suppose, are destined for motherhood.

Deep down, I know grandma would want me to have this child. I imagine perceptive words. *"You might feel wretched and doubtful at the moment, but that child's a blessing."* Or is it my voice of reason. Maybe, but mostly, I believe grandma Blu speaks to me no matter how impossible that sounds. If only I could talk to mom with such ease, but I can't, not after all the years of animosity. How could she place her career before her children? How selfish! Well, Nik, now you're just like mom, pregnant with a career. How will I do this alone? No matter what, this child will never be second to my wants. I won't be like mom.

13

The Morning After

I DON'T REMEMBER much about last night, or how I made it upstairs to bed. But I can tell by the heaviness of my head, sour grape taste in my mouth, and abdominal distress, I had too much to drink. My eyeballs hurt with the rush of light, aggravating my pounding head. I close them quickly and lie unmoving; surprised I'm still dressed and entangled in clothing. I imagine falling into bed, too drunk to undress and dissolving into a deep-intoxicated coma. Now regretting my date with the bottle, I lie hungover trying to recall remnants of last night, displaced with alcohol-damaged brain cells.

Slowly, the night saunters into my memory—the conversation with Catrina, the photo of Senator Greg Murphy and his family. Had I spoken to someone on the phone? A vague memory of a male voice, I can't grasp, hides behind fuzzy memories. *Did I talk to CJ?* Then I remember the flirtatious texting back and forth and grimace, hoping the conversation wasn't too raunchy. *God, I'll never drink again.*

I'm so thirsty; I could drink a gallon of water. Holding my head and rising from bed, blood explodes like a thunderous bass drum in my brain. I exit the bed, step softly toward the door, and trudge down to the kitchen for water. Taking a bottle from the fridge, I guzzle the entire container. With a squint, I stand, oblivious to time, only wanting the pounding to stop. I scoff at the empty culprit on the counter. *That's what you get for drinking the entire bottle.* Under the purple-stained wineglass lies a note from Nikki.

Someone's been drinking, and I bet right about now you're suffering. Add a touch of cayenne pepper to ginger tea or your coffee. It'll help the hangover. By the way, I hope you don't mind that I answered your cell last night. A detective Pennington returned your call. Allie, is something wrong? It's not like you to drink that much wine. If you need to talk, I'm here. Call me.

Love Ya, Sis

She answered my phone! That perturbs me more than the call from Pennington. Did she read my texts too? Suddenly I'm horrified, remembering last night's texting with CJ. Had I texted anything out of character? Detective Pennington? Why did he call back? Maybe he's curious how I got his unlisted number and why I hung up so fast. Looking around the room, I spy the mobile near my laptop and rush to retrieve my text messages. I gasp at the lengthy exchange with CJ, surprised I could type in my drunken state, but I'm more surprised at questions fueled with alcoholic daring.

Allie: "So, CJ what do you look like?"

CJ: "If I tell you I'm tall, dark, and handsome, would that make this conversation more desirable?"

Allie: "Well, I'm certain if I'd say I'm out of shape with pimples, your interest in this conversation would wane fast."

CJ: "Ah, you didn't answer my question, but your presumption is wrong. I'm not interested in just physical features. Attraction goes much deeper than that. I'm intrigued by intellect, your spirit, not your looks."

Allie: "I sense dishonesty. Not many men feel that way. But you have to admit physical attraction is important at first."

CJ: "Yes, that's true, but you could be the most beautiful woman in the world and still have an ugly soul. Inner beauty is much more appealing."

Allie: "Well, I'm certain physical features are ninety percent of the attraction."

CJ: "Fifty percent."

Allie: "Well, you're unique."

CJ: "You didn't answer my question."

Allie: "What was that?"

CJ: "If I were tall, dark, and handsome would this conversation be more desirable?"

Allie: "Honestly, looks are important. But I'm certain I could be attracted to something other than looks."

CJ: "Have you ever been?"

Allie: "Honestly, no. I sound superficial, but I'm not."

CJ: "No, you just haven't found the right soul yet."

Allie: "So, what do you look like?"

Allie! Where are you going with this conversation? What did you say? *I can't read this.* I place the phone back on the table, and then quickly retrieve it, ready to delete the entire conversation, but I can't. Ignorance is bliss. I plead drunken innocence. The mischievous child again, Grandma' Blu's reprimands enter my mind. *"Take responsibility for your actions, Allie."* So, with a pounding headache, I continue to read uneasily.

CJ: "I'll give you some basics, but why don't we keep our physical features to a minimum and get to know each other's minds instead."

Allie: "You're such an intellect."

CJ: "Well, I'm six feet, with an athletic build."

Allie: "That's all ... Come on give me one feature that would help me find you in a room full of strangers."

CJ: "I have raven hair, brown eyes, and if you need to find me in a room full of strangers, check my wrist for a quill pen tattoo."

Allie: "That will help. The tattoo is one feature we have in common. I have a small purple butterfly on my shoulder, a dare from my college days. Also, I'm five feet seven, brunette, slim built. I'm keeping it simple."

CJ: "I'm still picturing you in that white flowing skirt sitting in the breakfast nook, like a willowy dancer. You probably wear your clothing as an artistic expression of your soul. And I suspect you have brown piercing eyes that give away every emotion, and the spirited style of your skirt means you probably wear your hair natural and as loose as your clothing."

Allie: "Hmm, you're rather perceptive. My eyes are brown. And yes, I wear my heart on my bohemian sleeve. So, are you married? Do you have kids?"

CJ: "I knew that was coming, and the answer is no and nope. I've sworn off dating for a while."

Allie: "Why?"

CJ: "Let's just say, the last relationship left an emotional scar."

Allie: "Sorry to hear that."

CJ: "Anyone in your life ... Kids?"

Allie: "There was a year ago. But, like you, I've taken a break from the dating world, and no, no children."

CJ: "Another point we have in common."

Allie: "I have to tell you this is frustrating. I wish I could see you and hear your voice. You do realize we might not be attracted to each other in person. I mean there might be an instant spiritual attraction, but not sexual. OMG! I'm presumptuous tonight. I wasn't alluding to anything other than a friendship. I have to confess I've been drinking, and I get overly frisky when I do."

CJ: "I'm already attracted. I like frisky."

Allie: "Now, you're lying. You don't even know me."

CJ: "Well, I already like your spirit, your words, your friskiness, your morality. I sense a battle of wills when we talk. You want to say what you feel, but the goodness in you always wins. I bet you wish you could let go and just enjoy, perhaps be a little sexier than you're used to, enjoy a little fun with me. But you can't. You need a stimulant such as alcohol to overcome inhibitions. But I admire your desire to be virtuous. See, I'm already attracted to you."

Allie: "That sounds like a dare, and you can't possibly perceive my character with just words. But I have to say you're rather clever, but I disagree on one point. Of course, alcohol reduces inhibitions, but I don't need it to be sexy, especially with someone I'm attracted to."

CJ: "I sense defensiveness. I'm only saying what I've perceived from our brief conversations. I also sense your trepidation, which is normal, and I understand your reason for holding back. You probably wonder if I'm some online psycho, but I hope you're starting to warm up to me a little."

Allie: "A little, but not enough, as you say to be sexier. Anyway, what do you mean by that? Should I be flirting, talking about my sex life, what turns me on? And why do you men always go there! What's wrong with just getting to know each other without the sexual equation? OMG! I've had too much to drink. The room is spinning."

CJ: "Wow, and oh, boy! How much did you drink?"

Allie: "I'm embarrassed to say."

CJ: "I've had my share of drunken nights with an entire case of beer. It can't be any worse than that."

Allie: "I drank the entire bottle of wine, and I'm not bragging."

CJ: "Ouch! You're not going to like yourself much in the morning. Drink plenty of water before bed."

God Allie, you're pitiful! I'm shocked by his perceptions of my brown eyes, willowy figure, and my battle of wills. Either he's psychic, or he's found a picture of me on the web. *He couldn't have!* I'd deleted the photo on my blog before we met online. And my Facebook account has been closed for months. *Allie, he doesn't know your name.* With relief, I sigh and continue reading the remaining text, flinching with each word as the conversation grows more intense, sexual innuendos apparent on each side. After the diatribe about keeping the conversation friendly, it appears I'd stimulated a sexier conversation about my wine-stained lips. *Oh, no!* I sent him a picture of my purple lips. *God Allie!* I'm embarrassed but relieved it was just my lips and not my entire face. I scowl at my brazen drunken state.

As I read further, I notice I'd revealed worries about Patrice's manuscript, and then the texting stopped abruptly. I wonder why. A fuzzy image of me dropping the phone, rushing to the bathroom, and throwing up, confirms what I'd suspected from my raw throat.

CJ's sent a final text at 11:04 p.m. I'm touched that he's concerned about my safety. Feeling ashamed of the entire drunken exchange, I hope I haven't scared him away. I begin to type a remorseful text, fearing he's deleted or blocked me from existence. "Thanks for your concern. I'm fine, except for the excruciating hangover. I apologize for my embarrassing drunken behavior and hope I didn't give you the wrong impression."

I wonder if I would engage in the sexy exchange without alcohol. And honestly, I don't know. In my sickened state, I don't deliberate further. Instead, I follow Nikki's advice; make coffee with a touch of cayenne pepper, and hope it eases my discomfort. It doesn't help that my pores reek of wine. But the putrid roses nauseates me more than the alcohol. Needing to vanquish wine from my pores, I head to the bathroom and linger under the shower's pulsing stream until a calypso ringtone sounds downstairs. A frenzy of thoughts breaks the momentary calm. So, I towel off, dress, and head downstairs. My cell displays one missed call from Nikki and a text message from CJ.

CJ: "Your behavior didn't repel me. On the contrary, I enjoyed our conversation. I suspect you're hurting right now. I hope you're drinking plenty of water. After our discussion about Undaunted's mysterious manuscript, I did some digging of my own. As I told you last night, Undaunted's been following my site for over a year and responds to all my posts. Sometimes I feel she's lurking in the background. When you told me she'd deleted her blog, I checked to confirm. The site was removed, which makes me even more curious, especially after she'd blogged for so long.

When you told me Undaunted's real name, I grew more alarmed. Two years ago, Patrice Jensen, a student in the District of Columbia, disappeared. The address you gave me is the last place she was seen. Patrice Jensen can't possibly be the manuscript's author unless she wrote the story before disappearing. You need to be cautious of Undaunted."

14

Three Revelations

YOU NEED TO BE CAUTIOUS OF UNDAUNTED herald like a road sign, danger ahead, advance with caution. I wonder what menacing face will appear around the dangerous curve. *Patrice went missing* repeats like a broken record. I've been dealing with the ghost of someone long gone, or someone who's assumed her identity. If Patrice Jensen is missing, who is Undaunted? Then it hits me. Patrice and Belle are the same woman. She'd lied about her name two years ago, but why? Immediately, I'm alarmed about everything, and everyone even CJ. As much as I want to trust him, it's too risky. My mind whirls with fearful questions, trying to decipher Undaunted's motive. There's a reason she sent me the manuscript, but at the moment, cayenne pepper's temporary relief fades and nausea returns, squelching all logic.

Nikki's second suggestion, ginger tea, leads me to the cabinet, only to discover an empty box. Then I remember the green-leafed carton she'd slipped in her tote three mornings ago. I creep upstairs to her room and into her immaculate closet, rummage every purse, clutch, tote, and satchel, determined to preserve order. It's been years since I've gone through Nikki's closet. The last time I was sixteen and borrowed and never returned a beautiful fringe scarf which she never missed. Curiously, I'm feeling like lil' sis again as I eye every space and corner.

Behind price-tagged clothing on the top shelf, juts the edge of a small leather tote. Why isn't it with the other bags? Stretching and tugging at the strap, the bag, and its contents spill onto the floor. Wide-eyed, I stare at three pregnancy magazines, *Pregnancy for Dummies*, and a box of ginger tea at my feet. Instantly, Nik's recent illness, lack of appetite, weight loss, evasive behavior, and ginger tea makes sense. *She's pregnant!*

It's morning sickness, not a stomach virus as I'd presumed. There's no debating the obvious. Considering Nik's aversion to childbearing, she must be devastated. *Poor Nik.* She's never wanted children, but I've always believed she will make a great mother. This could be the best mishap in Nik's thirty-two years. *Auntie Allie* sounds nice, but I know Nik isn't feeling the same about being a mother. It's hard to conceive Nik pregnant and wearing maternity clothes. And a large belly will certainly impede her demanding schedule. Despite physical changes, I wonder about her mental state and hope she hasn't considered ending the pregnancy. *No, she wouldn't!* She's too conscientious and would never terminate a life.

Spying the folded page in *Pregnancy for Dummies,* I open the book to the second trimester. Is she that far along? Is Shane the father? Well, Nik, you're in a fine mess now. I grab two tea bags, place the book and magazines in their hiding place, ready to rush straight to the phone and call Nikki. But I hesitate, realizing she'd hidden the books for a reason. She doesn't want me to know. Can I keep my mouth shut? One facial twitch and Nik will read me like a book. Anyway, she can't keep this secret forever. She'll have to tell me when she starts showing.

Downstairs, the cell phone rings Ryan's ringtone. How soon he'd slipped my mind. Just a day ago, I was eager to start his manuscript, but worries of Undaunted obliterated all thoughts of Ryan. I drift downstairs and return his call with an apology. I'm soon relieved to find it's just a courtesy call, letting me know he received my link and paid for the editing. However, I'm puzzled when Ryan asks if I'm okay. His sudden familiarity and detection of subtle nuances in my voice after short conversations is surprising. I consider whether he'll think I'm a lush if I reveal I'm hungover. There you go again, worrying about what other's think, so I say with unease, "I'm a tad hungover." *A tad ... How about immensely!*

"Ah, as my cast-ironed stomach father would swear, you need the hair of the dog that bit ya," he chuckled, "but that's never worked for me. Plain old aspirin and water are the best cure. I hope a night of fun justifies the hangover?" He inquired.

The fondness his voice holds is a surprising contrast to resentment present a month ago when he'd explained his father sent the manuscript. "No, just plain stupidity," I faulted.

"Sometimes we need an elixir for our ails, especially after a long, exhausting day."

"That was the intent last night, but I overdid it."

"Well, I've had my moments, especially during college years ... You know, wild frat parties, waking up the next morning an amnesiac and wondering what mayhem I'd caused. I have to say; discovering misdeeds from frat brothers was a bit awkward. Those were crazy fun times, but I don't miss the brutal hangovers. I'm sure you've had some drunken misdeeds in college."

"Not many, maybe one or two," I replied, recalling the off-campus party and the blackout. The strange outer-body sensation as I climbed dangerous stairs wasn't from alcohol but drugs. I've tried many times to recapture the familiar voice pulling me through swirling halls toward that room, and vague figures moving swiftly across the room when I opened the door. I was asleep on my feet, with no control of my body, senses withered, and then blackness. Now that moment is a distant, inaccessible memory.

Oddly, my mind revisits Romance Literature 301, catching a curious blonde's strange stare across the room, her smile an impish curve. Class ended, and Belle approached not like a woman should another woman, but with a playful sexiness used on men. I was chagrined, stunned by her bold invitation. Although bothered by her sensual behavior, her audaciousness was intriguing. Belle wasn't interested in other's perception of her. That's what caught my attention.

"Two isn't bad," Ryan said.

"No, but it's enough and embarrassing."

"It can't be that serious."

"It's one of those moments parents warn their daughters about, and no woman should find herself in. But I was a naïve student looking to have fun."

"Hmmm … I'm afraid to ask?"

"No, it wasn't anything like a physical assault, just too much alcohol, passing out, and waking with a nasty bump on the head … But I'm rather ashamed of what followed."

"What happened?"

"I'll make a long story short. I had two strong drinks at an off-campus party, and bewilderingly, I woke the next morning with a bruised head, wondering how I made it to my dorm."

"Sounds like a classic drunken blackout. I've woken in obscurity and suspect many people have at least one episode in their lives," he said as if to assuage my shame.

But have they ever passed out and been carried home by a total stranger, I muse shamefully? I don't think he'd appease me If he knew a strange man, an upper-classman I'd never met, drove me to my dorm and disappear as quickly as he'd appeared. A night I can only attest through my roommate's eyes that an attractive senior delivered me to my bed and showed great concern for my bruised head. For months, I wondered how he'd located my dorm. I concluded he'd found my college I.D. in my purse. All I could picture was my unconscious body searched by a stranger in his car. He could have done anything to me, and I wouldn't have known. The entire junior year, I imagined him secreted on campus, watching and aware of what I'll never remember.

"So, you don't recall anything before the blackout?"

"Nope, not even leaving the party, nothing…"

"After two drinks you shouldn't have blacked out. I suspect your drink was spiked."

"I wondered about that later. I didn't see any reason to worry. I felt fine the next day, but that night taught me never to accept invitations or drinks from suspicious strangers. The rest of my college years, I surrounded myself with like-minded people and only accepted drinks in capped bottles."

"So, you became a prudent student."

"Yep, suspicious of everyone..."

"I've always wondered about the mind and how lost memories return years later. There's a possibility that night will awaken."

"After all this time, I doubt it."

"Well, memories have a way of receding until something ignites them. The brain does an incredible job of shielding us from pain."

"Pain ... No, blacking out and a strange man carrying me to my room is just plain embarrassing. But for months, I worried about that night. Images of unspeakable horrors plagued my junior year. It was like staring through a keyhole into a dark room, straining to see an imperceptible image, but the outline melted with the dark. It's there, just undetectable."

"Maybe there's nothing to see because nothing ever happened."

"Perhaps. Anyway, I finally gave up trying. Whatever it was, it's gone."

"Sometimes, you have to let go of the past."

"Are you speaking from experience?"

"I am."

I wonder what painful memories he's relinquished. "Ryan, I realized a few moments ago when you mentioned your father that I know so little about you. It appears you're close," I said, seizing the chance to unearth his past and dismiss the vexing blackout.

"Closer than most, especially since my brother's death. We've grown closer."

"Oh, I'm sorry. Was his death recent?"

"You know, I owe you an apology for not explaining the book is based on my brother's life."

"No apologies. But I must admit, I thought the novel was about you."

"Somewhat, but it's mainly Kyle's story. It's taken me time to get over his death. We were close. But that all changed after the first tour of duty. Kyle wasn't the same man. He came back from war restless and lacking interest in his old life. I guess war does that to a person. After six months at home, he decided to return for a second tour of duty. It was a deadly decision. He was there only a month when his tank was hit, killing him and several crewmembers. I dove into my writing which was the outlet I needed to mourn his death."

"It must have been devastating for his wife." Or is the romance fictional? The love interest was so compelling. Had he abandoned her for war in real life? Ryan grows silent, and I believe I've spoken out of turn. Just as I'm about to speak, a heavy sigh winds my ear.

"It was ... well, I'd written the book while Kyle was at war and Kerri, his wife was pregnant with their first child."

I sense a struggle for words and assert gently, "You don't have to talk about this right now." But his words come fast when he reveals Kyle and Kerri met in high school and they were inseparable until the war. He pauses. The acute silence vibrates devastation and heartbreak. My heart sinks at once when he reveals preeclampsia claimed Kerri's life during childbirth. Mirabella, the baby, was born premature and lived only a day.

"Ryan, I'm so sorry." I can't imagine his pain, and from my suffering, I know words can't describe his grief. *I'm sorry for your loss; my thoughts are with you and your family;* are simple condolences I hate to express. So, I say nothing else, hoping my silence doesn't appear heartless. On the contrary, empathy, undetectable through the phone, is palpable. The loss of a family, their memory eternalized in a novel has left me wordless. I desist with further questions.

"Wow ... I'm sorry. I didn't mean to burden or inflict you with my problems in your current state—"

"No—no," I insist. "Nothing you say can make this hangover worse." I recognize qualities in Ryan inherent in myself—reluctance to inflict personal pain on others. He probably holds every emotion at bay, never expressing his troubles. I'm touched he's concerned about my discomfort, but he deserves all the sympathy. His pain is far greater than my self-inflicted hangover. Now, I'm confident it was heartache I witnessed in my office when he mentioned the novel is for his brother.

"We should talk when you're feeling better—"

"Ryan, I've been meaning to thank you for keeping me as your editor. Your trust means a lot to me."

"And again, Ms. Bertrand, I wouldn't want anyone else handling my manuscript but you."

I smile, reflecting on his disinterest when I called him months ago. *We're making strides Mr. McThursten.*

15

Unearthing Penelope

GIVEN ALL THAT'S HAPPENED this morning, I hadn't noticed rain falling outside. An hour before Ryan called, I'd wanted to jump in bed, cover my head, and forget the world existed. But after three revelations, Undaunted's false identity, Nikki's pregnancy, and Ryan's story about his brother, I can't go back to sleep. And the off-campus party returns like an old annoying wound. In just twenty-four hours, I've revealed my secret to two people and didn't die of shame.

I approach the rain-dribbled window, and a verdant watercolor painting appears. Except for occasional sun peeking through rolling clouds, it looks like early evening. I slump hungover into the breakfast nook and watch the teenage dog walker command more control of the canine pack. *He's learning.* Soon, thoughts turn to Literature 301 and the curious blonde. Two years ago, her abandonment left me angry and baffled. But what I didn't know at the time was she'd vanished off the face of the earth. I was eager to give her a piece of my mind the next time I saw her, but she never returned to class. In a way, I was relieved she was gone. Her presence would have been a constant reminder of what I couldn't recall, but I can't help worrying she'd met a horrible fate.

For months, I rationalized Belle's sudden disappearance as foul play. I thought perhaps a kidnapping by sex traffickers who shipped her off to a foreign land. Second, given her brazenness, I pictured her approaching the wrong person and instantly meeting death. The most obvious cause is she ran away, leaving behind a dreary life. But suspicion and concern drew sinister conclusions intensified by fuzzy moments before I blacked out. I'd tried to recapture the dark shadow moving across that room, but my vision dwindled as the figure approached. But without a doubt, the shadowy images were men.

Okay, Allie, stop. I rest my head against the wall and sip the ginger tea. But I can't shut my mind off, and thoughts turn to Undaunted. At once, I check her blog. The glaring message appears surreal—*Undaunted's defunct, nonexistent*—but I still have her cell number. Recalling CJ's text, I realize the person I'd spoken to wasn't Patrice. Then who was she? After a night of drunken worries, I need answers to mounting suspicions. I dial Patrice's number and the phone rings once, followed by a prerecorded message. "This number has been disconnected." *Disconnected!* That's the second time in a month my heart twitched with that recording, first when I called Grandma Blu after the layoff, now this. I dial the number a second time, hoping Undaunted will answer with a cheery voice. But once again, the electronic recording dashes my wish. This is incredible, a defunct blog, a disconnected phone, and a suspicious author who's abandoned and left me with a chilling manuscript.

Did she delete the blog and disconnect her phone intentionally or has something happened to her? I'll never know. Then I remember the PayPal purchase. I have her address on file. Quickly, I retrieve the information and wonder if the address is as phony as her name. Ninety Windsor Street, Chevy Chase, Maryland. I cut and paste the information into Google Earth. A white, two-story Dutch Colonial surrounded by flowers appears like a dream. The address is real, but is it someone else's home? Ahead of the driveway sits a mailbox with an illegible name. Hedges cover the last two letters, enlarging the screen doesn't help. *Is it Undaunted's home?*

Opening Senator Murphy's website, I search for more clues. For some reason, I linger on his daughter's face. Her eyes are sad, her smile forced. Did she feign happiness just for that moment? Her name evokes childhood memories of grade school and a classmate named Penelope. A name that became synonymous with cantaloupe, and later, puki-poppy-seed when students discovered Poppy was her family nickname. Often, when I hear Penelope, that childish jeer resonates immutable. Curiously, Senator Murphy's daughter appears as I've always pictured someone named Penelope—brunette, big-eyed, undefined, round features with a reserved smile, just like my classmate.

Penelope … Poppy…

My mind echoes. *"Damn it, Poppy! What's taking so long?"* The man I'd heard when I spoke to Undaunted emphatically said, Poppy. I'm sure of it! Could Senator Murphy's daughter be *Undaunted*? Is the surname on the mailbox Murphy? Swiftly, I type Penelope Murphy into the browser. Several results appear, but only one is revealing. On Penelope's Facebook account, the main page displays a brunette with unsmiling eyes. On the sidebar, a history of photos shows her past. One picture catches my attention—Penelope sitting with a blonde on a vast expanse of lawn reads *BFF's For Life*. The background screams a familiar setting, a place I'd visited many times before classes, Emsworth University's quad. The two women grin with their foreheads pressed together. Penelope's smile is demure, the blonde's mischievous. My eyes swell with clarity. Unmistakably, it's Belle's smile. Penelope's friend is the blonde from Romance Literature 301, and her name is Patrice Jensen.

16

Another Piece Of The Puzzle

AN INVISIBLE THREAT FESTERS, warning and urging me to recapture lost memories scattered in cerebral crevices. Undaunted's blog, the mysterious manuscript, and the campus photo of Patrice and Penelope are only frazzles—pieces of a daunting puzzle. There's a reason Penelope's resurfaced two years later with her friend's stolen online identity. I sense a scheme intended to unearth Patrice's disappearance. She's providing small clues, guiding me closer to Patrice. Detective Pennington, Senator Murphy, is the PayPal address also evidence?

Penelope didn't want to publish the novel. It's a subtle entrapment. She knows something about that party, and if she does, it's because she was there. God, if only I could remember. I don't have a choice but to follow the next clue. I dial information for Patrice Jensen's number at Ninety Windsor Street, Chevy Chase, Maryland. The operator reveals the address belongs to Doctor Mark and Connie Jensen. Another piece of the puzzle fits. I suppose they're Patrice's parents or relatives. Hesitantly, I dial the number. A woman answers and warily I ask, "Is this Mrs. Jensen?"

"Yes. Who is this?"

"I'm looking for Penelope." Then I realize my mistake and quickly state, "Patrice."

"Who are you?" The woman asked, taken aback.

Recalling the photo on Penelope's Facebook account, I reply, "I'm an old friend from school." Well, we were classmates. Reflexively, I repent my deceit.

"Patrice … It's been years since she lived here. Did you say Emsworth?"

"Yes, we attended Emsworth together."

"She's not here." Her voice sounded through my ears like words echoing in multi-chambers.

A confused pause and heartbreak ensue with the mention of her vanished daughter. Right away, I want to end the call, but I persist deceitfully. "I'm sorry to bother you, but do you know where I can reach her?"

"My daughter's been gone for a long time. When did you say you were in class together?"

She said gone, not missing or dead, which makes me believe she hasn't forsaken her daughter. "I apologize. After so many years, it must be strange receiving a call out of the blue. I was just going through the school directory and saw Patrice's name. She was in my junior literature class, and I just thought I'd reconnect."

"That sounds about right … That was around the time my daughter went missing."

"Oh, I had no idea." I feigned surprise, and frown disquiet, certain my pretext has aroused silent heartbreak. "I'm so sorry." Wary of pressing on, I bite my lip and ask quietly, "Was she ever found?"

"No. For two years we've tried, but Patrice simply vanished without a trace. We hired private detectives but with little success. Frankly, I'm surprised you hadn't heard. There were posters all over the University when she went missing. For months we placed them everywhere, hoping someone would come forward with information. You said you were in her junior literature class; didn't you notice when she didn't return to school?"

Yes, I had. I'd wanted Patrice to return so I could chew her out for abandoning me. I answered in my head. "No, I hadn't noticed the posters. I wish I had. When she didn't show up for class, I thought she'd dropped the course. And I wouldn't remember posters because shortly after, winter break began." That's partially true. I remembered the posters but was too consumed with my memory loss. I never stopped to read them. And two weeks later, I left for winter break. When I returned, I noticed the posters but never paid attention. I was paranoid about people from that party and seldom roamed the campus after winter break but stayed in my dorm or the library studying. I heard talk about a missing student, but never thought it was Belle. Now I wonder if I'd known it was her, would I have gone to the police. I was the last person to see her and hold a piece of information that could have led to her discovery. Now, after two years, there's no possibility of finding her. But Patrice's mother deserves the truth. If I reveal I was with her daughter the night she disappeared, I'll only appear suspect.

Awkwardly, I express sorrow for her loss, words I've uttered twice today. My dishonesty causes a pang of guilt, but regardless, I need to know Penelope's motive. Determinedly, I continue, hoping precise questions will enlighten obscurity. "Your daughter was a wonderful writer."

"Yes, she was ... She was following in her parent's footsteps. My husband and I teach literature at Emsworth University."

"Oh," I said. How could I forget Professor Jensen, who taught Introduction to Romance Literature during my first semester? I had no idea he was Patrice's father. I can't picture Patrice raised by scholars. I deliberate parenting skills applied to affect the brazen woman I'd met. Are the Jensen's artsy, liberal types, allowing Patrice many freedoms or strict authoritarians? Either style could conceivably mold audacious Patrice. After all, freedom and rebellion stem from the same root. I recall Albert Camus' words. "The only way to deal with an unfree world is to become so absolutely free, that your very existence is an act of rebellion." Patrice either had too much or too little parental control. She exerted a brassy persona to attract or repel attention. Nevertheless, she was a rebel undaunted by peer's opinions of her overt sexuality. Undaunted. Was her blog title another act of defiance? Mrs. Jensen's voice ruptures deep thought.

"It's strange you mentioned her writing. She was working on her first novel before she disappeared. She never told us what the story was about, and we never found the manuscript. It vanished as simply as she had."

And it's landed in my hands. I imagine Patrice's parents searching her dorm room, probing computer files, and notebooks, with no success. Penelope must have found the manuscript and deleted all traces of the novel. "That's strange ... Did you question any of Patrice's friends? I assume Penelope knew about the manuscript."

"Did you know Poppy?"

I play ignorant, pretending I've never heard the name. "Poppy?"

"Oh, of course, you wouldn't know. Penelope preferred her nickname. She always thought Penelope sound old-fashioned, so we've always called her Poppy."

"I see. I didn't know Penelope, but I understand she and Patrice were close. She must have been devastated by the loss."

"Yes. Patrice and Poppy were childhood friends. She was like family. We did question all Patrice's friends, but no one knew about the manuscript. Poppy is just as confused and devastated as we are. The Murphy's were wonderful throughout the ordeal, they even hired a detective, but no clues ever surfaced."

"I'm sorry you never discovered what happened to her."

"I've tried to remain positive and hope one day she'll come home. But after two years, the chance grows ever slight. You said you only knew her from class. So, you weren't friends?"

"No, but I remember Patrice's classwork. She was a talented writer." And that's the truth after reading her manuscript, but I can't attest to her character. Regardless, Patrice's mother has suffered enough. She needs to know her daughter was a gifted writer.

"The chance you'll remember is improbable, but I have to ask if there was anything odd about Patrice before she went missing? Did she appear troubled?"

Troubled. No, just provocative and mischievous, I think. But I do recall how quiet Patrice appeared behind the wheel as she drove to the party. In fact, her silence left me anxious. But I can't tell Mrs. Jensen. "No, nothing, it was so long ago."

"I didn't think you would remember."

It strikes me Mrs. Jensen is still searching for Patrice. Wouldn't any mother continue until they have proof, a body or some evidence of their child's death? But after two years, her faith must be dwindling. "Given what you've been through, I hate to ask. But as I stated, I'm trying to reconnect with old classmates and arrange a class reunion. I would love to invite Penelope, someone who was close to Patrice. The student directory lists her old number. Would you have her new number?" I asked tentatively, prepared for a prudent refusal. However, and surprisingly, she obliges. I'm puzzled she would without further scrutiny, but relieved more lies aren't necessary. I thank her and end the call with condolences that have probably soured.

At once, I dial Penelope's number, expecting the cheery tone from two days ago. The voice I believed was Patrice Jensen's. Voicemail confirms it was Penelope Murphy I'd spoken to, but I don't leave a message. She can't know I'm aware of her real identity. Although pleased to prove Penelope (Poppy) Murphy is Undaunted, my conscience screams trouble! But I'm anxious to unearth Penelope's charade.

Just as I question the apparent farce, I ponder how Penelope found my blog. She couldn't have known my identity because I'd deleted my bio and picture. Had she seen my site before anonymity? I try to recall Undaunted's first comment, but time blur indistinguishable, days meld into one. I backtrack to a crucial point. The day of the layoff, I'd written the rebuking post about McClelland. The next morning my blog overflowed with comments, and Undaunted's was one of them. The date of my blog's anonymity strikes with precision, a month after the layoff.

Penelope must have seen my photo. She hadn't stumbled on my blog accidentally. CJ said she'd been a follower for a year. Did she find me on his blog? I'm so confused! Did CJ know my name, my face, before that first coffee sip? No, he couldn't have. His first text came a day after I deleted my name and photo. I know it did. He discovered me through his faithful follower, Undaunted.

The laptop pings a new email. The subject line reads 1414 Kalorama Road. The room vibrates a static quiet. For the third time in a month the anonymous email screams from the screen.

I KNOW YOU WERE THERE. I SAW HUNTER CARRY YOU OUT.

Part Two
Where It All Began

17

Hunter

FROM EMSWORTH STUDENT Newspaper's window, I gaze at students dawdling on the campus quad then I notice her again. The stunning junior with large fawn eyes and bee-stung lips I'd wanted to bite at first sight. She glides across the quad in ankle boots and a mid-calf skirt swishing about tone legs. Underneath a leather jacket, dangling necklaces overlay an Indian tie-dyed T-shirt. Her style, I believe, Boho chic suits her graceful figure. To the window's edge, my eyes follow her frame until she fades inside the campus post office, and then someone else catches my attention.

For two days, I've secretly watched the probing-eyed blond roguishly stalk campus, hunting unsuspecting victims. No one would ever suspect her foul intentions; especially given her parents are honorable Emsworth Professors. Since the anonymous letter appeared on my desk two days ago, exposing a slew of student recruitment into the seamy world of escorts, I've pondered the mystery informant's identity and motive.

Later that same day, inside my mailbox, I found another note addressed to Hunter, my newspaper alias. No one uses that name but student reporters, a penname after my childhood pet, a Redbone Coonhound named Hunter. My friends always said I have a knack for trailing a story to its truthful origins, thus the alias. The anonymous tipster has given me another trail to follow. The letter declared a blonde would strike Friday at 9:00 p.m., arriving in a black XJR Jaguar in front of Darnall Hall.

Since I joined the campus newspaper three years ago; no story has captured my attention as much as this, especially knowing the fallout will taint the school's reputation. Zealously ready to achieve journalistic excellence before graduation, I snatch the opportunity without hesitation and prepare to camouflage, pursue, and expose the ruse. I can't let them induct another student.

* * *

Friday 9:00 PM

Ready to pursue, I watch Darnall Hall's front door spring open, slinging light into the wintry night and revealing an attractive silhouette, but night hides her facial features. She pulls her jacket tight against the cold and darts toward the waiting Jaguar. Uncertain, she pauses, stoops, then peers through tinted windows. The car door opens, dangling an expensive leather invitation. Now confident, she smiles and slides inside, pulling a sculpted leg adorned in black-stiletto-ankle boot inside and closing the door behind her. I recognize those shoes and realize she's the fawn-eyed student, Allison. Immediately, I want to race from the car and expose the treacherous blonde, but I can't blow my cover. Okay, this is going to be tricky, but I have to get her away from that party. For a moment, I wait until the car drives several feet then follow off campus grounds onto Georgetown's narrow streets.

Cruising Potomac Parkway Northwest to Waterside Drive, I suspect the passenger ahead is anxious about her destination when the car traverses Kalorama's residential, cobbled streets. The mystery informant's letter revealed students are told the party's held in a private home, but never the locale. I'm curious whether the informant's a misled recruit, now, bent on revenge.

Red lights flare. Gracefully, the car swerves into a private drive. The home's main level stirs with silhouettes shifting through obscured windows. The Jaguar crawls through retracting jowls, disappearing behind a side alley. Continuing past several houses, I park, wait, and deliberate my next move. When ten minutes pass and no one enters the home, I reread my source's note.

1414 Kalorama Road's patrons are wealthy politicians and business-men. Arrive well-dressed, and when asked, you're an entrepreneur. At the entrance, the code word is Pennington.

I glance in the rearview mirror at a well-groomed, twenty-two-year-old dressed in a black, tailored rental suit.

Will they believe I'm thirty?

I take a deep breath and open the car door.

18
Poppy

Friday 9: 15 PM

FROM A DISTANCE, I watch the Jaguar appear and swivel into the private driveway. I'm sure the silver Range Rover trailing behind is Hunter. Earlier, I worried he wouldn't show up but hoped journalistic curiosity would win, and it did. I slump into my seat as Hunter's car approaches, watching him park two cars behind. In the side-view mirror, lights dim. He peers ahead at women and men entering the home, as I've done for an hour, anxious to view a man called Pennington. But I wouldn't know him if I saw him. The only facets of Pennington I've gathered are his address, car, and name. When Patrice told me his name is Ted Pennington, I snickered then frowned at her deceit. Everyone knows Pennington is a teddy bear or is it Paddington. Anyway, it sounds suspicious. Why would she believe I'm that gullible? But when she refused to reveal Ted's physical features, I suspected the name a pseudonym, concealing his true identity.

Patrice and I've never kept secrets from each other. Thus the affair was a total surprise. I felt betrayal and jealousy, which I've never felt deeply. I was downright bitter someone else was usurping Patrice's time and worried she'd retreat further from my reach. After two years at EU, a mysterious man transformed our friendship and her appearance, a sudden transformation which caused great concerned. The modest girl-next-door fell asleep one night and woke brazen Patrice. I suspect Pennington's the root of her dramatic change.

I grew more concerned when I'd entered the dorm room and stumbled on Patrice's private conversation. Her voice was alarmingly wrong. I paused, pressed my ear to the bathroom door, and listened to her plead to Teddy. I was ashamed of both eavesdropping and Patrice's degradation. I tiptoed out of the room, waited several minutes, and then reentered just as she exited the bathroom.

She'd smiled, masking inner turmoil. Horrified, I'd gasped and glared at the reddish-purple splotches covering her underwear-clad body. Some were greenish-yellow bruises faded from days of healing. She appeared just as shocked and quickly threw on a robe. Her pretext of slipping down rain-slick steps was a blatant lie. A simple fall wouldn't account for the patchwork bruises covering her body. I couldn't straighten my pinched brows or close my agape mouth. Embarrassed, Patrice moved toward the bathroom and stated she needed a shower. As soon as the water squished from the spigot, I swiped Pennington's number from her caller I. D, thus the start of an investigation that's led me here tonight.

A year ago, the idea of spying on my best friend from a car would be inconceivable. College was supposed to be fun, independence from our families. Although I preferred to get away from Washington, preferably California, Patrice pleaded and convinced me to attend Emsworth University. Frankly, wanting to attend the University where her parents teach was a surprise. After years under their scrutiny, I thought she'd be eager to escape their reach. The idyllic first year we'd planned never happened. As months progressed, we rarely saw each other. Patrice vanished most nights, slipping into the dorm at dawn, just as I prepared for class. She never appeared drunk or stoned, but she was high on something. And, I could only guess the potent substance was sex. But after witnessing the bruises, I worried sex had turned abusive or rough.

Consumed with worry, I began probing—searching the dorm room with hopes of uncovering the alien substance invading Patrice's body.

I found no evidence of drugs, but something possibly more harmful, a shocking computer file labeled Pennington. Correspondences detailed a three-year illicit affair before Patrice reached legal age. There was no doubt in my mind Patrice chose Emsworth to remain close to her lover. Emails revealed Teddy's broken marriage and a naive girl's first love. A subfolder label *Undaunted* spilled stinging poetry of a lover's mental and physical abuse. In the same folder, I found an unfinished novel, the novel she'd mentioned writing, but never disclosed the storyline. Now, I understand why. I snooped through emails which grew darker, exposing not only a passionate affair but also an ignoble business.

I couldn't imagine Patrice deceitfully leading students into Pennington's hands. *She wouldn't!* And if she had, it couldn't be because of love. There must be another compelling reason. I'd searched through all her email to the last one dated a month ago. Different from the rest, it exploded with Patrice's threats to expose Pennington's business if he didn't leave his wife. Cunningly, his emails pacified persuasively, and I imagine Patrice fell for false promises.

The girl I'd known, virtuous to the point of prudish, would never partake in unethical behavior. Desperate to disprove a shocking discovery, I trailed Pennington's expensive Jaguar from Kalorama Road for weeks. After several trips, I witnessed nothing unusual until I showed up outside her classroom. A disturbing picture of a shameless temptress inviting an unsuspecting classmate to party appeared aberrant. A few steps away, I hid around the corner, pretending to search for something in my schoolbag while listening to Patrice's lies, and feigned exuberance, extolling an awesome time to be had at an off-campus party. She practically hypnotized her classmate into saying yes, although the bewildered student wavered, she accepted the invitation.

Patrice's following words, crafted like a well-rehearsed movie line, sped from her mouth, preventing the girl from changing her mind. "Where's your dorm? I'll pick you up at nine. I'll be the sexy girl driving the black Jaguar," she'd said, cocking her head to one side and twirling a strand of hair.

Like a dazed deer in headlights, the young woman replied, "Um, at nine … Okay. I'm at Darnell Hall." And like a seasoned professional, Patrice closed the deal swiftly. "See you Friday at nine, Allison."

At that moment, I felt obligated to run after the duped student, and warn, stay away from the party. But Patrice trailed behind her as she left the building. I had to do something. Then Professor Jensen's office appeared. I'd imagined stomping inside; disclosing his daughter's sordid affair but Patrice's parents would only silence the matter and protect their daughter's reputation.

Mulling over tactics to thwart Patrice, I'd strayed aimlessly into the student lounge when suddenly a copy of the student newspaper sparked an idea. Without a doubt, Hunter, the student reporter who'd exposed drug abuse and sexual misdemeanors on campus, would be interested in the recruitment of students as escorts. What better way to crack the escort service than lead him straight to them? So, I'd continued to the student newspaper. The office door was wide open. Two students, glued to their computer consoles, barely looked up as I stepped inside. At the near right appeared a desk with Hunter's name. I ambled over and snuck a letter into a wire file holder. Later that day, I placed a note inside his mailbox, leading him to the denizen of deceit.

It's been ten minutes since Hunter parked, and I wonder why he hasn't budged. Just as I glance at the side view mirror, an attractive six-foot frame wearing a black double-breasted coat and black tailored suit steps from the car. As I'd prescribed, he's assumed the role of a young entrepreneur handsomely. He should have no problem getting through the door. Hunter moves toward the home haltingly. There's an urgent need to whisper out the window, code name Pennington, but I can't reveal my identity.

He stops.

I worry.

He turns toward the car. I slump lower and watch him pull something from his inner pocket, place it around his neck, and tuck it beneath his shirt. Now more determined, he moves toward the private entrance. At the door, he straightens and presses the doorbell. I hope the information I've given him will get him in. Right about now, he's probably sweating bullets. The door opens, and a man dressed in a dark suit stands solidly.

19

Code Word Pennington

THE CLOSER I GET, the more fearful I become. Oblivious to what lies beyond those doors, I imagine dangerous criminals ready to interrogate rigorously before allowing me into their private sanctum. And if they discover the hidden camera, circumstances could get nasty. I'm ill-equipped to protect myself against God knows what. Will they question my age? Young men buying sex is not an anomaly. It happens all the time, though it's never been a desire of mine. I've often imagined men's humiliation, bidding physical pleasure from strangers. Such brief discomfort can't match women's degradation, tendering flesh for survival.

The closest I've come to an escort, call girl, whatever they call themselves was my brother's bachelor's party. The tawdry act stirred sadness, not lust. I was sorry to see women display their bodies with such shameless disregard. Inside the looming home, I'm sure exploits are tamer, a more sophisticated persuasion. I picture the unsuspecting, fawn-eyed student's horror, discovering Patrice's treachery and luring predators ready to prey. The thought's enraging. I hasten my pace toward the expensive address. The transgressors aren't average criminals if they can afford a home that lists in the millions. *Sometimes wealth is begotten with unlawful acts* I remind myself.

I pluck up at the door, imagining an impenetrable fortress opened only with the intangible Pennington key. I hope my informant is right and the code hasn't changed. Since the mysterious letter appeared, I've pondered my source's ability to cipher the secret password. I can only assume an affiliation, perhaps an ex-client or escort. I've also considered the letter a prank, but after observing Patrice Jensen's campus antics, I'm certain the escort business is legitimate.

Assuming a demeanor of sophistication and wealth, I stiffen and press the glowing doorbell. A few seconds later, the door unlocks, revealing a man perhaps in his mid-thirties. His midnight black suit looks too expensive for security. And his athletic physique tells me the gym is his second home. His eyes measure mine in height. He stands mum with a steady gaze, a muted exhort forces "Pennington," from my mouth.

With a curious stare, he stands silent. I assume it's my age he's questioning and brace for a barrage of questions and insistence for identification.

"Cell phone?" He asked deadpan and then explains, "No cameras or recorders allowed in the home. A precaution we take to protect our guest's privacy," he said extending his hand.

Of course, I'd anticipated safeguards and left my mobile in the car. A wise move, I think at that moment, believing he may have searched the phone for more information. "No worries here, I didn't bring it with me," I replied, patting my coat as if this would assure him.

"Can you remove your coat?"

I do as he asked.

He approaches a mere inch from my face, searching both outer and inner pockets.

"Extend your arms," he commanded.

Again, I do as he says, hoping he overlooks the dual-purpose cross about my neck. Beneath cubic zirconia stones hides miniature lens. Unless examined thoroughly, the small camera is undetectable. I stiffen as he pads my suit jacket inside out. His fingers graze the cross's metallic imprints.

He stops.

I brace for discovery.

"Open your shirt," he said with laser eyes roving my face.

I'm fucked if he's a trained profiler, able to detect the subtlest facial and body changes. Behavioral psychology, a prerequisite course I took a year ago, is finally useful. I recall facial cues indicative of liars—increased pupils, high-pitched voice, firm lips, unblinking eyes. So, I do the opposite, blink several times, relax my lips, appear as casual as possible, and unbutton my shirt, exposing the backward-facing cross.

"Catholic boy?" He smirks as if a private joke charged his mind. Turning the cross face forward, he sweeps the edges with his thumb. "No need to repent your sins here," he said, glancing at the cross. "This is all good."

I blink twice trying to relax my face, but every muscle tenses forming a trickle of sweat down my collar and a lip quiver, which I suppress with a firm bite of my molars. Out of one eye, a woman pauses in the foyer. Odd, she drops her head and hair cascades, covering her face. Perhaps she's embarrassed to be seen. I look away when the chain releases from his hand smacking my chest. He grins and pads my waist down to my ankles.

"All right, you're okay," he said finally. "You realize this is a referral business. We keep a tightly knit group here. Before I let you through, I need the name of your contact."

Shit! Contact? The letter didn't mention a contact name. Did my informant forget? *No, impossible.* A client or escort would know a reference is required, which refutes my earlier belief. The informant is an outsider. *Damn, I'm shit out of luck!* I'm not getting through that door tonight. For a moment, I accept defeat, and the next, I'm a master of deceit. "My contact is a discreet man, and I respect his privacy. But I can assure you, he's a mutual friend, and even closer friend of your employee, Patrice Jensen," I said arrogantly.

"If you're referring to Mr. Murphy, he's an important associate, as well as Patrice. You wouldn't know the young woman's name or their affiliation unless you knew them personally. You see, inside these walls, our girls are all called Belle."

What the f…! He bought it! I didn't know Patrice's lover before this point, but I do now, and I've deceived my way through. I contain a grin and listen to the next mandate which sounds absurdly like a scheme fitting a James Bond movie—cloak-and-dagger, espionage stuff. But it's not absurd given my charade as a wealthy entrepreneur and my hidden spy camera.

"When you're inside the home, your name is Pennington. It's your prerogative to reveal your real name to the girls, but we suggest you don't. Thank you, Mr. Pennington," he said, turning his body and revealing the straps of a leather gun holster. I shake my head in understanding and step inside, hoping I make it out alive.

20

Patrice

I SENSE ALLISON'S HESITANCY. She tensed the minute the car slid into the garage and the door shut. I've had this reaction from other recruits entering a strange home with a person they hardly know. I've put myself in their place many times, imagining their fear as the car crawls inside, surprised to find the party is in a private home, not a campus house or fraternity. Only one girl freaked out and demanded I take her back to the dorm. I fear from Allison's worried expression she'll do the same.

To relieve Allison's worry, I feign excitement and a party-girl vibe. "Loosen up! I said, shaking her shoulders playfully. "This is going to be fun!" I take her hand and tighten my grip around her slack resistance. "Come on," I squealed with a warm smile. "You're going to meet some awesome people tonight. You're special. Not many students get invites to these parties. It's a small, discreet group of people. You'll see what I mean." Allison's grip tightens, and she follows silent and wide-eyed into the home and through the kitchen pantry. I swing her arm like two schoolgirls, plaster a reassuring smile, and guide her around the back of the kitchen. Finally, she speaks.

"Is this your family's home?"

"No, it belongs to a friend."

"Why is it so quiet? Where's the party?"

"It's in the next room, come on," I said entwining my arm in hers and guiding her toward the billiard room ahead. My cell phone vibrates in my hand. I glance at the unexpected text from Ted.

Patrice, I need to see you immediately. I'm waiting in our special place.

Hmm, he never calls me Patrice. And why is he here? I thought he had a business dinner tonight. Maybe I got the date wrong, or he slipped out early. He couldn't have caught me at a worse time. I never leave recruits alone their first night. But I'm dying to see him. Allison's a big girl. I'm sure she'll be okay with another associate, although it's my job to make her feel comfortable and paint a rosy picture of fun evenings entertaining wealthy clientele. No one does it better than me. I talk recruits up and persuade them about a well-paid opportunity they'd never find as students. And to assuage their concern, discreetly, I insist it's their choice to provide personal services.

Don't get me wrong, I have some scruples, though acquired from wayward parents. Raised in a white, Dutch Colonial in Chevy Chase, Maryland, a home painted dreamy pastel, with white wainscoting. I lived in a quintessential Jane Austen English cottage—rooms overrun with flowers, romantic décor, and erudite books. My parents provided a simple life on their modest university salary, but money was never scarce. My father born of wealth inherited a trust fund he seldom touches. He invested wisely and splurged on special occasions—summer vacations, dance and equestrian classes, birthdays, holidays, and now my college tuition.

Loving to the point of annoying, my parents never argue, but I've sensed discontent. At moments, I thought words would unleash explosive, but mom would walk away and return stoic. Dad, the constant pacifier, would brighten momentary silence with some horrendous joke, or comical tale. My parents, cordial to the point of discomfort, hide discontent well. I suspect for my benefit. Years later, our private universe, camouflaged pastel—flowers, aromatic meals, worldly conversations, and treasured novels—burst foul when I discovered my loving parent's philandering ways. I justified their deceit quietly, never showing any disquiet. An innate psychologist, I theorized their shared passion—love for literature and their daughter—wasn't enough to satisfy passionate needs. I believed secret lovers kept them together all these years. My parent's marital deceit taught me an occasional lie is necessary, and marriage doesn't bound sexual needs.

Philandering parents and countless romantic novels launched teenage promiscuity. At the age of fifteen, my first sexual experience occurred with a man old enough to be my father, my dad's best friend. I fell painfully in love with a man who introduced me to another world, befitting my ideology. There was no pursuer in this chase, merely a secret tango of stolen glances; coy smiles, light touches, and occasional hugs which appeared innocent. One summer day, when my parents and his family vacationed together at Shelter Cove Marina on Hilton Head South Carolina, incessant flirtation turned physical. I'll never forget the adrenaline rush as he took me in the Nordhaven yacht. Below deck, the small bunk heaved with our quick actions. Above, his wife and my parent's voices, tinged with Mojito bliss, echoed audibly. My innocent clawing, frantic beneath his experienced touch, climaxed in a delightful squeal, and a rush that brought no relief, only exasperation, an insatiable need.

We dressed quickly and emerged on deck. My mother waved me toward a middle-aged clutch of professors, who couldn't dispense with university talk on vacation. Mom smiled, brushed windblown hair from my eyes, and placed a cold drink in my hand. The scent of orange blossoms escaped on a breeze from glistening, suntanned bodies. Without an ounce of remorse, I delighted in my newfound identity, my lost virginity. Several times that summer my new lover and I stole away to hidden places, but those moments were never enough. In the middle of the night, we'd find relief on a dark beach. For three summers on Shelter Cove, the clandestine affair persisted. Not even my father suspected the illicit union with his best friend. That was my first deceit.

With time, I've reconciled morality and promiscuity with philosophical studies. After all, didn't Maslow identify intimacy as a psychological necessity on the Hierarchy of Needs? As I see it, sex is as much a priority as food, water, and security. We're providing a service much like Starbucks just not on every corner. After two years of inducting recruits, I'm finding the mission rather thrilling. I'm not doing this for Ted, but to fulfill an unquenchable thirst. I suspect the adrenaline rush from my first sexual encounter triggered a surge I can't switch off.

Before I approach a target, I consider the client's needs—a young, attractive face and physique. For days, I play a mental game of studying and discerning students inclined or disinclined to participate. I have to say, I've become an expert. With the right words, I can sway a few reluctant recruits. I'm not forcing their arms, just dangling a tease too sweet to resist. Generally, I induct twenty percent of the students I recruit. The other eighty percent are too ethical for an affair they perceive degrading. But sometimes the intellectual ones are money hungry and will leap at a chance to make a thousand bucks each night.

But I suspect Allison might be a difficult persuasion, which is why I hate to leave her side. I can only imagine her alarm with my abandonment, but Ted's urgent text message commanded I come immediately to our special place, a room on the second floor. After our last heated exchange, I believe he's ready to forgive angry threats to reveal an illicit three-year affair with an underage girl if he didn't abide by my wishes. Threats I've made on several occasions with no real intent are merely a lover's tantrum for attention. He knows I would never jeopardize our affair. My threats are innocent longings for something unattainable. Besides, I refuse to ruin a family, a lifelong friendship, and my parent's reputation. The discovery of Ted's real identity would shatter Poppy's world. For her sake, I wish I could walk away, end it all, but it's too late.

I'll leave Allison just for a few minutes. She'll be okay with one of the girls. I lead her toward the bar and smile my sweetest apology. "Allison, I have to take care of an urgent matter." I motion toward a girl sitting at the bar and say, "I'm leaving you in good hands until I get back." Leaning into the inquisitive girl, I whisper, "Recruit." She shakes her head in understanding. I smile at Allison and say, "I'll be back in a jiffy." I see unease in her face as she stares around the room. I bet she expected a fraternity party with students running around drunk and unruly not a tame scene with older men. I turn and hasten out of the room.

At the front door, Ethan frisks an attractive, twentyish looking man. *Hmm, unusual.* Most of the patrons are forty and older. You seldom see twenty-year-old men in these halls. This is an older man's game. I'm sure he's a referral, and if he's not, Ethan won't let him through that door. If he's legitimate, the girls will get a thrill seeing an attractive young man tonight. Unnoticed, I waltz past the foyer, eyeing the young man's frozen expression, and continue upstairs.

As I ascend to the second floor, I imagine Ted waiting with another expensive item—his usual apology after a fight. I'm excited to see what he's bought this time, and ready to apologize for my horrendous outburst. I open the door, surprised the room is dark. In an obscured corner, Ted's sits silently. The honeyed fragrance of roses pervades the space. Another peace offering, I think. Before the door shuts, the black dress Ted bought at some posh boutique in Georgetown falls to my ankles, and light from the hallway casts my shadow floor-to-ceiling across the room. Moonlight's pale glow colors the charcoal room milky gray. I assume the unlit space another erotic game.

I take one step slipping out of one and then the second heel. Something soft squashes beneath my foot and pricks my toe. I sense roses scattered about the floor. A romantic gesture? But Ted's not the sentimental type. The loud silence is alarming as I drift toward his dark shadow. Why hasn't he spoken?

"Ted?"

A step from the chair, I stop when a familiar scent of orange blossoms sends a warning, but much too late, as the silhouette unfolds fearful.

She lunges from the chair hurling rapid jabs, voice spewing fury. "How could you do this to me? How could you..." echoes with each consecutive blow, "How could you? How could you!"

Her actions are swift, startling. I barely register the pain from the first blow. Moonlight through the window ignites my assailant's rage. Her hard, steel jabs seize my breath. I can't run or scream. I catch her wrist. She doesn't resist but stands fixed and silent with feral eyes shining sheer horror. I slide down her legs, collapsing to the floor. Silently trembling, she watches my naked, bleeding flesh.

She's waiting for me to die. I'm not afraid. I've always believed I would die young.

I tilt my head and meet her eyes. I want her to see my demise—an eternally engraved image, a tormenting ghost—an inescapable, haunting memory. In the dark, her eyes are visibly moist. My blood drips like syrup from her trembling blade.

She shudders and mouths inaudible words lost in an ocean of surging blood. The essence of orange blossoms arises, evoking a breezy summer day atop a glistening white yacht. A strange calm besets me. I've always believed death would claim me sooner than most, but not this soon, not here, not tonight, and not by those hands.

21

A Silent Witness

FOR A MOMENT, I watch Hunter at the front door until light floods the side lawn. A laughing couple, plainly drunk, staggers from the backyard. The spirited man pulls the giddy woman behind tall bushes, that shake, and shimmy with their actions. The patio's soft glow teases, inviting a stroll through the open gate.

Why not?

I could pass for a recruit. The designer cashmere, sweater-dress I'm wearing looks better than some of the girl's outfits. I remove my wool cap, brush my hair, and apply a fresh coat of makeup with one final assessment of my face. I've unwittingly convinced myself to enter the house, before considering the danger, a rash move I might regret later. Taking a deep breath, I exit the car into the brisk night; adjust the black leather belt around my hips and race toward the home.

The drunken couple moves about in shadows. They're no threat; they're hiding from discovery too. I keep my eyes fixed on security, padding Hunter's coat at the front door. Finally, out of view, I walk past quivering foliage, and the fervent couple too busy to notice as I rush toward the back entrance.

On the side patio, low voices drone nearby. I peek around the corner, spying sparse couples scattered about a large backyard, talking and re-clining under high propane heaters. Farther out past the patio, people sit around a burning fire. I look about at several doors. Entering the main patio is too risky. Someone will know I'm not one of the girls. To my left, a side door is ajar.

I wander into a long butler's pantry ending at a narrow stairway. Several passages emerge but only one I can enter unnoticed, a passage leading into the kitchen. On the counter, I swipe a drink from a tray to appear inconspicuous. Just as I round the kitchen, Patrice exits a room toward the foyer. I'm shocked by her outfit, a shamelessly tight black dress that reveals every curve, and heels at least four inches high. The bed-head hair she wears often falls in straight, shiny blond strands. If I hadn't seen her profile, I wouldn't have recognized her.

I follow Patrice down the hall and pause when I see a man examining a chain around Hunter's neck at the front door. Is that what he pulled from his pocket when I watched from the car? Why did he decide at the last minute to wear it? I lower my head, letting my hair hide my face. Hunter catches me with one eye and then turns his gaze to the probing man. Did he recognize me? He couldn't have. Besides, he doesn't know who I am. For all he's concerned, I'm just an escort. I rush past the foyer into the stairwell, and upstairs.

I've lost Patrice. She could be in any of the rooms lining the long corridor. I wander toward a small alcove with a seating area, and frit about, feeling insanely stupid with no clue of what to do next. Before I left the car, I should have thought this through clearly. Did I think I could just walk in, confront Patrice, and convince her to come with me? *Silly!* She'll be livid I've snuck inside, and second, mortified I've discovered her secret. Angry and defiant, she'll probably tell me to leave. That I know, she'll do, but I also realize embarrassment will ensue with my discovery. More than anything, I need to convince Patrice how dangerous and unethical this is, but I suspect my worries won't sway her judgment. At least being inside this house gives me an idea of what occurs here, although I'll never have an accurate view of what transpires in private between escort and patron.

I hope Hunter made it past security. Curious, I stroll toward the staircase and peek over the balustrade. They're gone. *Did he make it in?* Just as I'm about to check downstairs, a sharp cry resounds down the corridor. I cringe. Several sharp groans timbres close, in a room near the alcove. My flesh crawls as cries grow louder. Angry, clipped words escape intense with every moan—a woman's pain.

An unmistakable voice sounds from the room, its feral tone sending a chill through me. I move nearer as guttural words and moans pierce the wooden door. Then there's silence. Footsteps move further into the room. A faucet runs, and water splashes from an adjacent door then stop. Steps resume, growing farther away, resounding as if they're moving downstairs. I waver at the door, fearing the other side. The room is dark and quiet, except for the door creak as I enter.

A floral musk fills the air. My eyes adjust to the dark, widening in horror. I cup my mouth, muting a scream, wary of danger lurking inside the house. Moonlight illuminates shivering naked flesh. Choppy wheezes escape her breath. In disbelief, I approach tangling my shoe in something on the floor. The black dress and stiletto heels she wore moments ago, confirm what my mind refutes.

"Patrice!"

I kneel and lift her head, wincing at oozing blood. She shivers through wheezing breath, and whispers a name, confirming the undeniable voice I'd heard on the other side of the door. *Why! My* mind screams. "Patrice, I'm so sorry ... sorry," I utter through blinding tears. "Why would she do this to you?" She whispers inaudible words. Then she shudders with three loud gasps. Before I can lower my ears to her lips, footsteps approach from the back of the room and the hallway. Quickly, I slide under the bed, pull covers to the floor, and hide from danger.

22
A Harrowing Escape

THE GUN HOLSTER is unnerving but doesn't prevent me from advancing into an impressive foyer. Nonetheless, I'm mindful of danger close behind. Quiet chatter whirls about gothic halls and hidden spaces. Vigilant of every room and passageway, I stroll along a winding staircase and wander past a great room exploding with an abstract painting above the fireplace. Adjusting the miniature camera forward, I meander under high archways, past a formal dining room, open kitchen, and arrive at a spherical chamber boasting a sizable satin sectional. Two odd couples, like father and daughter, sit at opposite ends, engaged in private chatter. Both men appear older than fifty, and the two young women, eighteen or nineteen. The scene looks innocent, but I bet the conversation isn't.

Beyond patio doors, voices emanate from the night and firelight reveals guests in scattered spaces. A man stands at the threshold, like a guard dutifully at his post, gazing at an artificially lit backyard. I blink twice at a blond man seated in an oversized wicker chair. I'm sure I've seen his face before, but at the moment, it slips my mind. A thick-boned man enters the courtyard and whispers in his ear. The blond man springs from the chair and summons a bald man in the corner. He approaches with a perplexed expression that swiftly turns to shock. With a brisk stride, the two men leave the patio, rushing toward the foyer. The blond man slumps in the chair, grabs a glass from the table, drums his fingers rapidly, and swallows the drink in a single gulp with an ensuing headshake. He sits upright and looks around the patio, then bounds from the chair. I assume rushing to an urgent matter the linebacker and bald man headed minutes ago.

Something's going on.

Voices stream from hidden spaces and pinging pool balls resonate around the three-level home. Out of nowhere, a man barrels down a back staircase into my chest. "Whoa, buddy," I said, staggering from the impact.

With a flit of an eye, he rushes to the basement.

That's rude. Just knock me over. An excuse me would have been acceptable.

Voices pull me toward a spacious billiard room and open bar. Men and women move about coupled and uncoupled, prowlers on the hunt for a quarry come to mind. Soon, I realize pursuers are both male and female as I search for the fawn-eyed student, meeting several women's suggestive glances. I ignore them and look away, finding beside me, stealthier than a navy seal, the man who frisked me at the door. I smile and pretend interest in the scene.

"Whatever your preference," he said.

And I'm sure it's not the alcohol he alludes to. I nod with understanding. He smiles a half-grin. The thick-boned man who rushed from the patio moments ago approaches, and whispers quick words in his ear. I watch the two men move swiftly through the crowd and out of the room. Recalling the scene on the patio, I'm certain something dire is occurring under this roof.

I gaze at Allison, remembering the first time I'd heard her name on the campus quad, a name too simple for an exotic face. A man crosses the room toward the bar, addresses the young woman next to Allison, and throws them both a smile. He mouths a few words at the girl, and she slides from the stool. She whispers into Allison's ear then waltzes from the room with the man.

Allison glances about with skittish eyes and grimaces at the deer head trophy mounted over the fireplace. A dead ringer for Leo Lord, a well-known attorney to Washington bigwigs, swoops into the empty stool, and whispers in her ear. She smiles disinterest, looks away, and fidgets with her drink. Covertly, I ensure the camera is faced forward, confident I'll capture similar noteworthy patrons in the room. The man leans closer. Annoyed, Allison averts her eyes, searching around the room. I wonder if she's looking for Patrice Jensen. Roguishly grinning, the Leo Lord replica refills her drink. I perceive his licentious intent. Protective instincts swell as I watch the scene unfold. Allison takes the glass with a polite smile but avoids the man's enamored gaze.

A young woman, I'm sure I've seen before, rises from the dark, masculine, leather sofa in the center of the room. She approaches, blocking the scene at the bar.

"Do I know you?" she asked with an uncertain smile.

"I don't think so." Straightaway, I assume she's seen me on campus. Then I remember the noisy girl from the library whose cell phone tweeted every other minute. She'd appeared annoyed, gathered her books, and fled the library in a huff. I'm positive it was her. On the nape of her neck lies a small Chinese tattoo. As I'd sat behind her in the library, I'd wondered what it meant. Tonight, her hair covers the enigmatic symbol.

"You're a pleasing sight. Not many men your age attend these parties. It's mostly older, wealthy types, you know, the lonely one's looking for a young woman's company, an escape from the wife. So, you're not old, and you're too young to be married—"

"But I could be a wealthy philanthropist venturing to help a young woman pay her college tuition," I said, eyes drifting back and forth from her face to the bar.

"Hmmm," she purred. "You can help me any day," she said, placing her hand on my arm.

Her bold words are unoriginal and her closeness intrusive. Although she lacks grace, I'm sure her act arouses much attention. Her persona is that of a child playing a poorly rehearsed role. She cocks her head and forces a smile. I want to tell her to stop. You don't have to do this. But I can't draw suspicion. Her coy eyes roam an unsteady line from my eyes to my mouth. I guess she's waiting for me to respond with interest. I'm assuming she's a recent recruit from her nervousness. I sway sideways and look toward the bar, torn between rescuing Allison from the leech beside her and uncovering the story in this home. As long as I keep her in view, she's safe. So, I turn my attention to the young woman stroking my arm. "What brings a young woman like you here?"

"Similar reasons as yours," she said straightforward.

"And what's that?"

"Pleasure and good company."

"That's a dangerous assumption. My reasons could be more nefarious. I might be a deranged man seeking depraved fantasies," I said with unflinching eyes.

She laughs.

Seriously! I think. I don't smile, hoping she understands the gravity of my words. But she doesn't. Do any of the escorts worry about potential danger?

"If that's your preference, I can direct you to someone with the same preference," she said, looking at a seemingly bored woman in the corner.

I say nothing and smile, all the while scrutinizing the man leaning into Allison's ear. Perturbed, Allison takes a sip of the drink and looks away. Her eyes meet mine for an instant. I swerve from view, catching the inquisitive glare of the woman invading my space. "How did you discover this place?" I asked.

"I didn't. They discovered me."

"Being an escort doesn't bother you?"

"I hate that question," she said swiftly. "When you look around this room, what does it remind you of?"

Her vehemence surprises me, and I realize she's heard this question before. I glance around the room, studying the small crowd. "If I had no idea what occurs here, I would say I'd walked into an upscale bar."

"Exactly! The only difference is the crowds more polite, and each party knows it's a business deal. There're no lies, expectations, or heartbreak involved. It's just one exchange for another. But judgmental people label it immoral behavior."

"There's a significant difference—the exchange of money for sex. In a bar, it's just two people meeting, and sex isn't the main priority. But if they hook-up, its mutual attraction not money bringing them together."

"That's a big misconception. Most of these men want company or someone to share special occasions with. And if each party agrees to sex, there's nothing wrong with that. It's another need and two willing people. The girls aren't forced to do anything they don't want, and no one's keeping me here against my will. If I choose to leave, I can. Honestly, I like meeting successful men. They're interesting and respectable."

Respectable ... If that were true, they wouldn't be here, I think. How naïve is she? She's already rationalized her role. Not wanting to appear suspect, I change the topic quickly. "This house is ridiculous. Who's the owner?"

"We're not told. The owner's a mystery as well as the guest. Honestly, I prefer anonymity," she said, touching my cross. "Nice ... Are you Catholic?"

For the second time tonight, the cross rouses religious interest. "No." I said too fast. The scene at the bar spikes my concern. Visibly upset, Allison unpeels a lecherous hand from her thigh, leaves the bar, and stumbles into another room.

"So, what's your interest tonight?" She asked.

I force a smile and detach her hand from my chest. "Sorry, but tonight I have other interests. Take care of yourself." *Take care of yourself.* You should have said you need to leave here and never return. But I don't and move toward the exit Allison slipped moments before into a room which loops back toward the foyer. On shaky stilettos, I find her climbing the stairs. After thirty minutes in the home, she can't be drunk. Is she searching for Patrice or a bathroom? There's an instant protective urge to swoop her off her feet and carry her from this place, but I imagine she'll protest fearfully. I stay at the bottom of the stairs until she ascends to the landing, watching her uncertain left to right glances. Something catches her attention, and Allison wobbles out of view. *Perhaps she's found Patrice.*

With caution, I climb the stairs, uncertain of what's above. I pause, listening for sounds on the second floor, *nothing.* Arriving at the landing, I catch Allison's crimson dress before she enters the room. A thump sounds. A man rushes from the hall alcove into the room. The door closes quickly.

Whoa! Something's wrong!

Rushing down the corridor, angry, clipped whispers sail around the hall. A shrill scraping trails across floors, screeching to a halt. Approaching footsteps alert someone's nearing the door. I scuttle into an adjacent room, instantly, aware I've entered an adjoining bathroom. The bedroom door opens a slow, hesitant creak then closes. I stare through a slit at two men entering the corridor. They wobble side-to-side carrying a long object, sidling toward the stairs. From my angle, the item is imprecise. I wait, watch, and listen as they climb to the third floor and jump when my hip bumps the bathroom sink sending a butcher knife sliding into the ceramic bowl. Curious, red stains stream into the drain. *Is it blood?*

Anxiously, I move past the bathroom and dressing room toward a gothic style bedroom with dark cherry walls and floors. Allison's crimson dress appears a bloodstain on a four-poster bed swathed in white quilts. I move closer, fearing the door bursting open, thwarting my efforts with a lethal bullet. Beneath my shoes, something crunches. *What happened here?* The room's disarray and apparent signs of a struggle send a warning. Roses litter the entire space as if a bouquet was tossed into the air, scattering helter-skelter. Bedspreads cascade, sliding messily to the floor. Skewed chairs sit at odd angles, and a candelabrum in front of the fireplace has fallen from the mantel where an identical one remains.

I rush to the bed littered with tattered rose petals and lean over Allison's body. Her ribs rise and fall with breath warming my face. A nasty red bruise on her forehead can only be from the thump I heard when she entered the room. She must have fallen and bumped her head, or someone knocked her unconscious. The swelling is slight, so I assume it's a harmless bruise. But she'll feel it in the morning. A thick, dark splotch stains the front of her crimson dress. I run my finger along the spot. It's wet, and colors my finger red. I sniff detecting the metallic scent of blood.

It can't be from the scrap on her head. She's not bleeding. On the edge of the bed, bloodstains appear irregular. Alarmed, I turn Allison from her side to her back, checking from her neck down to her shoes. There's no apparent injury.

She moans.

Glazed eyes open, catching mine for a quick second then roll into her head. She's not drunk, but drugged! Staring about the room, I'm alarmed by the detectible crime scene. *What happened in here?* There's no time to think, we have to get out of this house, but getting Allison past the sentinel at the door might be difficult. It dawns on me they'll return, and when they find her missing, they're bound to search the house.

I've got to get her up!

Given her drugged stupor, there's only one way out, and that's to carry her through the door. I deliberate a position that won't impede my speed. The fireman carriage I'd learned from my brother may prove difficult. Without further thought, I scoop her into an old-fashion bridal carriage, lumber past the dressing room, through the bathroom, and then I notice another space down the never-ending suite.

Past the bath lies a study. From what I remember of these old homes, this was a servant's quarter years ago, gutted into one big master suite. At the back of the room stairs confirm my suspicion, stairs servants used to enter and exit the home. Then I remember the collision as the man rushed down the back staircase. And if I'm right, these are the same stairs that lead to the kitchen and a servant's entrance.

With Allison in my arms, I lumber to the stairs, halting at the perilously steep stairwell. I need a free hand to prevent a tumble to the bottom. The fireman's carriage is the only way down the steps. Lowering Allison's legs to the floor and leaning her into my chest, her eyes open, lips curl an irresistible smile, followed by an uncontrollable head roll. Her bee-stung lips, moist and soft, brush mine with drug-induced willingness. I've imagined kissing her many times but not like this, unaware of what she's doing. Instant guilt assails me, and at once, I release my lips from hers. She moans a protest.

"No, I want to, but not here, not now, Allison," I whisper inches from her lips, and straighten her stance.

Quickly, before willpower dwindles, I inch my leg between hers, squat and drape her over my shoulder. With one hand securing her in place, the other firm on the banister, I descend the stairs slowly but worry when voices and movement sound from behind. *They've found her missing.*

I descend the stairs quicker when frictionless loafers send me sliding forward. I grasp the banister tighter, impeding a catapult to the bottom. Landing on one knee, the other angled behind, Allison slips—a heavy cape down my spine. A rush of adrenaline bolsters my strength and spikes my pulse with fear of discovery. Straining, I hold my balance under her weight and readjust her body forward. Angling sideways, I step cautiously, listening to voices below and behind grow closer. At the bottom of the stairs, a narrow hallway parallels the kitchen through a butler's pantry ending at a side door.

Marble floors, shiny with gloss, may prove difficult in frictionless shoes. On unstable footing, I hurry toward the exit, when Allison begins to stir, twitching above my shoulder. She tries to resist, entangling her hand with the chain around my neck, pulling and strangling my throat. With one hand, I grip her thighs firmly, and with the other hand, release the chain from her grasp. She stops moving, falling lax across my back. The broken chain slips, sending the spy camera pinging on marble floors. Breathless, I turn in my tracks and try to bend and pick it up. *Forget it. There's no time!* Heedlessly, I bend forward. She slips, and I toppled, catching my fall with one hand. *Impossible!* Angry voices approach from the stairwell. *Damn! Leave it!* I gain my balance, and speed toward the door, praying we're not stopped by armed resistance.

Part Three
Memories Awakened

23
Hermoso Principe Caballerosa

Present-Day

I KNOW YOU WERE THERE. I saw Hunter carry you out. Eleven words leave me outraged. The thought of strangers watching a man carry me unconscious is embarrassing and unnerving. How many others saw him lug me from that house? For two years I've imagined curious onlookers gazing at my unconscious body, assuming I was drunk. *But I wasn't, I had two drinks damn it!* Allie, there are worst things to worry about. Why does my tormentor want me to remember that house? What happened to Belle?

Hunter. Finally, after two years, I know the mystery man's name. For months, I've tried to recall his touch, smell, or voice, anything to jolt my memory. The attractive man my roommate Lisa described visited my dreams with a kiss for months, which oddly, felt real. Many nights, I'd stand with him in front of a large window above a stairwell. His shadowy figure would recede and reappear in different shapes as if my mind was reconstructing his image. I've questioned whether the mystery man, I now know as Hunter, kissed me while I was unconscious. Why else would the images persist over and over? Eventually, the dream stopped, but now, it's like a scene from a movie I can't forget.

I don't recall ever meeting a student named Hunter, but I'm sure Emsworth University enrolled many students with that name. Immediately, I race upstairs in search of the Alumni Directory, find it on the bookshelf, and bring it to the dining room table. I've never bothered looking inside. Every year, when I receive an updated directory, I store it away with other school memorabilia. Lisa said Hunter was a senior, a year ahead of my class. Surprisingly, there were nine students named Hunter, but none fit my roommate's description of a raven-haired hottie. The only one who saw Hunter bring me to the dorm was Lisa. I'll never forget her enamored declaration. "Hermoso principe caballerosa!" She'd swooned over the handsome, chivalrous senior who'd brought me to the dorm. Lisa is a protective friend and never told a soul about that night. She'd occasionally joke in private but stopped when she realized it disturbed me.

It's been eight months since I've spoken to Lisa. The last time we talked, she was still in Washington, D.C., working for a Public Relations firm. Without her, I wouldn't have survived my junior year. Her innate ability to strengthen others helped me through my ordeal. I've always believed she was a godsend, placed in my life at the right time. Lisa is a lioness and protective of all her friends and loved ones. She'd make an excellent life coach or psychiatrist. I've always wondered why she chose a career in Public Relations. I guess her ability to inspire others is just as valuable in PR.

In my contacts, I find Lisa's number and hope it hasn't changed. We promised to stay in touch and visit as often as possible. But after we started working, life got in the way of that promise. Too busy with our careers, phone calls grew sporadic and then stopped altogether. I've always meant to call her, but never found the right time, until now. After eight months, she'll be surprised to hear my voice.

"Hello."

God, how I've missed her voice, I hadn't realized how much until she said hello. "Hello, roomie."

"Allie? Oh my God, where have you been? Do you know I've tried to reach you for months? I couldn't remember the firm you worked for, and your cell phone number changed. I even tried Louisiana, but I couldn't remember the town your mother lives in."

"Lisa, I'm sorry. With the job I got so busy, and after the layoff, I needed time to rethink life, but I've meant to call you with my new number."

"I'm sorry about the layoff. What're you doing now?"

"I've decided to freelance until I figure out the next step. How about you? Are you still in PR?"

"You're not going to believe it!"

"Don't tell me you're now CEO of your company."

"I'm CEO of my own life," she said with a chuckle. "Guess what?" She asked, prompting a stab in the dark. I picture a big grin and raised brows, waiting for a response. But before I fathom a guess, she screeches through the phone.

"I'm married!"

"Are you serious? When did this happen?" Marriage is not what I expected. In school, Lisa always said she'd wait until her thirties to marry. She wanted a career before settling down.

"Allie, I wanted you as my Maid of Honor, but I couldn't reach you. Instead, I had to settle for the second-best, but the wedding would have been more special with you there."

"Darn! I've always wanted to be a Maid of Honor." And that's the truth, even though I've no desire to rush into marriage, I love the idea of supporting a friend on such a special occasion. "So, when did the wedding take place?"

"For sixty-five days, I've been Mrs. Casales, and happily free of my job at the PR Firm."

"You quit?"

"As soon as I married, I left. Andrew bought this cozy old restaurant in Georgetown, and we've been fixing it up for months."

"That's great! You always liked cooking. You'll make a great restaurant owner." Perhaps she figured out earlier than most what she wants in life. "I'm so happy for you!"

"There's something else?"

"Don't tell me you're pregnant?"

"Yep!"

"Oh my God, I was just kidding! You're pregnant already? How many months?"

"A little over two months, it wasn't planned, it happened during the honeymoon. Neither one of us wanted to start the marriage with a baby. But we are, and I can't be more thrilled."

"Wow! Congratulations!"

"I still can't believe it. I guess it'll sink in when my belly starts showing. I'm planning a baby shower, so you have to come."

"I will. Just let me know when and I'll jump in the car with gifts and cheer."

"So, Allie, is there anyone in your life?"

"Nah, I'm blissfully single at the moment. Lisa, I hate to bring this up again, especially with all your good news. But I need your sharp memory." I remember the promise I made the last day of school, to put this all behind me and move on. I don't want Lisa to think I'm obsessing about this again. But she was the only one who saw Hunter that night.

"My mind isn't as sharp as it was in school, but I hope I can help."

"Do you remember the night I blacked out at the off-campus party and the guy who brought me to the dorm?"

"Yea, how can I forget? Why do you ask?"

"Well, I just discovered his first name is Hunter."

"Oh, is your memory coming back?"

"No, and I can't go into details right now. But I'm hoping you remember someone named Hunter from school."

"Hunter ... That sounds familiar."

"No one fits his description in the alumni directory. Do you recall anything unique about him?"

"It's been so long. As I told you before, he was attractive, raven hair, brown eyes; about six feet. He carried himself with a self-possession you don't see in men that age. But other than hair and eye coloring, I can't remember any other traits. Oh, I was surprised when he switched languages. At the time, I thought he was politely acknowledging my nationality. He told me to be safe and look after you in Spanish. So, he could be Latino."

"You never mentioned that."

"I didn't? I thought I had."

"Well, I wish I knew where to find him. He's possibly the only person who can shed some light on what happened that night. I'm so tired of guessing."

"Allie, it's been two years, if you don't remember now, I don't think you ever will. You have to let go."

"I wish I could, but it's not that simple. Remember the girl who disappeared junior year?"

"Yeah, it was all over campus."

"Well, she's the girl who invited me to the party."

"Why didn't you tell me?"

"At the time, I didn't know it was her. Whoever saw me with Patrice that night, believes I know what happened, but I don't."

"So, you think Hunter can help?"

"He was there and must have seen something."

"I don't know why, but his name rings a bell. Hmmm, the yearbook must have a picture of Hunter. I'll look through my school albums and see what I can find."

"Maybe it sounds familiar because he was in one of your classes."

"No, I would have remembered him. I never saw him before that night. But I think there was a guy named Hunter associated with a student club. It'll come to me. Let me do some digging, and I'll get back to you."

"Thanks, Lisa. It's so good hearing your voice!"

"Well, you'll be hearing it more often. You should come to D.C. We can catch up, and you can see our new house in Foggy Bottom, not too far from the University. We acquired this cute baby-blue row house with our new marital status. From what I remember, you had a fascination with row homes."

"I do. And when I get the chance, I'd love to see it."

"You're not working now, so it's the perfect time to come down. I'd love your company. Andrew's always at the restaurant, and I'm banned from the site now that I'm pregnant. It gets lonely here sometimes. All I've been doing is fixing up the house and preparing for the baby. I could use a friend right about now."

"I could use a break from the city. Let me sleep on it, and I'll let you know tomorrow." The idea of jumping in my car, leaving New York and my worries behind is tempting, but surely, my problems will stalk me to Washington, D.C., the place this mess started.

24
Impromptu Getaway

IT DOESN'T TAKE LONG to make up my mind. As soon as the call ended, the duplex's walls cave in followed by an anxiety attack and an urgent need to flee. Then I realize the District of Columbia is where I need to be, close to campus so I can dig up information about Hunter. The proximity of Kalorama Road might jolt my memory.

Promptly, I call Lisa back, accept her invitation, pack an overnight bag, and leave Nikki a note. Running away to D.C. is impulsive and uncharacteristic, but I'm tired of feeling anxious and guessing. I can't spend my life wondering about that night. I need to know what happened. Without further thought, I escape to the garage and my steel gray Audi, which I haven't driven since the layoff.

Exiting the city, my breath grows lighter, and my head clearer, watching skyscrapers dwindle from view. I bypass I-95's dull, flat roads and nerve-racking gridlock, opting for I-78's scenic route. A route I'd traveled four years to and from school. I believed I'd settle in the District of Columbia, Maryland or Virginia when I graduated, but when mom inherited Grandma Blu's home and moved back to Louisiana, Nikki and I got the condo. Prime New York City real estate we were happy to own. But, now, in a heartbeat, I'd move to escape the congested city, a city I once loved, crushes like a claustrophobic box. I guess I've changed, as all my friends have. And given Nikki's pregnancy, moving to D.C. is a good idea. She'll need the second bedroom for the baby. I know there's slim chance Nikki will change her mind and marry the baby's father, but I hope as her belly grows, she'll outgrow her fear of marriage.

* * *

Four hours later, I'm in D.C. I don't go straight to Lisa's but peruse old roads, spy old haunts, wind the car towards the University's grounds, exit toward Foggy Bottom, and cruise until I find the periwinkle row house with a bright red door between a pastel yellow and green home. Lisa must have been sitting at the window because the door flings open before I exit the car.

There she stands a little heavier, but otherwise, she still looks the same. Below-the-shoulder length hair she sported in college is now a pixy cut exposing her slender neck. The haircut surrounds her small face, making her look almost like a child in adult clothing. Her long, thick hair was her best feature. Why the drastic haircut? I exit the car, wave excitedly, and cross the street. I practically run up the narrow red-brick path, beaming ear-to-ear as Lisa jumps up and down with joy. She grabs my shoulders with a tight squeeze, and my eyes moisten. No other friend solicits these emotions.

We kiss on the cheek and examine each other as if it's been fifty, not two years since we last saw each other. Strangely, it feels just days ago we cried at graduation. After four years together, parting ways for our new lives was difficult. Lisa pushes overgrown bangs from her wide-set, brown eyes, and smiles elatedly.

"I love the new look," I said, but miss her thick Spanish waves.

"It was time for a change, but I regret it now," she said displeased and brushing her bangs from her eyes. "I'm letting it grow out again."

"We've all had hairstyle regrets," I said, glancing at her belly. The loose T-shirt dress hides any hint of pregnancy.

"The house is beautiful Lisa!"

"It's still work-in-progress, but we love it, especially given its only walking distance to Rock Creek Park. Remember I always said I'd buy a house right near the park. Well, I got my wish."

Buying a row house close to the park was my dream. Somehow, Lisa's forgotten the wish list I created in college. My vision was to become an editor with a major newspaper, buy a Victorian row house with a home office overlooking the park, and find a man who shares my passions. Perhaps it was a mutual ambition, a goal she accomplished two years after graduation. I've taken a detour, but my dream has never changed. "You did, and you're lucky, not many row homes are on the market."

"I guess you can say it was luck. Three years ago, Andrew inherited the home from his uncle when he moved back to Spain. He'd had enough of Washington and wanted to go back to his roots in Valencia. Andrew's like his son, so it was only natural to leave the house to him."

"Ah! Well, that's favorable," I said humorously. "Where would we be without relatives with real estate?"

"Living in small apartments in neighborhoods we hate," Lisa said, fanning her face with her hand. "Whew! It's an oven out here, come inside."

"Wow, this is gorgeous," I said, welcoming the cold blast of air from the air-conditioner, and the spicy aroma drifting from the kitchen. The long, narrow space is typical row house architecture. The main floor's layout runs in one straight line from the front door to the kitchen. They've gutted eighteenth-century features for a modern style, and down the hall are signs of more renovations. Slipcovered furnishings and powder blue walls give the home a classic feel. From the living room to the kitchen, recessed lighting covers the ceiling. Along the steep, white staircase, lays a small dining area opened to a beautiful kitchen. Through the open backdoor, sits a rectangular patio boasting an outdoor eating area shaded by foliage, and surrounded by a tall, tan picket fence, securing the backyard from adjacent neighbors. This is undoubtedly Lisa's taste, but I can't attest to her husband's style.

"So, who is this Andrew you married?"

"You know him."

"I do?"

"Uh-huh," she said, sauntering toward the mantelpiece, removing, and handing me a framed, black-and-white, wedding photo of two amorous people. "Remember the guy we sat next to junior year at a Hoya football game?"

"No."

"Yes, you do. You were upset because Andrew kept looking at me even though his girlfriend was beside him."

"Oh, yeah ... Now I remember," I said, staring at the photo, recalling Andrew's flirtatious back-and-forth smiles at Lisa. "I felt so sorry for his oblivious girlfriend. She had no idea he was giving you the eye. She looked so sweet snuggled into his side with her head on his shoulder. I wanted to scream turn around every time he glanced at you. If she hadn't been so involved in the football game, she probably would have smacked him across the face if she'd caught him," I said with a chuckle. *I hope he's matured and is more respectful of Lisa.* "Wait, you guys never hooked up in school."

"Yes, we did, during senior year. But it was only that one time, I swear. When I found out Andrew was still seeing his girlfriend, I refuse to return any of his phone calls. That's why I never told you about him. I didn't see the point."

"So how did you end up married two years later?"

"Three months after graduation, we bumped into each other at a restaurant in Georgetown. Shortly after, we started dating, and now I'm Mrs. Casales," she said, gleefully wiggling her fingers.

There's that waving motion. It saddens me when engaged, or newlyweds display their rings like some prized trophy, believing marriage is a passage to a blissful life. Most married people I've met look miserable. Mom wasn't happy. I've never had any desire to sport an engagement or wedding ring on my finger. Will I turn into one of these gloating women when it happens? Perhaps there's a little Nikki in me after all. I've never pictured Lisa flashing a wedding ring. She's changed as well. Maybe outside secure campus walls, reality dictates our lives.

"I guess it was love at first sight, meant to be," I said.

"I guess so … Wow! You haven't changed a bit, Allie. You look great."

I recall the dark circles under my eyes this morning and disagree. "I've looked better. I haven't been sleeping well lately."

"No, you look great. I'm serious. But you do look a little tired." Lisa leads me through the dining room into the kitchen, undergoing remodeling. Cooking utensils, bowls of ingredients, and a camera lay on one counter. In the stove, something spicy is roasting. From the refrigerator, she removes a jug of ice tea and brings it to the plastic-protected island. "Sorry about the plastic. We just installed new cabinets and the granite island. Painters are coming in this week, so we covered everything for protection."

"No worries. The kitchen looks beautiful. I'm sure when it's finished, it will look stunning."

"This has been my life for several months. If I didn't have remodeling to keep me busy, I'd die of boredom."

From what I remember of Lisa in school, she was always busy with student projects. I never understood how she juggled so many tasks with her studies, but she made it look effortless. She said employers love extracurricular activities on resumes. She was right. I remember recruiter's asking what clubs and affiliations I joined on campus. I'd wanted to write for the student newspaper but never got around to it. I'll always regret not having that experience. I guess life will hold many regrets as I grow older. Lisa was such a ball of fire in school; I'm sure leaving a career was a tough decision. She fills two frosty glasses and sits with an ambiguous grin. Without any warning, she's smiling and crying simultaneously.

"What's wrong?"

"Nothing, I'm just glad you're here. It feels good having company after spending days alone in this house. All my friends are busy with their careers, and Andrew gets home late every day. I miss having someone to talk to besides my mother on the phone."

"Why did you quit your job?"

"I hated PR. It was just a job until I figured out what to do next. After the wedding and getting pregnant, I decided it was time to quit. Allie, don't laugh, but I honestly like the idea of being a housewife."

I do laugh because, in school, Lisa stated defiantly, I'll never become a stay-at-home mom. Never say never, is what I'd replied. And I was right. "I'm sorry; I'm not laughing at you, just the irony of the situation. So, if you enjoy this life, why are you crying?"

"I'm just hormonal. Lately, I cry at everything. The other day I cried during a cat food commercial. I'm so ridiculous lately."

I laugh again, picturing Lisa on the couch and a cute kitten causing her to weep. "Hormones will do that. Sounds like me before my period is due. I start crying about the silliest things. But I imagine pregnancy hormones are worst. Anyway, you'll make a great mom, Lisa. If this life makes you happy, then this is what you should do and stop worrying about what others think."

"I knew you'd say that. That's what I love about you, Allie. You allow people to be who they are without harsh judgment. If I'd said I want to be a mountain climber, you would have said go for it," she replied with a chuckle. "Okay, enough about me. What's going on with you?" Lisa asked, wiping her eyes and sitting straight in the backless chair. "And why can't you let go of that horrible night?"

I recall Lisa's reactions in dire moments at school. Fear and danger paralyze her into a contemplative state as she weighed her options. I imagine she will digest my problem and consider a rational solution. But there's only one answer this time, remembering that night. I sigh deeply. "I can't let go of that night because someone won't let me forget."

"What do you mean?"

"For months, I'd received emails with a single question. What happened at 1414 Kalorama Road? The email freaked me out the first time. I thought it might be a prank until I started receiving one every month. I became paranoid and believed someone was watching me. Then the emails grew more insistent as if they wanted me to remember." I continue telling Lisa everything about the party and Undaunted's manuscript, watching her eyes grow wider.

"And you don't want to go to the police?"

"No!" I said, shaking my head. "That's the worse move I could make, not until I know more."

"Have you thought about hypnosis? Therapists help amnesiacs recall memories all the time."

"At this point, I'm open to any suggestions."

"Andrew has friends at the hospital. I'm sure he could get a referral."

"I don't know Lisa. I'm not ready for that just yet."

"Yet! It's been two years, and you still can't remember. A hypnotist is your best alternative."

"I'm not saying no, just not before I visit that house and talk to Hunter."

Sniffing the air, she rises and rushes to the oven. "What makes you think you can get inside that house?"

I take a sip of iced tea, hanging on her words as she checks the roasting chicken. "I'll think of some way to get in."

Closing the oven, she struts pensively toward the chair. "I don't know, Allie," she said with pinched brows and a noisy sip of the iced tea. "It's too risky. Besides, if this Pennington's the homeowner, he might not want a stranger roaming about his property. Allie, you don't know who you're dealing with. What if they're criminals and they recognize you. It's too dangerous."

"Or he might not recognize me. It's a chance I'll have to take. And besides, he's a detective, remember?"

"You think just because he's a detective he's not involved in wrongdoing? Think again, Allie. They're some of the worst criminals."

25

Interview With Danger

NO MATTER HOW GRAND and inviting, this place gives me the creeps. But the home has held me in captivation since I invaded its premises as a student journalist under the guise of a wealthy entrepreneur. How clueless I was at twenty-two, throwing myself into danger. I could be dead. I never imagined, two years later, I'd still be searching for Patrice Jensen, and she'd usurp my mental energy. All I know is Patrice went into that house and never came out. Is her body still on the property? I've often asked myself that question given what I saw from the bathroom that night—a long object two men carried upstairs. Was it Patrice's body?

Many times, I've plotted ways to break inside, but today, I won't have to. After two years, I'll walk through the door as a guest, not under pretense. Shortly after Patrice went missing, I discovered the homeowner's name, a powerful well-respected man in the District of Columbia who can silence a hungry reporter without remorse.

Parking the car on a familiar curb, I sit behind the wheel reflecting on senior year at EU. Even now, the Dean's directives make me angry as he'd clamped down on the student newspaper, threatening suspension if I published one more allegation. An action he took when a maelstrom of inquiries from worried parents, demanded Emsworth's take precaution against student's lecherous pursuits. Defiantly persistent, I refused to abandon a focused investigation when I'm right. I tempered my hotheadedness, assumed compliance, ignored warnings, and searched for proof to substantiate my claim.

With no more clues, I hit a dead end until one came during a moment of defeat—the names of Emsworth's board of directors on University letterhead. Curiously, searching the Internet, I struck gold; discovering Franklin Emsworth, a prominent benefactor, board member, and great-grandson of the University's founder owns 1414 Kalorama Road. Eager to prove my claim, I'd dialed the Dean's office without forethought. Franklin's a powerful man, and I knew the Dean would challenge my accusations. And he did. He'd argued the party was just a typical gathering of friends and business associates—associates who'd probably deny wrongdoing to protect their reputations.

Despite the Dean's rebuttal, I know the truth. I saw Patrice enter that home. The only credible evidence slipped from my neck when I raced from the property. The miniature camera easily discovered in view on white marble floors. Soon after that night parties ceased, but I'd suspected they didn't desist, just moved to another location.

For months, I pondered the school's silence. Were they protecting the University or Franklin? The board knew more than they'd revealed to the press. Why else the intensive censoring of the campus newspaper. I suspect 1414 Kalorama Road's influential patrons colluded, covering up a crime that could destroy them all.

Now, here I am again, wiser, and no longer a school reporter, but a professional investigative journalist with the Washington Post, uncensored, and without University demands. However, I'm certain Franklin Emsworth kept close tabs on my efforts. But after two years, why's he finally granted an interview? Without a doubt, he's aware I'm the student who tried to expose his illegal business.

Vigilantly, I approach 1414 Kalorama Road, ring the doorbell and wait for a man I've extensively researched to answer. For months, I've gathered information from acquaintances and business associates, molding an arrogant man exploiting his family's name and wealth. Over the years, Franklin's many university endowments appear self-aggrandizing means to gain control, and perhaps, the Dean's reason for ending my investigation.

In a year, I've uncovered Franklin's transgressions and various foibles—young women, excessive drinking, gambling, and other unseemly exploits. Besides his family's wealth, Franklin built his fortune as a Real Estate Developer. Married three times, he'd never had children. All three wives divorced him because of philandering ways, leaving the marriage wealthier than they'd been as single women. Regardless, he's never without a woman on his arm, usually conspicuously young. No, he's not a paragon of respectability I've concluded, but a weak man with a shameful past. Will he see through my ploy?

Franklin believes the interview is about the University endowment, but the grant is merely a prelude, a prologue to a murderous conclusion I'm desperate to prove. The door opens. Franklin greets me with a standoffish "Welcome," and leads me down the hallway with a self-important air one sometimes sees in the wealthy. Although he'd granted an interview, his disdain and disinterest are apparent. With his pompous attitude, I expect a summons to pour him a drink at any moment.

In the foyer hallway, hangs a photo gallery filled with family members. The pictures weren't there the night of the party. Black and white photos engraved with names display his family's lineage—father, grandfather, and great-grandfather hang respectively in rows—Riley, Richard, and Kane Emsworth. Suspended on a continuous panel are photos of his mother, aunts, and uncles. Fortuitously, a familiar name jumps from the wall—Pennington Emsworth. Pennington, the alias patrons of his illicit service used to hide their identity belonged to Franklin's uncle, another clue to Franklin's complicity.

On the back patio, Franklin guides me to a table. He sits across from me wearing a short-sleeved shirt, chinos, and a smirk. He appears younger than his sixty-four years. Not entirely gray, fading blond hair disguise silvery strands, except at his temples. Neither thin nor fat, he's solid for a man his age. Though his belly, pouching beneath a fresh-pressed, lavender shirt, hadn't escaped time's spoils. He studies me through dark rims, framing blue eyes etched with raccoon shadows. A sun-kissed tan speaks of days on the beach or travel to some distant island. I broached the topic of his recent endowment toward EU's Business School, but he rudely interrupts.

"I can tell you're a whiskey man. Can I offer you a drink?" He asked while summoning a man I recognize as the fortress who'd frisked me two years ago. He smirks my way.

He remembers me.

Immediately, I sense trickery. The fortress returns with two whiskey glasses and a smile of recognition.

"Ethan this is the man from the Washington Post I spoke about earlier, he's doing a piece on the endowment," he said watching my expression closely and drumming his fingers on the table.

"Yes, I recognize Mr. McThursten," Ethan said as blankly as he had while interrogating me that cold night. At the moment, I sense deceit. Franklin granted me an interview for one reason, to intimidate me. And from the salivating grin, I bet Ethan has informed his employer I was a guest the night Patrice disappeared. I exhale deeply, place the notepad and pen on the table, and wait for the game to begin. In my satchel, my trusty mobile is recording every word. Skeptically, I take the drink from Ethan's hand and place it on the table. Cocking a one-sided grin in my direction, he leaves the patio. Poker-faced, I wait for Emsworth to speak.

"You see Mr. McThursten, or should I call you Hunter? I know who you are, and I know this little interview is not about my endowments. So, drop the pretense. Did you think you'd find some clue about Patrice here, or did you think you could walk into my home and intimidate me? If I were you, I'd be careful. Many a coonhound has met its death chasing a large quarry," he said with malice.

The moment he mentioned coonhound, I knew he'd done some background investigation of his own. Only students who worked on the student newspaper knew the story behind my alias.

"I've granted you an interview with one stipulation. I control the questions. And I'm certain you came prepared with essential who, what, where, why, and when questions. Since you know the first three, I'll answer the why inquiry." He pauses with a whiskey sip and places the tumbler with a resounding thud. "As you know, the University is my family's alma mater, and the Emsworth's believed education a necessity much as food and water. In the tradition of my father, grandfather, and his father before, I support the University. Is this what you want to know? Does it answer the 'why' Ryan?"

Ire charge my mind and scorching words stockpile ready to spew a burning retort. With clenched teeth and fist, I clear indignation from my throat. "Partially," I replied steely. "Why did you choose the business department over math and science?"

"Hmmm, that should be an easy guess knowing my family's history, Ryan," he said, placing laced fingers on his bulging belly. "But for the record, I'll explain." Nodding his head toward the pen and pad, he jests, "Aren't you going to write this down?"

"No," I said, lifting one brow. "I have a damn good memory."

"I bet you do Mr. McThursten," he sneered with another whiskey sip. "Well, as you know, the University made a great impact on my family. And as an influential businessman; I'm committed to helping Emsworth build an exemplary curriculum for future business leaders." He leans back further with a scowl forming. "Is that enough for your article, Mr. McThursten or do you prefer to hear about my parties? The one you attended under the ruse of a wealthy entrepreneur?"

Mentally, I answer yes, ignore his intimidating expression, and hold his gaze.

"You see Ryan, I've known about you for a while." From his pant pocket, he removes the miniature camera and places it on the table. "Does this look familiar?" He asked, swallowing the remaining whiskey and sitting upright. "Mr. McThursten these parties are years in the making and didn't start with me, but powerful men who'd take you out in an instant. I'm certain you wouldn't want anything happening to your ailing father in Alexandria or the attractive editor from New York. I believe her name is Allison Bertrand. So, heed this as a warning, you continue down this road, you're going to get some peo-

E. Denise Billups

ple hurt, including yourself. If I were you, I'd point that coonhound nose in another direction, preferably toward a smaller quarry that won't kill you. Now, if I've answered all the questions for your article, I have more pressing matters to attend."

The mention of my father and Allison pushed a blazing button, and an urge to reach across the table and strangle the whiskey out of him. I thrive when provoked by unscrupulous aggressors which only make me more determined, and a damn good if not foolish reporter. I clench my jaw and remain calm, refusing to give him a satisfactory, angry response. Instead, I reply casually. "I imagine you wrestle with many demons at night. It must be hell knowing you've destroyed a young girl's life and her family."

His smile is chilling, his reply, impassive. His eyes veer somewhere else. "Yes, I've wrestled with many demons, and most successful businessmen do, but Patrice Jensen's not one of them," he said, steering his gaze behind my seat. For a moment, he sits dazed. I turn to see what caught his attention, staring past a quaint vine-covered guesthouse, the pond, and the empty backyard, but there's nothing to explain his odd expression. He lowers his gaze and drums his fingers on the table. Words speed from his mouth, "That young woman destroyed her own life long before Emsworth." As if pulled by strings, he springs from the chair. "Now," he said, and signals toward the patio door with his hand, "Good luck with your article and I don't want to see you near my home again, Mr. McThursten. I might not be so polite the next time," he said with a squint of his eye.

I rise from the chair perplexed by the strange expression crossing his face. Any doubt I had, vanished with Franklin's odd behavior. At the moment, I'm a hundred percent sure Patrice met her death by his hand or directive. As I turn to leave, the spot I believe Franklin stared moments ago catches my attention, an odd triangular rose garden on the side of the home where I'd escaped with Allison. A garden hadn't been there the night of the party. And Emsworth doesn't strike me as the rose garden type.

155

He pauses at the front door with his hand on the knob, and says, "You should make better use of your time at the Post, chase another story and forget Patrice Jensen." When Franklin opens the door, Ethan appears with a sarcastic grin on the other side. Swiftly, he snatches my satchel, rummages through the interior, and withdraws my mobile. A malicious grin rips across Franklin's face.

"Did you think I'd let you leave without checking?" He asked, taking the phone from Ethan's hands.

As he'd done the night of the party, Ethan pads every inch of my body with a grin. "No cross this time, my friend. What happened, you lose faith?" Ethan asked with a smirk and a final pat on my chest.

Franklin quickly erases the interview on my mobile and bestows my phone unsmiling. "Good day, Mr. McThursten," he said, closing the door at my back, leaving me hotter than hell.

Great, that was just lovely. What an ass! But I'm not walking away empty-handed, the suspicious rose garden and the look on Franklin's face reek of mischief. Recalling the picture on Franklin's foyer wall, another piece of the mystery slowly unfolds, his uncle's name—Pennington.

26
Tattered Clues

I'VE SETTLED INTO A COMFORT zone which always comes easy around Lisa. Like sisters, I don't worry about how to act or what to say in her presence. It's been this way since our first meeting in the dorm when a petite, spunky girl with massive brown hair greeted me with a warm grin. Shockingly, she rushed over, screaming, "Hello roomie," and hugged me tightly, like old friends, not strangers. We spent the entire first day talking and decorating our rooms as the noisy dormitory buzzed with newcomers. She made my first day, and the next four years easy and fun. I glance at Lisa, a few steps away, preparing dinner in the kitchen, and grin. *Life is strange.* I would never have guessed the first day of college I'd find my best friend.

The entire afternoon, I've lounged on Lisa's covered patio, digging through school memorabilia. Several overhead fans circulate aromas of Spain through patio doors, garlic, onions, and saffron, causing my mouth to water. It's been weeks since I've had a well-cooked meal. I'm amazed at Lisa's cooking skills. In school, it was usually greasy takeout or bland cafeteria food. In the kitchen, Lisa snaps photos of ingredients, and maneuver about colorful bowls filled with spices and chopped vegetables she used to prepare the dish. Pictures for a cookbook she's publishing titled *The Smells of Spain*. That's the Lisa I remember, always busy with some project.

On the patio table, lays a thick, red binder filled with recipes Lisa's mother collected throughout the years. Historical facts are written on multicolored sticky notes, dressing the binder's edge. Lisa's intensive research reminds me of the Storytelling Epicurean. I haven't thought about the blogger in days, not since I bought ingredients for the Polenta Lasagna recipe, the day I met Mrs. Edelstein. I wonder if she was referring to Lisa when she stated, *"She'll show herself soon."* No, she couldn't have been. We've been friends since freshman year. Ms. Edelstein said I'd known the woman a short time. After everything I've experienced lately, I believe she meant Patrice Jensen. I shake Mrs. Edelstein from thought and return to the cookbook.

"Lisa, these recipes are incredible, and your research is wonderful. You should start a cooking blog," I said, projecting my voice toward the kitchen.

"I thought about it..." she said, joining me on the patio. Sitting beside me, she stares at the box of school memorabilia. "Ooh! I forgot about this," she said, pulling a tattered article from a beat-up book, marked up with yellow highlights. "Allie, look at this. Remember the scandal about a student escort service on campus?"

"What! No, I don't." She hands me the tattered article ripped carelessly from a newspaper. "When did this happen?"

"During junior year, a student reporter exposed the story. The article revealed an EU student was recruiting unsuspecting undergrads. After the first article, there were no more articles published. Oddly, the Dean didn't notify students with precautionary measures. After a while, I figured they expelled the student or silenced the story to protect the school. For days, I pondered the mystery recruiter. She could have been a classmate or someone we knew." Lisa chuckles. Her eyes narrow, and her mouth puckers. "Don't laugh, but for days, I played this stupid game, studying faces, trying to determine who they were. How ridiculous, it could have been anyone."

"Where was I when this was happening? Why didn't you mention it?"

"I thought I had. Oh, wait; it was the month of your blackout. You went back to New York for two weeks. I had to talk you into coming back to school remember. I believe I mentioned it once, but you were so upset about your memory loss, you probably forgot."

"Hmmm..." I continue to read the article with growing alarm about a young woman who invites unsuspecting students to off-campus parties and tries to recruit them. High-profile men of D.C. are suspected patrons. "Lisa, this is weird."

"What?"

"I think Belle—Patrice is the person the journalist is talking about."

"Why do you believe that?"

"For one, she invited me to an off-campus party just as the article states. Second, I never spoke to Patrice the entire semester, why the sudden interest in me? I knew something was odd about that party. The moment I stepped from Patrice's car, I felt something was wrong. The men were older, and all the women were college age..."

My mind clicks, opening memories of a billiard room.

A graying man with bright white teeth approaches calling to the girl beside me. She smiles and leaves me alone at the bar. Why did Belle bring me here? As I sip the sugary drink, unease fills my mind as I stare about the room which looks like a gentleman's club, not a home. A man in the corner won't stop staring. I look away and fidget with my drink. My eyes bounce around the room, studying the cherry coffered ceiling and Tiffany lamps hanging above the pool table. Several men in the corner are now staring. Where's Belle? I glance toward the large windows facing a covered patio. I hope she comes back before one of them comes over.

A girl sitting on the dark leather sofa in the center of the room stands and walks over to a man. Her figure covers most of his body, but he appears younger than the other men. Pool balls ping and crash. I jump, glancing at two people moving about the pool table, as they concentrate on still balls. An antler over the fireplace catches my eye, and I grimace at the beautiful animal killed for display. A man in the corner moves across the room in my direction. I need to leave. This doesn't feel right. A sudden movement startles me. I look over, and a man slides into the chair beside me. He whispers in my ear, smelling of whiskey and cologne.

"*Hi beautiful, can I call you Belle, my name's Pennington.*"

My mind snaps shut, trapping memories inside cerebral walls again.

"Oh, wow!"

"What?"

"His name was Pennington."

"Who?"

"A man at the party introduced himself as Pennington."

"Did you remember that just now?"

"Yes." *High-powered men of D.C. . . .* I think reflectively. "This sounds suspiciously like Patrice Jensen's manuscript. Why did you keep this article?"

"I don't know. I was reading the campus newspaper in the cafeteria and ripped it out. I must have had some reason for keeping it, but now I don't remember."

I look for the reporter's name, noticing it was ripped off at the top. "There's no name, do you remember who wrote this?"

"I don't think I ever knew. Why?"

"If I had a name, I could contact him or her and find out about that night and Patrice."

"That shouldn't be a problem."

"What do you mean?"

"Allie, the school library archives all the student papers. And I remember the month was December of our junior year. That'll make the article and journalist name easy to find."

"Lisa, you're right! Why didn't I think of that?"

"Because you're not thinking clearly. You're too consumed with what you can't remember. You're not thinking logically."

"True." But how can I reason when part of my brain is asleep. "Tomorrow I'll visit the library." The idea of someone deceitfully trying to recruit me makes me sick! Agitated, I sigh and slump low in the chair. The spicy scent from the kitchen mixes with a sweet floral scent. "Are you wearing perfume?" I asked, sniffing the air.

"No, I thought you were," Lisa said.

"Nope."

"It roses. Maybe it's coming from the neighbor's garden, but I've never smelled their flowers this strongly on the patio before. It's probably the heatwave."

"Possibly..." Suddenly, I remember Ryan's visit to McClelland. The strange scent and chill faded the moment he left my office. I hadn't thought about the peculiar aura until now. I place the tattered article on the table, staring at it for a minute when an unwelcome force grips my chest. A phantasmagoria swirls in my eye's periphery, sweeping a chill along my face, neck, and arm. Something flutters on the table. I turn, and the Washington Post newspaper flaps open. *Was it the ceiling fan?* I stare up at the swirling blades then back at the paper opened to an image of Senator Murphy and his wife clad in black over a casket. Penelope Murphy's photo seizes my attention, and the caption sends me spinning.

The Tragic Suicide of Senator Murphy's Daughter

"No!"

"Allie?"

A pressure grips my chest. The room spins, and nausea rushes up my core. "Bathroom," I screamed.

"In the hall," Lisa said stunned.

She follows as I race into the narrow, angled powder room under the staircase. Swiftly I shut the door. Bile floods my mouth. I drop to the floor, spit into the toilet, grip the bowl, and breathe forcefully in-and-out, in-and-out until the room stops spinning and my heart steadies. A chill brush alongside me. I shiver. The sweet smell of roses engulfs and lingers in the powder blue room. Fearfully, I rise, trembling and sensing a presence around me.

This is not an anxiety attack. Whatever it is, it's growing stronger, colder, and sweeter, as if it's taking form. A frigid breeze swirls then fades. The air is normal again. I grab the sink, breathing in-and-out several more times. Can my mind conjure external sensations? Gold vines climb the wall. The room twirls making me dizzier, and I close my eyes for a moment.

"You okay, Allie?" Lisa asked outside the door.

"I'm fine." Turning on the faucet, I swish my mouth with water, dry my hands on Lisa's adorable floral hand towels, and neatly arrange them on the towel rack. I study my face in the mirror, running my fingers along messy brows and whisper, "You're okay." Taking a deep breath, I exit the powder room to Lisa's worried expression.

"You sure you're not the pregnant one?"

I try to laugh, but I can't.

"What just happened, Allie?"

"It's hard to explain," I said sauntering toward the patio table, lifting the sweating tumbler, taking a sip of ice tea, and returning to my seat.

Quietly, Lisa sits beside me with scrunched brows, staring inquisitively.

I sigh and meet her inquiring eyes. "For a while, I've had anxiety attacks. They just appear without warning. Or maybe something triggers them, but I don't know what. Lisa, it's the weirdest feeling. It's like an external force encloses me, and grips my chest."

"Have you gone to the doctor?"

"I did, junior-year during winter break and was diagnosed with acute anxiety. The doctor said it probably stems from my memory loss. Lisa, that's why I stayed in New York longer. It was hard coming back to school. Every time I thought about that room, I'd have a full-fledged attack."

"And this has been going on since the party?"

"Soon after ... It's like something trying to break through my mind. The moment I get close, I get these darn attacks."

"Then it's obviously linked to memory loss."

"That's what the doctor said. After graduation, the attacks stopped and returned after McClelland's layoff. It's probably just stress-related." I want to believe that's true, but the strange cold aura that surrounds me before the attack is external, not physiological, but something else. And the research I read on memory loss didn't coincide with my symptoms.

"Just now, before it happened, you were so calm. What brought on the attack?"

"This," I said, staring at the paper. "All this time I've been chasing a ghost."

Lisa's brows knit. "Huh? Okay, explain."

"She's dead."

"Who's dead?"

"Look at this."

"I read it earlier. I don't understand how a young woman can take her life like that. It's horrible! Nothing in this world warrants suicide. It's too sad."

"Lisa, look at the name. It's Senator Murphy's daughter, Penelope Murphy, the author who sent me the manuscript."

Lisa's mouth drops open.

"This is why I haven't been able to reach her."

Lisa stares at the photo hard, studying Penelope's face and her grief-stricken family. "This explains why her blog is gone, and her phone disconnected."

"Something's not right. Why would Penelope kill herself? It doesn't make sense." I begin to question everything, the fear in her voice when we spoke, the unfinished manuscript, the man who called her name on the phone. Who was he? Is this why she sent me the manuscript? Was she so overcome by her friend's murder she'd kill herself? Something more sinister enters my mind. Did Penelope find incriminating evidence that would get her killed? Do they know about the manuscript and that she sent it to me? *Oh, God!*

27
Ethan Cleary

AGAIN, ANGER REARS at Franklin's malice and Ethan's provoking hands padding me down like a criminal. For a moment, I almost lost it, but I didn't let them goad me into an angry display. It would have felt damn good punching both in the face, but with two against one, it's a fight I wouldn't have won. I'd rather keep my front teeth a little longer than give scumbag Emsworth the satisfaction.

Enraged, I leave the house, blazing hotter than D. C.'s heatwave. Placing my cell phone in my satchel, I stomped down the private driveway toward my jeep, when a whirring sound behind me. Over my shoulder, a black Mercedes backs into the street, the car Ethan entered a year ago. I'm sure he's behind the wheel and wonder where he goes when he leaves Franklin. I know nothing about Ethan other than he's Franklin's right-hand-man. Ethan's more of a mystery than Patrice. Curious, I jump in my car and follow at a distance. When he turns at the light, I speed up, following onto 17th Street N.W. Another rash decision, but my ire is red-hot, blazing to singe the culprit in front of me.

For ten minutes, I trail two cars behind the Mercedes, keeping my jeep out of view. Seven minutes later, Ethan turns onto Florida Avenue N.W, straight onto 24th Street in the Bloomingdale area. Several feet ahead, a garage door lifts and the Mercedes swings into a private parking space behind a three-story Victorian row house. I slow to a crawl and wait until the garage door descends before passing.

Circling the street, the front of the impressive slate-colored home appears. I surmise Franklin pays Ethan a hefty salary to live in this part of town where Victorian row homes list in the millions or perhaps it belongs to Franklin. After all, he is a real estate developer. Whatever the case, I can't imagine a single man living alone in a large three-story Victorian. Perhaps he's married. I never pegged Ethan the marrying type, more of a player, but I could be wrong. Are his wife and children waiting inside?

I keep driving past the home and park curbside, gathering my nerves for the daring next move. It's a dangerous decision, but it doesn't stop me from traversing the lawn straight to the front steps. The wall-mounted mailbox reads E. Cleary. E for Ethan, I presume. So, this is where he lives. Now that I have his address and last name, it will be a breeze digging up his history. Trying to look inconspicuous, I walk at a casual pace for neighbors who may be spying out their window. If Ethan Cleary discovers I followed him home, I'm sure it won't be a pretty picture. Back in the car, I head to the office, eager to unearth Ethan's past.

* * *

I access LexisNexis Accurint and find information about Ethan's family members, his current and previous addresses, motor vehicle registration, and his current employer, Emsworth Commercial Realtor. Records show he's thirty-nine years old, divorced with one child, which explains the large home in Bloomingdales. I'm surprised to find he's a graduate of Emsworth University, but not surprised he was an All-American athlete, scouted by a professional football team. I pegged him for an athlete or gym rat the night he frisked me. No criminal past, or misdemeanors, only a few parking tickets, he's squeaky-clean, at least on public record. Ethan was born in the District of Columbia and raised by his parents Theresa and Bret Cleary. Hmm, given their ages, I'd say they're his grandparents. Another family member, fifty-four-year-old Charlotte Cleary, is more likely his mother or aunt. The last relatives are his ex-wife, Claire Reilly and his six-year-old son, Stephen.

I consider calling Ethan's parents, using the endowment article on Franklin and his employees as a pretext to accrue more info. But journalistic duty pricks my conscience. I don't want to mislead Ethan's family, and there's nothing worse than an unethical journalist. Then again, the endowment article is legitimate, though its real intent is to sniff out Franklin. If uncovering a wrong means using every means to obtain facts, then I'll use every source I can. Nonetheless, Ethan's family may not be cooperative. I imagine a polite no, and a quick hang up. But it's worth a try. I dial the number, and an elderly woman answers with a croaky cough before she says hello in a hoarse voice. At eighty-five, I expected Mrs. Cleary to sound feeble, but her voice reveals she's either a smoker or ill.

"Mrs. Cleary?"

"Yes, who's calling?"

"You don't know me. I'm a reporter with the Washington Post. I'm looking for Charlotte, your daughter." If she's not her daughter, I'll find out in a moment.

"Charlotte doesn't live here, and she hasn't lived here or in D. C. for some time. What's this about?" She asked with a sputtering cough.

"I'm writing a story on Franklin Emsworth's university endowment as well as a write-up on his loyal employees. I was hoping to speak with Ethan's relatives and find out about his family life and childhood in D. C."

"Why didn't you get this information from Ethan himself? And Charlotte won't talk to you. She despises Franklin and the whole Emsworth clan. Besides, she hasn't spoken to Ethan or his father in years."

"His father?"

"Franklin."

Booyah! I whoop inwardly with a swift downward pump of my elbow and clenched fist. *Scumbag Franklin is Ethan's father!* I beam with another silent Booyah! And Mrs. Cleary rambles right on.

"Charlotte left D. C. to get away from that man and his family. My husband and I raised Ethan as our own. Anything you want to know you can ask us."

"I apologize. I had no idea." Right away, I sense she's the chatty type and perhaps gullible, providing information to a total stranger over the phone. I've met seniors like Mrs. Cleary and felt protective as I would with my grandparents or any senior for that matter. Momentarily, I feel like a dishonest reporter, wrenching information from a gullible old woman. Before I allow her to go any further, I interrupt. "Mrs. Cleary, I have to inform you any information you provide is on the record."

"I could care less. You can tell Mr. Emsworth yourself; Theresa May Cleary told the world what a spineless piece of shit he is. He's despicable! Got my Charlotte pregnant at fifteen and didn't lift a finger to raise his son. When Ethan turned around and went to work for the bastard I was outraged. I'll never understand, but there's nothing we could've done to stop him. What did you say this story's about?"

The tone of her voice leaves me stunned. I've never heard such a foul mouth on a woman her age. But I detect she's holding a major grudge against Franklin and could be the source of his undoing if given the right forum. "The article is about Mr. Emsworth's donations to the University."

"That's about the only good that man's done."

I agree inwardly and try not to laugh. "If you don't mind me asking, how did your daughter meet Franklin?"

"Emsworth's party... It still behooves me how a fifteen-year-old was allowed in. Those parties were for gentlemen if you know what I mean, no place for a fifteen-year-old girl."

"Did you ever find out how she got in?"

"I suspect Franklin's uncle invited her, but as I said, Charlotte wouldn't talk about it. We didn't know about the party until much later. If we had, my husband and I would have called the authorities and had Pennington and his twenty-five-year-old nephew arrested for child molestation. Sadly, we found out much too late when she was already with child."

The name Pennington again confirms the picture I saw on Franklin's wall. And given Ethan's age, these parties' have been going on for more than thirty-nine years. "Your daughter was a minor. You didn't need her consent to go to the police."

"We should have ... But Charlotte threw a fit and said she didn't want to press charges or have anything else to do with Franklin. We suspect something terrible happened inside that house, but she refused to talk and never mentioned it again. And with the Emsworth's power in D.C., I knew nothing would come of our complaint. We thought it best to protect Charlotte and remain quiet. Over the years, I believe they threatened my daughter into silence. Anyway, if we weren't such religious people, I would have marched her down to the clinic. But we're devout Catholics and couldn't do that to a child, even Franklin Emsworth's child. I just hope the boy we raised doesn't turn out like his father being mixed up in his business and all—"

"Terry, who the hell are you talking to?" A man interjected sharply. I assume it's Mr. Cleary.

"It's a reporter at the Post?"

"You talk too much, give me that darn phone," he grumbled. "That's family business, and Charlotte asked you to keep quiet about it."

For a second, muted voices rustle through the phone. I assume Mr. Cleary is trying to take the receiver but fails when his voice retreats with expletives in the distance. Finally, I've found someone who despises Franklin as much as I do and wouldn't mind putting him behind bars. Too bad the statute of limitation for statutory rape in D.C. is fifteen years. Sex with minors would certainly land Franklin in prison for a while. But it's damn good proof of his other transgressions. "Mrs. Cleary?"

"Sorry, that's my cantankerous, cowardly husband afraid to challenge Franklin," she said, raising her voice for Mr. Cleary to hear. "But

I'm too old and not many years left on this planet to give a damn if you know what I mean."

"I do … Mrs. Cleary, I'd like to speak to your daughter. Is it okay if I contact her?" From what she's revealed, Charlotte will be just as eager to see Franklin locked away, but perhaps reluctant to talk.

"She won't talk to ya. And the last we heard from her was six months ago. She's moved down to Alexandria with her new husband. She's listed as Charlotte Harrington."

Hmm, she's right in my own backyard.

"I hope she'll be as helpful as you have."

"I doubt it. You'll be wasting your time on that one."

"It's worth a shot. Mrs. Cleary, you've been a gem. Thank you." I want to say watch out for my story in the Post, but imagine her pain discovering the grandson she raised is indeed involved in Franklin's misdeeds. So, instead, I thank her for her time and hang up.

So, my daring adventure to Bloomingdale paid off. Ethan's not just an employee, but Franklin's illegitimate son. A son Franklin conceived out of wedlock at the age of twenty-five with a fifteen-year-old. Sounds familiar. Franklin's always had a thing for younger women. But why employ a son he abandoned as a child to do his dirty biddings? My instincts are screaming Charlotte Cleary has information that could ruin Franklin, information that might lead straight to Patrice.

Her mother was right. The directory lists her daughter as Charlotte and David Harrington in Alexandria, Virginia. After two rings, a man answers the phone.

"Hi, I'm calling from the Washington Post. May I speak to your wife?"

"She's out back. Can you hold on a second?"

"Sure." I wonder if Charlotte's mother is right. Will she refuse to talk or be open about Franklin when I tell her my suspicions? I'm hoping the latter.

"Hello."

"Charlotte, my name is Ryan McThursten. I'm a reporter with the Washington Post."

"I know my husband told me. How can I help you?"

"I'm writing a story about a student named Patrice Jensen who went missing two years ago from Emsworth University." I realize I didn't use the endowment story I'd told her mother. But given Theresa Cleary's loathing of Franklin, she'll probably jump on the bandwagon to have him convicted in Patrice Jensen's case.

"Yes, poor girl. Has she been found?"

"Unfortunately, no, it's still an active investigation." I pause before mentioning Franklin's name uncertain how she'll react. So, I state slow and firm, "I suspect Franklin Emsworth played a part in her disappearance."

"There's nothing I want to hear about that man. I'm sorry about the young woman, but I can't help you."

"Please don't hang up yet. I understand your history with Franklin, but I think you'll want to hear what I have to say, and if you still feel the same, I'll understand."

"Nothing will change my mind, but I'll listen."

"Two years ago, when I was a student reporter, there were rumors of a student escort service. I believe Franklin Emsworth is at the center of it." I continue telling her about the party, and my infiltration, as well as what I saw in the home. The entire time, she remains quiet until I mentioned Allison's suspected drugging and blackout. On the other end, I hear sniffling. "Mrs. Harrington, are you okay? Did I say something to upset you?"

"She was drugged ... So was I."

28

Ryan's Deceit

CLICK-CLACK, CLICK-CLACK, click-clack, click-clack... I throw the pillow over my head, blocking sounds of footsteps downstairs. A muted click-clack continues outside. I remove the pillow, turn sideways and try to go back to sleep. Pressing my face into the pillow, a hint of mulled-wine, maybe cloves, fill my senses. A chill taps my back like fingers down my spine. Swiftly, I turn my head, lift my nose in the air, and sniff the pungent odor hovering and falling around me. It's everywhere, even on my skin and clothing. I lower my nose toward the pillow and sheets. The sharp scent fades faint and stale like old blankets stored in antique trunks.

For days, the scent has grown stronger, and so have my anxiety attacks. Several instances of the strange aura arise. Ryan's visit at McClelland. The fall in the duplex. Lisa's patio and powder room. I reflect on the instant when I left my bed and call out to Nik from the second-floor landing. Before I raced down to the kitchen and slipped, I swear someone had moved about the duplex's main floor. Yesterday's episode in Lisa's powder room felt spectral. Though I've never felt a ghostly visit, Grandma Blu believed firmly in the spirit world. I've never. However, I'm starting to wonder if she was right.

I close my eyes, hoping the strange morning dissipates. For a moment, I savor quiet, but the smell keeps me awake. Unable to fall back to sleep, I squint at white crown molding encircling lavender walls toward large, bay windows and pause at white, slipcovered chairs bordering the fireplace. The cushion swells then flattens. I believe its sunrise casting shadows inside the room. Again, the cushion dips. I sit straight and stare at the chair, expecting another swell. *She'll show herself soon.* Words Mrs. Edelstein spoke, and her assistant said I should heed. "This is ridiculous," I mumbled, slinking back under the sheets.

Bang! Bang!

I gasp and spring upright with a frightful glance at the swaying balcony door. I locked that door last night after I'd stepped onto the private balcony for a few minutes of stargazing. When I came inside, I twisted the lock. I know I did. I slip off the bed toward the terrace, and a slight breeze sweeps inside the room but not strong enough to slam the door open. Vexed, I close and lock it as I had the previous night. Although I remember bolting the latch, I can't remember the rest of the evening. Sleep deprivation finally caught up. I suspect the moment my head hit the pillow, I'd fallen asleep, evident from the T-shirt and shorts I'm still wearing. On the bed, the iPad prompts memories of reading before I dozed off. And remnants of Lisa's spicy dinner frost my tongue, another sign of swift slumber. I always brush my teeth before bed but hadn't last night.

Then I remember Lisa's disappointed face when Andrew called explaining he would be home late. I wonder what time he finally came home. For Lisa's sake, I hope it wasn't too long after I headed to bed. We sat on the patio, eating, drinking, and catching up with each other's lives until ten o'clock. When the night grew late, I apologized and headed to bed. I felt terrible leaving her, but she understood, and said, "*You have plenty of time to meet Andrew in the morning.*" But with the sound of clacking shoes and the front door closing, I'm sure I've missed him again.

Buzz. . .thump, thump. I jump then laugh. *God, Allie!* I sigh and retrieve the thumping mobile from the silver-studded nightstand and squint at CJ's text.

How's it going? I miss our coffee moments. I assume you've been busy with freelancing. Have you received any more emails from Patrice?

I haven't spoken to CJ since the night I drank an entire bottle of wine, and I've forgotten our last conversation. Sliding against the headboard, I begin to type.

I've missed our coffee moments too. So much has happened since our last text. I'm in D.C. visiting my college roommate, Lisa. No, no more emails from Patrice, but I realize Undaunted can't possibly be her. I've discovered much since our last talk. Lisa kept a two-year-old university newspaper article about a student escort service. I believe Patrice was involved. I'm on a hunt today to find the journalist who wrote the story. Maybe he can provide more information on Patrice. I'm heading to Emsworth's Library to locate the original article.

After a few minutes of waiting for a response, I figure something pulled him away. Eager to get to the library, I refuse to wait any longer and head to the shower.

* * *

Ten minutes later, I check my mobile, still no response from CJ. He's probably busy at the coffee shop, I assume. I throw on one of my favorite tops, a white, laced gypsy style tunic, pair it with cut-off denim shorts, and comfy western ankle boots. I grab my hobo bag, and a breeze slips past me. I glance at the balcony door again. It's closed, and strangely, the floral scent is gone. Unnerved, I leave the room and enter the quiet hallway. There's no answer when I wrap softly on Lisa's door. I peek inside, finding her curled asleep in the ocean blue upholstered Colette bed. Silently, I pull the door closed and head out of the chilly home. On the front steps, my cell phone buzzes with CJ's response.

Be careful and keep me updated on what you find.

The mid-morning heat is stifling. I've stepped from the North Pole into the Sahara Desert. With the stifling humidity, it must be at least ninety degrees causing my top lips to bead with sweat in merely seconds. I scurry down the walkway, point the car keys toward the Audi, and cross the street with my tunic swaying in the wind. The balmy breeze offers no relief from the heatwave blanketing the District of Columbia. My thighs screech on the hot leather seat as I slide into the scorching interior. At once, I start the car, turn on the AC, and begin my quest toward Emsworth University.

* * *

Moments later, I'm strolling across EU's rectangular campus quad, recalling instances lingered on the grass between classes. It's remarkable how four years made a lasting impression. I feel I've never left this place. It's as much a home as New York City. I pause in the middle of the quad, examining surrounding buildings, and recalling classrooms within. Straight ahead, looms the four-level library shaped like a squat brick box, a place I spent countless days studying.

The musty scent of books attacks my nostrils when the revolving door thrust me inside, evoking memories of caffeine-induced wakefulness and long hours studying for exams. A distant memory of me glued to a laptop wearing a hoodie, and jeans with music streaming through my ears appear at a table near the window—my favorite spot. I wonder if I'd ever crossed Hunter's path amid rows of desk and shelves. He could have sat behind me during junior year, watching with knowledge of that night. I could have glanced his way, sat beside him, or smiled, never grasping his identity. But he would have known me.

I approach the librarian and ask to see the campus paper archives. Before she can ask, I flash my alumni card. She leads me into a side room, motions to a chair facing a large console between four computers. I approach and sit on the rock-hard chair as she opens campus newspapers stored on digital files.

"You can search by date, title, or author, and if you have any questions, please let me know," she said, leaving me to my task.

I type the date, and the computer queries its massive database producing an article for December ninth instantly. I enlarge the page, and a haunting name pops on the screen.

Hunter!

I sit in disbelief, unmoving, just staring at his name.

Of course! It makes sense! He's not only the mystery man who carried me home, but also the journalist who exposed the escort service. I should have known! Hunter was at 1414 Kalorama Road as an undercover journalist. Did he think I was an escort? God, I hope not! But if the intent was to recruit me, how did Hunter get me out? Wouldn't they have stopped him? I search Hunter's articles for a picture and surname. No last name, only Hunter.

I need to find him. I have to know what happened.

Grabbing a copy of Hunter's article from the printer, I head to the student newspaper. Finding the office closed for summer break, I continue to the Registrar, located in the main building. With urgency, I ask the elderly woman behind the desk if she can help me find a student named Hunter. She appears wary of giving out information. I assuage her concern and show my identification. "I'm a graduate." With an imploring face and pleading voice, I state, "It's urgent. I'm sure it'll be okay just to look up his last name."

"All right, I guess I can give you his name, but nothing more," she said, tilting her head and examining me over the rim of her glasses. Although she doesn't recognize me, I remember her. She was never friendly, and I assumed she hated her job, but now I see it's just her personality. Some people aren't warm, approachable types. I'm sure she has some redeeming qualities beneath her gruff exterior. Remembering Hunter was a senior my junior year, I give her the date he would have attended school.

"I have several Hunters graduating that year."

"He was a student journalist can you find him with that information."

"Sorry, I need his last name." Noticing my angst, she sighs and prints the list of names. "This is all I can do. Sorry."

I recognize the names from the alumni directory. They're not the Hunter I seek. "Is there someone at the student paper who'll remember Hunter?"

"Joseph Atwood has been the paper's editor for years. But he won't be back until the fall semester."

Joseph Atwood. How could I forget? My sophomore year, he interviewed me for a student reporter position. If I remember correctly, he's not only the editor of the newspaper but also a Professor of English Literature. I wonder if he'll recognize my name. He's probably forgotten the wishy-washy student who couldn't make up her mind to join the paper. "Would you have a number or email I can contact him."

The woman stares at me with deliberating eyes, releases another sigh and states, "I'm sure it'll be okay giving you his email." She looks through the computer and reads the address slowly, repeating it twice for accuracy as I type it on my phone.

"Thank you so much. You don't know how much this means." Straightaway, I send Joseph an email and leave my cell phone number, hoping he responds soon. Exiting the main building, I roam the campus quad for several minutes when my cell phone rings.

"Hello."

"Hi, Allison, this is Joe Atwood. I just received your email."

"Joe thanks for calling back so promptly. As I explained, I'm trying to locate one of your student reporters, but I only have his first name, Hunter."

"Yes, I remember Hunter, but that wasn't his real name. It was just a moniker he used for the paper. Hunter's real name is Ryan, Ryan McThursten."

My eyes pop, and my shoe skid with a sudden stop.

"Ms. Bertrand?"

"Did you say Ryan McThursten?"

"Yes."

No, he can't be the same Ryan McThursten. "Is he about six feet with raven hair, and brown eyes?"

"That about sums him up."

"I can't believe it…"

"I didn't catch that."

"Oh, I'm sorry. I believe I've met Mr. McThursten before. Would you happen to know where he lives now, or have a telephone number?"

"The last I remember; Ryan lives in Alexandria and works as a Journalist for the Washington Post. You can contact him there."

"Joe, thanks so much for your help." I don't bother telling him I'm the student who turned down the journalist position with EU's student paper. The thought slipped my mind the moment I heard Ryan's name. *I can't believe it!* All this time Ryan's the man who carried me from Kalorama Road. Why hasn't he told me? It's just odd unless he's hiding something. Did he send me those emails? Is he the anonymous sender, if so, why?

Something's not right.

The more I ponder his reasons, the more suspicious I become. If I'd reviewed Ryan's past when he signed with McClelland, I would have known long before now he was a student journalist, Emsworth graduate, and the mystery man who rescued me. Did Ryan know my identity the day I called inquiring about his manuscript? He couldn't have. He wouldn't have rudely hung up on me.

Catrina would have known Ryan lives in Alexandria. She made his travel arrangements. Did she also know he was a journalist at the Washington Post? Immediately I dial her number.

"Hi, Cat."

"Allie, what a coincidence, I was going to call you on my break. How's it going?"

"I had to get away for a while. I'm visiting my college roommate. Cat, is Ryan McThursten's information still on file?"

"I think we still have it. Why?"

"Do you know his address or home number?"

"Yea, but you're his editor now. Don't you have it?"

"Cat, I'm just trying to figure out if you knew before he showed up at McClelland, where he lived or whether you knew his occupation?"

"Of course, I did. I had to make the flight and hotel reservations remember? He lives in Alexandria. I knew he was a journalist only because his father gave me his work number at the Washington Post. Why are you asking about this now? Is something wrong?"

"Catrina, I feel so stupid. I didn't follow the normal due diligence because of the layoff. I didn't know any personal facts about Ryan. You're not going to believe it, but Ryan is the mystery man who rescued me from that off-campus party."

"What! Are you kidding? Why didn't he tell you?"

"I don't know, but I'm going to find out. I hate to cut you short, but I have to go. I'll call you later."

For a moment, I consider calling the Washington Post and demanding answers. But I don't. Instead, I play Ryan's charade, feign ignorance, and remain the faithful editor. If this is how he wants to play, then I'll play along. Keeping the pretense, I send him a text.

Ryan, what do you think about the revisions made to the manuscript? Please let me know. Call me soon.

I don't expect an immediate response. Ryan's deliberating his next move to keep me unsuspecting. I head back to my car and drive around with thoughts of Ryan, remembering the day he walked through my office door, and the odd sensation we'd met before. Now I know why he appeared familiar, even in my drugged state, some part of my brain retained a memory of his voice. Before I realize it, I'm approaching 1414 Kalorama Road.

29

Scrabble Tiles Murder

DESPITE THE BRUTAL HEATWAVE engulfing the District of Columbia, Washington Post employees shiver under sweaters and jackets as humming overhead vents release frigid air across the room. Unfazed by the cold, the chilly vents are mere pink noise as I sit at my desk drawing an inky loop around a newspaper ad and gazing at an unrelenting obsession—a timeworn folder thick with investigative research and six photos.

Moving the pictures about like Scrabble tiles, I try to form a logical conclusion among the six. The center tile is Patrice Jensen. *She looks so innocent.* I bet the Jensen's provided this shot to the press for that exact reason. A picture of a seventeen-year-old dressed in a gray T-shirt and jeans, with unruly blond strands falling about a makeup-free face paints a wholesome image. There's no hint of the edgy seductress I saw on campus, but a sweet, modest teenager. When did you start down the wrong path Patrice and if you'd known your life would end so soon, would you have lived life differently? What happened to you?

I surround Patrice's picture with photos of four suspects: Penelope Murphy, Senator Murphy, Mrs. Murphy, Franklin Emsworth, and Ethan Cleary, the man I now know as his son. If the pictures were letters, I'm sure they'd spell murder. *Which one of you is guilty?* I move the images about randomly, recalling a photo I'd seen a year ago when I interviewed Patrice's parents in Chevy Chase, Maryland. When my car approached the white, Dutch Colonial, I imagined a girl playing in the front yard. And before I reached the doorstep, I pictured a happy childhood in the quiet, upper-middle-class neighborhood. Did Patrice's neighbors see her grow up? Professor Jensen opened the door, and I stepped into another era. The home was reminiscent of a Jane Austen cottage.

Mrs. Jensen was gracious and the home charming. However, I couldn't picture Patrice living there. When she allowed me to visit Patrice's room, I'd speculated her bedroom would be different, but I was wrong. It was more Austenian than the other spaces. On a bookshelf, a beach photo of the Jensen's and Murphy's caught my attention. A sullen-faced Penelope sat frowning at her mother and father. Patrice, straddling a grown man's lap, appeared happy while her parents sat unwittingly staring at the ocean. I'd studied the photo closer and noticed the man with Patrice was Franklin Emsworth. No other items in the room captured Patrice's personality except her image eternalized between the white, wooden frame. Plainly, the photo had shown her flirting with Franklin. Maybe I'm wrong, but her parents had to be suspicious of their daughter's sexy pose on a grown man's lap.

During the interview, I established the Jensen's close association with the Murphy family and Franklin Emsworth. Mrs. Jensen explained they all traveled in the same circles and spent summer vacations together. I can't imagine her heartbreak discovering Patrice's underage affair with their supposedly good friend. Were they so involved in their own worlds they were inattentive to their child's life? No, that's not believable. If they were as close to Franklin, as they said, there must have been some sign of misbehavior or perhaps their friend's perfect character assuaged any suspicions. But a tinge of disgust flickered across Mrs. Jensen's face when she stared at the beach photo. It was then I'd realized she was aware of her daughter's inappropriate behavior. I ended the interview with no concrete information, but the picture and Mrs. Jensen's expression confirmed what I'd already known.

Placing Senator Murphy's picture on the right and Mrs. Murphy's on the left side of Patrice—husband, wife, and mistress—an angry lover or vengeful wife, yes, they'd be my first choice if they hadn't been at a political fundraiser the night of Franklin's party. But I haven't ruled them out yet. I slide Penelope's photo beneath Patrice's. She's still a mystery. Penelope was the only member of the Murphy family unaccounted for that night. From what I'd seen in the news, she became overwrought and fell into a deep depression. Soon after her friend went missing, Penelope vanished from public view. After many attempts to set up an interview, she refused every request. Her reluctance struck me strange. I would think she'd do anything to find her best friend unless she had something to hide.

I've always believed Penelope was the anonymous tipster. The day I found the informant's note on my desk, an EU reporter described a student who fit her description snooping around the newspaper. Penelope had a compelling motive to expose the escort business. Outraged if she discovered her best friend was seeing her father, revenge or something more deadly was her aim. Or perhaps she didn't know about her father, and her motive was to rescue Patrice from the seedy business.

Now with Penelope's suicide, I'll never know her real story. The way I see it, she was either consumed with guilt or depressed over her friend's death. The other assumption is she got too close to the truth, too close to Patrice's murderer and met a similar fate. It's all speculation, but one of my theories is right.

Penelope's death has left me with a daunting list of suspects, patrons, and escorts, who may never come forth with the truth. Anyone at Franklin's party could be guilty. High-powered Pennington's would rather see me dead than reveal information. And I'd only met one escort that night. When she discovered I'm a reporter, she refused to talk. Squinting at Franklin's photo, I place it above Patrice's image. I suspect he stands to lose the most. But why would he kill a critical member of his team? Had Patrice become a threat?

How could I miss the resemblance? Placing Franklin and Ethan's photos side-by-side, their mouth and eyes are similar except Ethan's not blonde but brunette. Unlike Franklin's square face, Ethan's face is oval, features from the Cleary side of the family I assume.

After speaking to his mother, Charlotte, I discovered she too had been Emsworth's victim. Drugged, just as Allison, she blacked out, losing and recalling only parts of her memory. But she's convinced Franklin raped her. For years, her shame prevented her from telling anyone, not even her family, which she asked me not to reveal. I hope somehow, after many years, she'll find the courage to come forward.

"Hey, Ry is there something about that paper you don't like, or you're just doodling?"

Jason's voice swoops in snatching Emsworth from thought and halting the oblivious destruction of the newspaper on my desk. An inky well carved clear through the paper blackens an announcement of 1414 Kalorama Road's open house. "Shit!" I reach for the Clorox Wipes and try to erase the stain, creating a bigger mess in the center of the desk.

"Dude, you looked miles away. You thinking about that file again?"

"Yep and this," I said waving the ink-stained newspaper at my stubble-faced coworker, whose wrinkled clothing reveals another night spent in the office. "You ever see a million-dollar home open for public viewing?"

"It's rare… Generally, upper-end homes sell to high-end, invite-only prospects. The owners don't want the public to know they're selling. Why'd you ask?"

"Well, either Emsworth doesn't know that, or he doesn't care," I said, showing Jason the ink-stained ad. "He's put his family home on the market with an open house viewing."

"Haven't you heard?" Jason asked, running a hand through his messy mane.

"What?"

"Last night Emsworth was admitted to the hospital for a mental breakdown or at least that's what my sources are saying. He's in the psych ward. When he entered the hospital, he was screaming about seeing something in his house. One of the hospital staff said he'd kept repeating over and over, 'she won't leave, she won't leave.' Freaky, huh?"

"You sure?"

"As sure as day."

"I just interviewed him a day ago, and he looked..." No, he didn't look fine, as I recall the odd look on his face as he stared at the rose garden.

"She won't leave... Anybody figure out what Franklin was talking about or who she is?"

"I asked my source the same question, but all she said was Franklin was home alone ... no one else was in the house but him. A neighbor saw him on the lawn screaming and having a fit, so they called the police, and the rest is history."

"Hmmm, something happened in that house. Franklin's not the type to break so easily."

"More information to use for your investigation. Maybe the Emsworth's are a bunch of loons. Maybe he did have something to do with that girl's disappearance."

"No, there's no history of mental illness in that family, just pure greed. But you know, with Franklin in the hospital, it's the perfect time to check out his house." The promise Franklin made a few days ago, enters my mind. "*Good luck with your article and I don't want to see you near my home again, Mr. McThursten. I might not be so polite the next time.*" But how's he going to know from his hospital bed unless his right-hand-man Ethan is there? But it's a chance I have to take.

Jason places the paper on the desk and gives me a severe eye. "I see the hackles rising, but I'd be careful going back to that house."

"Does a coonhound ever lose its trail?"

"No, but they've been shot chasing a target."

"Humpf," I grunt, "Well, I'll just have to keep an eye out for hunters." Just as I push the chair from the desk, my mobile tweets a text from Allison.

Ryan, what do you think about the revisions made to the manuscript? Please let me know. Call me soon.

If scumbag Emsworth knew she was back in town, it could mean trouble for both of us. Until I find incriminating evidence against Franklin, I have to keep my distance from Allison. I have to continue letting Emsworth believe we lost touch. After his revelation during the interview about Allison's career, I suspect he's been shadowing her for two years. But he doesn't know she's lost her memory. Even so, she still poses a threat. Seeing us together would only make it worse for her. Franklin would be suspicious of our union, believing we're in cahoots to implicate him in Patrice's disappearance.

I hope I can hold her off a little longer before she discovers my identity. There's no way for her to connect my pen-name Hunter to my real name. The school newspaper never carried my photo nor does the Washington Post. The perplexed expression on Allison's face when we shook hands at McClelland, tells me there was a hint of recognition. I came extremely close to telling her the truth, but the words wouldn't leave my mouth. Nonetheless, it's only a matter of time before Allison discovers my identity, but I hope not before I uncover Patrice's truth.

30
A Ghostly Awakening

THE FAIRYTALE HOME, akin to another era, looms in the distance. My stomach stirs dread as steeply pitched gable roofs, and octagonal chimney pots grow nearer. I ponder lives in wealthy communities, bound east to west by lavish mansions. Sculpted lawns flaunt peekaboo views of coveted estates desired by many, afforded by a privileged few. I admire the homes but not always the people who reside inside, especially not residents of 1414 Kalorama Road.

As the triangular portico grows closer, I can't believe what I see. An unexpected 'For Sale' sign mirages with TTR Sotheby's International Realtors splayed in majestic letters across a placard stuck on the lawn. It strikes me strange a million-dollar home is open for public viewing. Nonetheless, it's a stroke of luck, granting access without permission.

I drive past the private drive, crawl down the road, and park on the opposite side of the lane. For a few minutes, I deliberate entering, when from the side view mirror, a thirtyish looking woman exits a car. She tugs at a sheer dress showing the outline of her body. On woven-platform sandals, she walks around to a fiftyish looking man exiting the driver's side. She takes his hand, and they continue toward the house, stopping at the 'For Sale' sign wedged between sculpted hedges and verdant lawns. With a slow gait, they arrive at the private driveway. Immediately, I leave the car, realizing if I enter behind them, no one will notice my presence. I rush toward the couple and keep enough distance between us, but close enough to catch the end of the man's last sentence.

"...were right."

"I wouldn't believe it if I hadn't seen it with my own eyes. When Jane revealed the house is on the market, my immediate thought was why?" The woman said.

"His family's rolling in their graves," the man replied.

"Has he lost his mind? Angie said she'd rushed over to his lawn to see why he was screaming and swore she'd heard him say ghost, but she hadn't told anyone. I hope that's not the reason Franklin is selling his property. Why wouldn't he leave it to relatives?"

"What relatives? I don't believe he has any relatives left and Franklin never had any children," the man said as if he's on familiar terms with the owner. "Every woman he's ever married left the fool because he's a wolf."

"And rightly so given his philandering ways—"

"Pft!" The man hissed in disagreement. "They knew what they were getting into ... Downright gold diggers all of them. And they got a hefty chunk of money when they divorced him."

"Well, ghost or no ghost, I still say it's peculiar he's selling the house. It's been in the Emsworth's family for centuries. Ghost! Has the man lost his mind," she said, staring up at the approaching home with a snicker. "More than likely, Franklin was drinking heavily and saw his own shadow," she said.

Oh my, God! I freeze in disbelief. Franklin Emsworth? My brain explodes like fireworks. Unexpectedly, a question I've pondered two years has finally appeared. Franklin Emsworth, the grandson of Emsworth University's founder, not Detective Pennington, owns the house. A vivid image of Franklin speaking profound words of wisdom to my graduating class appears. I can't believe a well-respected man would engage in the escort business. But the proof is in front of me. He's the owner of the house. Impossible, he's too priggish to take part in a sleazy business. With his money, he can have any woman he wants. Why this?

Oh, no! This will destroy the University's reputation as well as Franklin's. A renowned figure in Washington's business community, he'd probably do anything to hide the escort service. *Anything. Would he kill?* The shocking news triggers a scary analysis that rings true. Would Franklin fake Patrice's disappearance to conceal the truth, hide her murder if it happened on his property? It would explain why she's still missing. The culprit or culprits covered up her murder, making Patrice appear a teenage runaway.

With rampant thoughts racing about my head, I'm frightfully aware of my precarious memory loss. Nonetheless, I must see inside that house. Ahead, the couple saunters along the circular driveway. I breathe deep and resume an alert stride, hoping no one recognizes me. I worry Emsworth saw me at the party, if so, will he remember me after two years? *But he's not home.* The woman ahead said he's in the hospital. That's a relief.

The couple moves through the stone-embellished door. I pause, watching people stroll about the interior. On hesitant feet, I cross over the threshold into a magnificent foyer I'd never entered when I arrived with Patrice through the garage. I've always wondered if Ryan escaped with me through the front door or some other passage. A familiar pine scent rises off shiny cherry balustrades. The home's gothic halls and steep arches gleam with dark, cherry walls. Down the long hallway, Oriental rugs span the length of dark, shiny wooden floors.

Hoping no one sees me; I move behind the couple and peek around labyrinthine hallways for security patrolling a treacherous domicile. Ahead, through an arched passage, three people scrutinizing the great room emerges. A high-pitched female voice echoes off empty walls.

"Such elaborate and solid masonry…"

A statuesque brunette wearing a navy gabardine pantsuit, crisp-white blouse, and Jimmy Choo, open-toed, stiletto pumps pushes swinging, blunt-cut, shoulder-length hair behind both ears. I'm sure an effort performed countless times a day. "Yes, these homes are lovely," she said, twisting a sizable diamond ring around her well-manicured fingers with an amicable smile. I notice the ring finger on her left hand adorns a silver Claddagh ring as she tugs escaping hair behind her ear again. Tiny crow-feet frame blue eyes and latent-smile lines deepen around bow lips as she addresses the middle-aged couple. "The English Tudor was popular among Washington's elite in the 1920s and 30s as well as the Colonial homes European Architects brought over in the late nineteenth century."

In awe of the architecture, the beguiled couple fingers the stone and wooden adornments. "We've traveled abroad and often see this style in Europe. The old country, as they say, made its way to the new world," she replied with a smile.

"With other traditions," the agent said. She continues elaborating on Tudor homes' exposed wood frameworks, casement windows, and something about timber I didn't catch. Her well-versed description of Tudor architecture shows a seasoned realtor, experienced in fine selling points.

Two couples roam about the great room. The man and woman I entered with grab a brochure and head toward the polished sales agent. They show no interest in viewing the home, and I assume they've been here before. His question springs loud and intrusive. "Why is Mr. Emsworth selling his family's home after so many years?"

The realtor caught off guard, turns with raised brows. "Hi, Jack. That's a question only Mr. Emsworth can answer. But it's not uncommon for a person to downsize to a smaller home. You do agree, this is a large home for just one man," she said, addressing everyone. Her furrowed brows reveal the question perturbed her a bit as she turns her gaze from Jack to his partner and approaches her with a light kiss on both cheeks. "I'm glad you both made it over. Jack, let me take care of these lovely folks, and I'll get back to you and Mandy."

Mandy moves to Jack's side, blocking the realtor from view. I'm confident she can't see me, so I grab a pamphlet, rush past the foyer toward the U-shaped staircase I once climbed on shaky stilettos. The second-floor hallway is lengthier than I remember. In the center, a sitting area divides the west and east corridors. A few steps farther, lay a small alcove decorated with twin sofas flanking a floor-to-ceiling window.

I've stepped into a dream. My mind swings to a fuzzy moment radiant with moonlight illuminating a shadowy figure moving toward me from an alcove. *"Sweetheart, are you okay?"* The funnel closes, my mind snaps shut. The memory fades to recessed memories, affecting a weightless instability as I wander past the alcove. Bygone whispers draw me toward the first door on the left, and here I am again. For a minute, I stand unmoving with my hand on the knob, fearful of what's on the other side.

The door clicks and creeks. The cavernous, gothic bedroom that adjoins several spaces appears large enough to fit three Manhattan studio apartments. The sight and smell wind me like a blow to the chest. I pause, studying the octagonal space, crystal chandelier dangling from cherry coffered ceilings, and lavender curtains cascading from three, tall, arched windows to chocolate, wooden floors. Dark walls and floors gleam with daylight. The solid four-poster bed blanketed in white coverlets beneath the chandelier is familiar. Except for the bed, plush lavender curtains, and candelabras on the mantel, the room is bare.

I wander close, willing a memory. A sudden sensation of flight sends my arms flailing like a limp rag doll. The floor rises fast, and the looming hearth's edge greets my forehead with a sharp graze.

It was the fireplace!

Startled by the flashback, I pause in the room's center, wondering what triggered the memory. How strange. All this time, I couldn't remember how I'd bruised my forehead. The sight of the fireplace must have sparked the memory. Like a ghost returned to its place of demise, I wander toward the windows, under a fold of lavender curtains, turn and examine the space with keen eyes. At the moment, the whirl and whisper of mist taking shape are inscrutable. Unaware of what's emerging, I walk through sunlight streaming through the windows. Buoyant dust particles stir fast, too fast. Fearfully, I stop and stare at the rapid charge. *It's nothing,* just dust I've disturbed, I reassure an anxious mind. My back crawls with a creeping sensation. I spin around to an empty room. "Okay Allie, get a grip."

Resting my hand on the mantel, I examine the empty chasm and ponder whether a fire burned that night. I can't remember. For a moment, the space spins and the unpleasant anxiousness swells, grating my memory. I try to squelch the aura and familiar angst I've lived with for months, intrusive energy invading my mind, a remote space refusing to open. I breathe deep, expel unease, and concentrate on a room I'll never see again. Turning in several circles, I absorb every vibration, smell, color, and sound, trying to conjure that night.

Like fingers, a gentle breeze ices my skin and raises hairs on my arms. Swiftly, I turn toward closed windows, searching for something a breeze can escape. *Impossible!* The only vent lies across the room. An overwhelming scent of roses whirls gossamer coils about me. My mind recognizes but refutes an invisible presence. It can't be real. It's just my imagination and the room making me anxious. Instantly, something seizes my consciousness. Spectral hands clamp my body, guiding a slow descent, lowering me safely to the floor.

My forehead grazes the fireplace's edge, but drugs numb any pain. Quick steps sound behind me with the click of the door. Two men whisper fast, clipped words.

"I thought you locked the door."

"No, I thought you did."

"Is she the recruit Patrice brought in tonight?"

"Yea, I think so."

"I just saw her in the hallway. She looked wasted."

My heart thunders in my chest as I try to move my numb limbs splayed across the floor's cold, wooden planks. But paralysis grips my body. Floor wax mixed with floral musk and something metallic fills my nostrils. I open my eyes to a blurry scene, sensing someone standing over me. There's motion in the corner. Someone else is here. I open my mouth, but I can't speak. Why aren't they helping me? Something rustles beside me.

Faint gasps roll in waves nearby. I try to move, but only my fingers are mobile. I stretch them wide; grazing something warm, moist, and

E. Denise Billups

velvety. Petals. Flowers. Through bleary eyes, a face blurs beneath blond strands. She's so close. Dark charcoal frames pained eyes. Red creases beneath a Nordic nose, a shade of red Patrice wore. I open my mouth, I think, but nothing comes out. A labored breath warms my face. She's in pain. Inaudible words fan hair across her lips, but I don't understand. Her hand grasps my wrist then slackens. Faint gasps dwindle. Her eyes close. She quiets.

Black loafers move across the room. Trouser hems, black as night, swayed on close approach. Another person remains still in the corner. Their figures waver imperceptible, flashing in and out of my fading vision.

He approaches. "Hey, hey you," he whispered.

He bends over.

I closed my eyes fearfully, feeling his hand touch my face, a finger under my nose searching for breath.

"She's out cold. We gotta get Patrice out of this room before someone else shows up." He pulls my clutch from my shoulder and the zipper sounds. "She has an Emsworth student I.D. Allison Bertrand is her name," he said, zipping the bag. He slides his hands under my shoulders, drags and leaves me on the floor near the bed. I open my eyes, catching a glint beneath. Large, brown, eyes glisten and lock with mine. She shakes her head wildly with frightened eyes and places a finger on her puckered lips. Her eyes, I've seen before.

A whir vibrates around me. Spectral hands release its icy grip, and the empty room comes into view. I gasp and spring upright. *Poppy!* It was Poppy under the bed! Her haunting wide eyes wet with frightful tears imprint my mind alarmingly. I realize why she appeared familiar in the photo. It's because I'd seen her here, under the bed with eyes sadder than her picture. Sensing another presence, I whip my head side-to-side, searching for the force that held me fixed. I know it's her. She wanted me to see what happened. I glance around, no longer denying what I've ignored for days. It's Patrice. I recall her grip on the floor before it slackened. She died next to me, holding my wrist. Is that why she's been with me all this time?

In the hall, the realtor's voice nears. I scamper from the floor, scoot toward the back, and stop at a steep staircase spiraling up and downstairs. A tall arched window adjoining the stairwell educes sudden arousal. *I've been here before.* Wooziness assaults my balance. My mind opens to a shadowy figure lowering me onto wobbly legs. I seize the fuzzy memory, willing a sharper image.

His face wavers close. My head rolls brushing his head then his lips, pressing light and then harder. I part my lips slightly. He opens his mouth and then quickly releases my eager kiss with words. "No, I want to, but not here, not now, Allison." He secures my body into his with a tight grip around my waist. My legs are jelly as he leans me into his chest. He stoops and lowers me over his shoulders.

The memory fades. His shadowy features blur in and out, but I know it was Ryan. The bedroom door opens, and I rush down the angled stairwell, darting headlong into a woman at the bottom, and knocking her onto a counter. A man races to her side. It's the couple I followed from the car into the home. She mouths angry words, but in my spinning mind, it sounds like gibberish. I apologize briskly, race toward the foyer, into the blistering afternoon sun. A sultry breeze melts spectral sensations and swipes pungent odors from my nostrils. I'm sure the sweet, metallic scent was blood and roses. I rush straight toward my car, arms wrapped around my quivering body.

My mind and body vibrate from awakened memories. *It was her, I felt her, I know it was!* The cold aura that appears before each anxiety attack was Patrice. She's been with me since I left Kalorama Road two years ago which explains the paranoia I've felt and dismissed as imaginings. It wasn't! It sounds impossible, but her presence is the only explanation that makes sense. Patrice wanted me to see her death. I wanted to believe the blood splotch on my dress that night was from my head wound. But even then, I realize the graze didn't bleed, only swelled to a lump. It was Patrice's blood, the metallic odor I sensed on the floor.

Why was Penelope in that room? Her horrified expression says she witnessed a ghastly scene. Now she's gone, and Patrice's killer remains a mystery. Was Penelope's fate murder, not suicide as the newspaper reported? *Could I be next?* The two men in that room know who I am, so why haven't they come after me? A shiver prickles my spine. Were the anonymous emails from Patrice and Poppy's murderer? And do they know about the manuscript? Did Hunter see Patrice's body when he took me from that room?

"*We gotta get Patrice out of this room before someone else shows up.*"

The two men must have hidden Patrice before Ryan arrived. Otherwise, I'm sure Ryan would have gone to the police unless he's involved. No, that doesn't make sense. He was trying to expose them. "Damn it!" What happened while I was unconscious?

I slide into the car, turn the ignition, and press my foot hard on the accelerator. My speeding mind halts fearfully with the sound of screeching wheels. A car zooms past, missing my bumper by inches. I back the car behind the intersection line, take a deep breath and silence my mind for a second. Looking left to right, I wonder what to do next. I can't go back to Lisa's. I need to think clearly. *They know who I am,* keep bouncing around my head, but why didn't they kill me that night. I stumbled on a murder scene. Surely the killer would have seen me as a threat and disposed of me as well. But why didn't they? I need to talk to Ryan.

31

The Rose Garden

FOR THE THIRD TIME, I cross Emsworth's property. Leerier this time of the muscular fortress, I stop and scour the front yard for Franklin's men, enter with slow steps, and then pause at the threshold. Although Franklin's in the hospital, I'm sure Ethan, his faithful servant, will keep his promise if I'm found intruding on the property again. Nearing the offensive spot where Franklin dismissed me after erasing my recording, a bitter taste slicks my tongue recalling his warning. I'm wary but enter regardless.

Toward the rear, voices rise and fall, I suspect chatter between the realtor and prospective home buyers. On the main floor, Emsworth has removed small personal items, leaving only large furniture unsavory visitors can't lift from the property. Cautiously, I wander the hall; surprised to find evidence of the current owner—the Emsworth family photo gallery and the infamous Pennington eliminated.

Eager to examine the odd rose garden, I advance toward the rear. I'm positive the flower bed wasn't there the night I escaped with Allison. I would have noticed. Passing the hall mirror, I halt and study my image, questioning whether I look like a wealthy homebuyer. The rich seldom look the part. It's always the less affluent dressed in labels they can't afford. Feigning interest in the home, I continue toward the rear, hoping there aren't many people in the backyard.

In the kitchen, stands a polished woman dressed in a slimming, navy pantsuit. Her carriage and mannerisms speak of wealth. An inward-pointing Claddagh ring adorns her finger, proclaiming her marital status in Irish tradition. She probably married money or comes from wealth, knowing nothing of the sordid details of life, only wealthy ideals, or perhaps she's Emsworth's relative. I'm sure Franklin hired the best to sell his family's property. I wonder what percentage of the fifteen-million-dollar proceeds she'll receive in commission, perhaps six or seven percent. A hefty sum for a home I'm sure will sell in an instant.

Noticing my entrance, she stops midsentence, "I'll be right with you. Please feel free to take a brochure," she said, pointing at the granite island. "Or look around if you like," she said, with a lifted brow and roving eyes. She grins bashfully followed by an awkward pause I've witnessed on women caught checking me out.

"Thank you, I will," I said, nodding my head.

With an apology, she resumes her sales pitch to a man and woman admiring the marble counters and floors.

As usual, I smirk at women's embarrassment when caught gawking. It's always the same, an instant attraction, curiosity, then a blush or nervous grin. I turn and notice she's found my rear end. She averts her eyes and fumbles with her hands. I smile and continue toward a passageway leading to the billiard-room that once contained an open bar, now empty, open space. An image of Allison appears timidly sipping a drink. *If only she knew.*

I wander toward the patio when the realtor addresses me again. "Do you care to see upstairs?"

"No, no. If it's okay, I'll continue the lower floor."

"Sure," she said with a smile and exits with the couple toward the front stairway.

I saunter toward the back, a place I'd fled from danger with Allison. A daring escape across slippery floors, which my polyurethane-soled oxfords now grip with a screech. I arrive at the backstairs where a man rammed into my chest. Instantly, the entire scene plays like a silent black and white movie in my mind. The odd-looking man was small in stature and wore a suit that was too big for his frame. His face was whiter than a ghost when he ran into me. I hadn't thought much of him that night, but now I'm convinced he'd seen or done something horrific. He'd glanced at me so fast; his face blurred. It was odd he didn't stop or apologize but continued to the basement. But I'd soon dismissed him with the scene on the patio taking precedence—a scene with a blonde man I now know was Franklin.

I've pondered the scene on the patio many times—Franklin's nervousness as he summoned two men, their quick exit—and concluded they'd rushed upstairs to erase a crime scene. And I bet the two men carried what I believe was Patrice's body to the third floor. It's the only logical conclusion. But who was the odd man rushing to the basement? Was he the perpetrator? Did I get it wrong? Those stairs lead directly to the room I'd found Allison. Given his ghostly pallor, he'd committed or witnessed something grisly. Why did he flee to the basement?

I head outside to the spot I sat a day ago. Now, here I am again, despite Franklin's warning, scrutinizing the suspicious garden that drew fear on his face and wary of the three-stories of whitewashed brick walls, angling like a medieval fortress over the open space. Countless windows sweep wall-to-wall, overlooking the patio from above. I cast an eye at dark windows, hoping no one's watching. Farther out in the yard, a woman, oblivious to my presence, studies a gaping lion's mouth spewing water into the fountain. I move out of sight, toward the rose garden, and immediately sense a drop in temperature. A few steps back, I was sweating from the ninety-degree weather, now I'm shivering. The space I stand feels like a refrigerator, and it's not because of the shade. A drastic drop in temperature, especially on a hot summer day, is impossible.

I grow closer and the air chillier. A cold breeze, reeking of decayed roses, cuffs my nostrils more potent than the scent a moment ago. White, frosted rose petals, wilted with fungus or root rot, explains the rotten odor. The garden's strange placement warns of something fouler than decayed flowers.

My mother, who took up gardening when my brother left for war, taught me the basics of horticulture. For days, after we received news of my brother's tour of duty, mom would fuss about the garden with gloves, shovel, and picks for hours. Flowers became her refuge from a war that stole her son. For hours on end, she'd plant, fertilize, and water seedlings as if she were nurturing a newborn child. In a way, I believe gardening soothed her worries. After a while, she created a beautiful plot of annuals, biennials, and perennials. She'd take pictures and send them to my brother with uplifting quotes to help him through his ordeal.

I remember the old wrought iron headboard she pulled from the garage. Instead of buying a real trellis, she placed the headboard behind the flower bed. She explained, *"It doesn't matter, just as long as the flowers get plenty of sunlight and have a trellis to climb as they grow."* She'd shown me how to build drainage to prevent fungi and root rot. I can still smell the sulfur of peat moss mixed with mulch. Gardening with mom became a silent prayer for my brother's return. In those moments, we barely spoke his name, but he was always in our thoughts. Mom wasn't religious, but during my brother's tour of duty, she resumed a Sunday morning ritual relinquished years ago, hoping a forsaken God, would hear her prayers. When we received notice of my brother's death, she never returned to church, abandoning a God that took her oldest son. But she'd continued her silent ritual of gardening, a solace for her grief.

Emerson's slipshod garden is the work of a novice. I'm amazed a man of his wealth wouldn't hire a professional. Any experienced Gardner knows better than to plant roses in the shade. Franklin's garden sits under the home's northwestern shadow, no possibility of sunlight. Noticing water puddles, I stoop to the ground and run my finger atop damp soil, a sure sign of improper drainage, which explains the rotten stench. But I can't account for the garden's inexplicable chill. The plot feels almost spectral. Maybe I've seen too much television, but I suspect something else besides roots lie beneath.

Fresh footprints trail the garden's edge. Someone's been here recently, perhaps a prospective buyer. The slender prints can only be a woman's, but why was she barefoot? The last print dips, spiraling underground. I step on the concaved spot, and the earth gives way, a sinkhole sucking my shoe beneath. I speculate improper drainage carved a void below, but instantly, suspect something else. Softly, I press my foot into the soil, and it sinks deeper, ending at something solid. When I bend to my knees, a prism of light scatters a diamond pattern along the tree, blinding my eyes.

On the second floor, a blonde woman's reflection glows faintly through the window then recedes from view. Has she been watching since I entered the garden? With my eyes fixed on the window, I rise, shake the soil from my pants and shoes, hoping to glimpse the woman who looked incredibly like Patrice Jensen. *Did I just see a ghost?* Again, an image appears, but it's someone with darker hair. She stands unmoving then flinches and moves down the staircase. I remember the tall arched window bordering the steep stairwell. The spot I kissed Allison.

Stomping loose soil from my pants, I rush back inside just as a woman races down the stairs, knocking another woman into the counter. Startled by the collision, the slumped over woman grouses abrasively, "What's wrong with you?"

"Are you okay?" A man said, coming to her aid, helping her off the counter.

Watching the scene unfold, I stop immediately, frozen in disbelief, absorbed in every inch of the woman who ran down the stairs. Cut-off denim shorts reveal tone slender brown legs, a bohemian lace top with tassels overlaid with turquoise beads swing from an elegant neck about her perky, braless bosom. Western ankle boots circle slim ankles. With a rash apology, she backs away, and turns, revealing a panicked expression.

Allison!

She swerves around quickly, misses my figure in the doorway, and hurries from the kitchen to the front entry. From the panicked exit, I imagine something happened upstairs. *Did she remember that night?* I follow from the kitchen down the hallway to the front door, watching her race toward a gray metallic Audi. When she starts the engine, I slip through the front door and race toward my car.

"What the fuck!" I circle the car, growing four times angrier with each punctured tire. *Who would do this?* Ethan's black Mercedes rolls past, stopping behind Allison's Audi at the traffic light. If Allison's car weren't ahead, I'd throw a rock at the tire slasher hidden behind tinted windows. My mobile rings, but before I pull it from my pocket, it stops. Allison's name appears then dissolves from the screen. *Why did she hang up?* At the traffic light, her car swerves right onto 17th Street N. W., and the Mercedes follows her tail.

Quickly, I dial the office. "Jason, I need your help. Pick me up at 1414 Kalorama road." Worried about Allison safety, I dial her number and hope she answers. I have to find out where she's heading. Knowing Emsworth, he's probably tracking her or something worst. The phone rings three times. Finally, she picks up.

32
Rock Creek Park

JUST AS I DIAL RYAN'S number another call comes through. I disconnect his call and take Lisa's. "Hello." The traffic light turns green, and I swerve onto 17th Street N. W., with no destination just needing to drive.

"Allie, are you at the university?"

"Not anymore, I was earlier."

"Are you okay? You sound strange."

That's an understatement. I'm downright alarmed! "Lisa, you're not going to believe this." *What am I doing?* I can't tell Lisa what happened. She'll surely think I've lost my mind.

"Believe what? Did you find the reporter's name?"

Yes, and I saw a ghost! I need to tell someone, voicing it will make it real. But I can't, not just yet. "I did."

"So, who is he?"

"Lisa, I can't believe it!"

"Allie, what! What's happened?"

"I'm so stupid!" I screech, banging my hand on the wheel. "All this time, he's been right under my nose. So stupid, stupid, stupid! We've been talking for months, Lisa. Hunter is the new author I just signed."

"Allie, calm down. Are you positive your author is Hunter?"

"I'm positive! Hunter's real name is Ryan. He's a writer I met at McClelland the day of the layoff. Lisa, I had the strangest feeling when he walked into my office. I felt I'd met him somewhere before. Now I know why. The entire meeting, I felt he was waiting to say something revealing, but he never did. Maybe I should have questioned him, but I didn't."

"Allie, are you sure and why didn't he tell you?"

"I've been asking myself that all morning. Why didn't Ryan just come out and say, hey, by the way, I'm the man who found you blacked out and rescued you from that house." I said in a nonchalant voice. A tone I assume Ryan would adopt in an awkward moment. "I've been talking to him for months, and he's never mentioned a word."

"Maybe he doesn't want to embarrass you or possibly doesn't recognize you, Allie."

"No, he knows me." The sensation of his kiss and his words of resistance sweeps my mind. *"No, I want to, but not here, not now, Allison."* He said my name. He knew who I was when he rescued me, but how? "Lisa, he must have found my I. D. in my clutch. Otherwise, he wouldn't have known where my dorm was."

"Okay, from what I recall, Hunter seemed sincere. He must have a good explanation for keeping this secret so long. Oh, wow, is his last name McThursten?"

"How did you know?"

"Everyone knows Ryan McThursten. He's a journalist at the Washington Post. When I discovered he's an EU graduate, I started following his stories, but I would never have guessed he's the hottie who brought you home."

"But didn't you recognize him from his photo?"

"His column doesn't show his photo, just his name. There's no way I could've known he's Hunter. Why don't you call him? He's gotta have his reasons for not mentioning that night."

What are your reasons, Ryan? Perhaps Lisa is right, but I can't imagine anything to justify his silence.

"Allie, you there?"

"Yeah … I'm here."

"Are you going to call Ryan?"

"No. You're right. Whatever Ryan's reason, I'll wait until he's ready to tell me."

"That's ridiculous, especially given your memory loss. Ryan might shed some light on that night. You need to call him now and get some answers."

"If he wanted me to know he would have told me by now. Whatever the reason, it must be significant to withhold a secret for so long." My rational mind tells me Ryan's known about Franklin Emsworth since school. But why hasn't he exposed him? Maybe he never found conclusive evidence. Am I his last link to Patrice? But why hasn't he interrogated me about that room?

"It's your call Allie, but I think it's ridiculous. How can you tolerate the unknown, especially when answers are just a phone call away?"

"I've dealt with the unknown for two years, another day or week won't matter."

"Okay … I just want this nightmare to end for you so you can get on with your life free of Patrice. Are you going back to that house?"

"I did already."

"Did you get in?"

"You won't believe it, but the owner is selling the house. There's an open viewing, so I walked right in without anyone noticing."

"Wow, what a coincidence. Did you remember anything?"

As much as I want to tell Lisa about Emsworth, and my awakened memories, I can't. She'll freak out and demand I go to the police. And I can't until I know who those men in the room were. "No, but I remembered how I got the nasty bump. I hit my head on the fireplace."

"Anything else?"

Yes, a ghost helped me remember. I can imagine how crazy that would sound. A ghost isn't that what that woman, Mandy said Emsworth was screaming about on his lawn? Maybe I'm not losing it. Patrice is still in that house, haunting her murderer.

"Allie, did you remember anything besides the fall?"

"No … nothing."

"See this is why you need to talk to Ryan."

"Lisa, you sound like a broken record. I'll talk to Ryan, but not just yet. I need to clear my head first."

"Why don't you come back to the house."

"No, I need to be alone for a while. Driving usually clears my head. I'll see you back at the house later." *Think clearly.* There's only one place that calms me, a place I often visited in college. I turn the car onto Columbia Road, and just as I enter Rock Creek Park, my cell phone rings. It's Ryan. "Hello."

"Allison, I just saw your number on my caller I. D." Ryan's voice streams potent through car speakers, rousing desire, irritation, and suspicion all at once. *Now I understand.* The recurring dream was real, although my mind conjured a more sensual kiss, it happened. I freaking kissed Ryan on the stairwell! Did I beg for more? How embarrassing!

It was the drug. I recall the article about date rape drugs detailing symptoms of memory loss and rendering victims helpless, willing, and sexually responsive. That explains my arousal; nonetheless, it doesn't lessen the shame. It's not Ryan I should direct my rancor toward, but the jerk who'd tainted my drink. I hope Ryan recognized drug-induced behavior and hadn't thought I was bold or shameless. Even in my vulnerable state, he'd shown decency. Well, he has some redeeming qualities, but I wish he'd tell me what he's hiding.

Slowly, irritation over Ryan's dishonesty builds, but no matter how puzzling, I'm sure his reasons are compelling. Anyway, I need to hear his voice to silence fearful thoughts.

Let it go, Allie.

Play ignorant until he's ready to tell you he's Hunter.

"Allison?"

"Ryan, I'm in the car. Sorry about hanging up. I had to take another call."

"Is everything okay?"

His concern reminds me of sympathy he'd shown the morning of my embarrassing hangover. In one phone call, I'd learned more about Ryan than any other time. We connected that morning when we spoke about the blackout and his brother's death. He was the second person I told about the party, but he'd already known. *The entire time he knew!* Why didn't you tell me then when we were spilling our guts about our problems? I inhale and exhale slowly, quieting rising anger. "I'm okay," I lied. "I'm just taking a drive." I bite my lips, wishing I could tell him I know he's Hunter. More than at any time, I need for him to be honest, especially now that I've recalled that night. I imagine him telling me my memory is wrong, nothing happened. My mind is playing tricks, trying to fill a blank space I can't account for. But after my experience, I know the truth.

"Visiting old haunts?" Ryan asked.

"Something like that..."

The car winds past Valley Trail where I'd often hiked with Lisa during school. Instantly an image of a man dressed in a vest, sweater, gray twill pants, and navy-blue scarf wrapped around his neck emerge from my memory—an alluring stranger I'd ventured Valley Trail with one autumn morning. "Yes, I just entered Rock Creek Park. I used to come here all the time when I was in school." His voice fades in and out. "Ryan ... Ryan?" The connection drops. I hang up, overcome with the sudden memory.

It feels like yesterday when I'd signed up for an autumn hike along Valley Trail with a nature group. Thirty minutes into the three-and-a-half-mile trek, I'd stopped to take pictures of fall foliage on Theodore Roosevelt Trail, when I felt a sudden push from behind. Before I slipped from the rocky ledge, someone grasped my waist, rescuing me from the creek below. I was stunned speechless when he pulled me into his chest. It happened so fast I didn't have time to react. He'd held me against his solid chest, his breath rapid at my back. Before I'd turned around, he'd apologized for his clumsy slip, which accounted for the sudden push I'd felt as he collided into my backside. Grateful for his swift action, I'd never considered him a threat.

When I'd turned around, an attractive man with an athletic built, prominent beneath a layered outfit left me stunned again. His handsome features kept me talking longer than usual with a stranger in a secluded park. We'd spoken effortlessly, admiring brilliant autumn colors from the rocky ledge. Surprised by his knowledge of trees, I'd assumed he was an Arborist or worked with the park's Nature Conservatory as he'd explained characteristics of various trees—tulip poplars, red maples, sycamores. An eager student, I'd listened to his description of green ash, black walnut, holly, black gum, and beech trees, which dripped deliciously off his tongue. Captivated by his attractiveness, I didn't care I'd fallen behind the nature group ahead.

Honestly, I didn't care to return to the group. I enjoyed his company and the devilish twinkle in his eyes. Oddly, his flirting intrigued rather than offended. Perhaps my hormones were in overdrive that day. We detoured from my group; a foolish move Grandma Blu would've reproofed. I swear I'd heard her voice screaming from Louisiana, "Don't be stupid, child," but I'd tuned out her imagined voice.

Eventually, we wandered off the path to another trail. "*You must see Boulder Bridge which Valley Trail bypasses*," Ethan had said. We stood atop the bridge, and I'd listened as he relayed a story about a ring President Theodore Roosevelt lost and never found. Underneath the water, I'd imagined shining jewelry stuck beneath rocks, finally discovered by future archaeologists, a piece of ancient history recovered in a long dried up creek.

Ethan Cleary was his name. We hiked together for hours that day, and neither of us cared to leave the park. A native of Washington D.C., he'd said he often visits the park on the weekends. When he'd asked my age, I replied twenty-one. I'll never forget his response. He'd paused with a long stare and said, "*You have much to learn.*" He revealed he was thirty-seven, but the sixteen-year age difference hadn't bothered me. I've always preferred the company of older men. Nikki said I'd marry my grandfather one day. And I'd replied, I hope so, he'll treat me well. Later that afternoon, Ethan drove me back to my dorm. He took my cell phone, skillfully typed his name and number in my contact list and extended an invitation to dinner that evening. I'd made a rash decision, but I didn't see harm sharing dinner in a public place. Our first meal was the beginning of many in my senior year.

I lost my virginity to Ethan Cleary. The sexual tension was there from the start and much too strong to ignore. My entire senior year, we shared occasional dinners, movies, and weekend hikes. Whenever we met, we enjoyed each other physically, but those dates grew infrequent with his work and my studies. I don't know what came over me in those brief months. But he'd made me feel more secure than I'd ever felt. He became a security blanket of sorts, which frazzled and thinned over time.

Although I'd enjoyed spending time with Ethan, I'd always sensed another side of him. He'd let me into his world through physical pleasure, but his past was off-limits. The moment I'd asked too many questions, he'd withdraw and not call for several days. Therefore, I kept my emotions at bay, not wanting to grow attached. Nonetheless, I'd allowed the affair to continue. The harder I tried to end the relationship, the more I'd wanted to see him.

Ethan was reluctant to reveal his past, but he'd asked many questions about my life in New York, my studies, and social life. He appeared concerned about frat and campus parties and cautioned against men at bars and social gatherings. I was stunned when he'd mentioned date rape drugs and tried not to flinch at his warning. But without a doubt, my face froze in shock when he'd spoken of the missing student. *"Girls don't disappear that long unless they run away or meet the wrong people."* His words contained an underlying message as he'd stared intently. When he'd mentioned a popular off-campus party on Kalorama Road, I'd stiffened. *"I've heard bad things about those parties. You should stay away. I wouldn't want anything happening to you,"* he'd said with a strange quirk in his lips.

At that moment, I'd wanted to tell him I attended the party a year ago, but I was still too ashamed to mention it. I'd merely said, *"Thanks for letting me know,"* and never let on about Kalorama Road. However, I wondered how he'd known and had asked. He explained he'd heard through friends but had never been. That was the last we spoke of Kalorama Road.

As months went by, I learned Ethan worked for his father, a Commercial Real Estate Developer. In bits and pieces, he revealed information about his family, his mother's teenage pregnancy, and his father's abandonment. He'd said as soon as he'd turned eighteen, he ignored his mother's wishes and sought out his father. Since college, he's worked for the family business. I'd suspected Ethan told me only what he'd wanted me to know. Most of his life remained a mystery.

Ethan and I saw each other on-and-off for eight months, but I'd hardly known him. Gradually, I'd withdrawn, concentrating on schoolwork before graduation. Our time together was amazing. As startling as our meeting was that autumn day, it ended unremarkably on a spring day. The blackout stained my junior year, and Ethan Cleary kindled my senior year. I've never mentioned him to anyone, not even Nikki or Lisa. Ethan is a secret I didn't want to share.

Lost in thought, I fail to notice the fast approaching Mercedes. It's the same car I saw behind me on Kalorama Road. It grows closer then slows down. My alarm ratchets to fear, wondering if they've followed me. Did someone recognize me at that house? I start to believe it's the men from the room now ready to kill me as they had Patrice and perhaps Poppy.

The car disappears around the bend. I'm relieved for a moment until the car reappears at a higher speed, trailing a close distance. Panicked, I grip the wheel, peering at tinted windows through the rearview mirror. The car speeds up and parallels mine. The driver taunts a dangerous game, speeding up and slowing down. I dare not glance over, afraid it's Patrice's murderer, trying to scare or kill me. The Mercedes decelerates, moving close behind.

Panicked, I pick up speed, wishing other cars were on the road, but the only car I'd seen passed me when I entered the park. I don't dare pull over; fearing they will do the same. I continue at high speed, hoping to pull away, but the Mercedes roars faster, approaching then pulling back just as it nears my bumper. If my memory is right, there's a dangerous curve approaching right before Boulder Bridge. At seventy miles per hour, I'll surely wreck the car, but I can't slow down. Just as the car winds the curve, a bump jolts the car and my heart.

This can't be happening...I'm in trouble!

The SUV butts with greater force, pushing the car onto the road's shoulder. My heart thunders, tires rumble, the wheel vibrates against my sweaty palms. With a third ram, the Audi zigzags, speeding toward a biker.

Oh, God, oh, God, oh, God! Please, don't let me hit him.

Dangerously, maneuvering right, I avoid a deadly crash. Approaching Boulder Bridge's abutment too fast, I swerve and the car barrels down the embankment toward a tree. I close my eyes and brace when the car door swipes the tree with a ripping screech. My head jostles about like a rag doll, swiveling several times with a final blinding bang into the wheel. Airbags explode. A sweeping breeze engulfs me. I'm disembodied air and light—peace replaces fear. From above, I watch the Audi careen and roll upside down in the creek.

33
The Coma

WE'RE TOO LATE. Ahead, flashing police and ambulance lights cause my heart to sink. All I think is *she's dead*! An image of Allison's bewildered face the day we met in her office flashes in my mind. She'll never know. I'll never get the chance to tell her the truth. On closer approach to Boulder Bridge, Jason slows the car, and EMT appears with Allison on the gurney. The cervical collar supporting her head and neck gives me hope. *She's still alive.* The gray Audi, crumpled on the passenger side, lie upside down in the creek.

"Jason, pull over!" I jump from the slowing car and run toward the ambulance.

"Is she okay?"

"She's alive but unconscious."

"What hospital are you taking her to? I'm a friend."

"Georgetown University Hospital," he said, closing the ambulance door.

Racing back to the car, a man pushing a bike catches up and runs beside me.

"You're her friend?"

"Yeah, why?"

"I saw the crash. A car rammed right into her bumper and just kept going," the biker said.

"Did you see the make of the car?"

"It was a black Mercedes as I told the police. I got the driver's license," he said, taking a card from his fanny pack.

He's confirmed my suspicions. The black Mercedes followed Allison from Kalorama Road.

"If you need a witness you can contact me at this number," he said, placing the card in my hand. "Poor girl, she swerved to avoid hitting me and lost control of the car. She was going too fast when the Mercedes rammed her from behind. She lost control of the car, and it scraped that tree over there and tumbled into the creek. I hope she's okay. She saved my life."

I turn and glance at the tree's bright cambium where the car stripped bark from the tree. But the Audi bore more damage than the tree, evidenced by it scraped sides and bent door. I imagine Allison's fear as the car rammed her off the road. What was she thinking right before she hit the tree? Was she still conscious when the car landed in the creek? I grow angrier knowing she could have died, and I'd never have the chance to tell her who I am. I rush back to Jason's car, and we follow the ambulance straight to the hospital.

* * *

After an hour of pacing the waiting room, and fearing a fatal update on Allison's condition, it dawns on me her family in New York doesn't know. But I don't have her home number or her roommate, Lisa's number. Catrina at McClelland is the only one I can contact. *I can't talk to her. She'll wonder how I know.* I give the phone to Jason, who tells Catrina about the accident and ask her to notify Allison's family.

Finally, the emergency doctor updates me on Allison's condition. "She's suffered a head wound and a broken arm. But she never came out of the coma. They've taken her to intensive care. EMT said the airbag saved her life," she reported with a reassuring smile.

"Thank you; I've informed Allison's family in New York."

Coma ... That's serious. Anger builds with the thought of Franklin in the same hospital. Did he orchestrate her accident from his hospital bed? Does he think Allison is dead? I grow more concern with his proximity. Is Allison safe in the same hospital? They can't possibly get into the intensive care ward. And if she's in a coma, she's no longer a threat. Immediately, I realize what I need to do.

34

I See What They See

"ALLISON, WAKE UP. I want to show you something. Wake up, wake up," two voices said together.

"I'm awake."

"Then open your eyes and see. You've been asleep too long. It's time to see again. Open your eyes. Don't be afraid," a voice reassured.

"Nikki, stop playing around ... leave me be, let me sleep."

"Allison..." Fingers colder than ice poke and pull at me. A chill licks my face. I try to move my head, but I can't.

"There's not much time. He needs your help."

"Who needs me?" I asked, trying to move my head.

"Come see..."

It's so cold. I shiver and reach for a blanket but slip.

I'm falling!

No, I'm floating!

I open my eyes with a gasp, noticing below my sleeping body. I'm in the hospital. *I'm above the room!* My heart races too fast, and I strain, trying to propel my body below. The machine beside the bed beeps louder and more frequent.

I'm dreaming.

I close my eyes and hope to wake in the bed below. Again, my eyes open above the room.

Am I dead?

My heart flutters, and I can't catch my breath. The machine below beeps incessantly. A woman dressed in blue top and pants rushes into the room, checks the noisy machines, adjusts the IV in my arm, and the fluid sack above. Glancing over her shoulder at the monitor, she studies my racing vitals. I feel her warm fingers as she checks the bandage at my hairline.

I'm still alive, but how can I see my body?

Nikki and Lisa rush through the door, followed by a white-coated, Indian doctor. Both their faces suffused with fear.

"She's okay. She's just dreaming," the nurse said with a reassuring glance. "She's in rim sleep, a dream state."

I notice the rapid movement of my eyelids, but I know I'm not dreaming if I can see everything so clear. "Nikki, Lisa," I call out, but they can't hear me.

"Is this normal," Nikki asked with a sullen tone I've heard before. A low timorous voice on the edge of tears, the same voice she had when we received news of Grandma Blu's illness. She's scared. Am I dying too? Is this why I can see my body? But I don't feel any pain. I don't feel anything but my thoughts.

The doctor's voice is clear. "She's physically fine, except for the coma. Car accidents like Allison's, generally cause a few broken bones, and neck and head traumas. She's lucky to have sustained only a broken arm. I've seen worse. We believed the head injury is the cause of the coma, but she sustained no swelling. There's no pressure on the brain to explain the coma," the doctor said perplexed.

"If there's no swelling, why is she still unconscious?" Nikki asked.

"Your sister's condition is puzzling. Generally, we see pressure from bleeding," he said, looking at a chart. We've run tests, and her blood pressure and blood sugar came back normal. There's no brain tumor or an aneurysm, which is good news. We can only speculate the blow to her head is the cause."

"How long do you believe she'll stay unconscious?" Lisa asked, approaching the bed and rubbing my hand. I see from her puffy eyes she's been crying, and I want to reach out and tell them I'm okay, but I can't.

"We'll have to wait and see what happens. Meantime, we will monitor Allison closely."

"I'm awake!" My mouth opens, but words are silent. By the expression on Lisa's face, I know she heard me.

"She's talking." Lisa leans close to my face and squeezes my hand tight. "Allie?"

"She's dreaming. It's common for coma patients to start talking," the doctor said.

"I'm awake! I'm not dreaming!" I scream. But they can't hear me. Something chilly gathers at my side, and two subtle figures flicker and hover close.

"Allison ... look," words unspoken enter my head, two distinct voices without sound.

I'm slipping away. A funnel grows long ending at a widening chasm of light. Two invisible hands interlock with mine. I'm no longer in the hospital but on a dark, moonlit street. A familiar Jaguar swerves into the private drive with Patrice behind the wheel and me beside her.

I'm dreaming. The doctor said I was dreaming. It's the bump on my head. But everything's so real and vivid.

"Allison, he's here."

Images unfold like a 3D movie. I feel the breezy autumn night and see the full moon above. The ground beneath my feet is solid and hard. But I don't know who's holding my hands. The movie swirl about me. I'm a part of it, a silent character. Penelope and Hunter, both on the same mission, move in different directions. I'm seeing through someone else's eyes, their journey inside that house. I sense both Poppy and Ryan's fears.

This can't be real.

Beep, beep, beep... Nikki and Lisa are talking near. Two icy hands grip tighter, pulling me away from their voices toward a dark patio filled with people in the night. I sense they can't see me.

"Allison, look..."

The patio disintegrates, and a long passage emerges. A man rushes from the basement and up to the second floor. His figure is odd, small and the ill-fitted black suit hangs on him.

"*Allison, Allison it's time to see,*" the voices fill my head.

My thoughts and memories are not my own but have merged with my invisible companions. Simultaneously, I'm everywhere, omnipresent, intersecting on several paths, a maze in my head. I'm Patrice exiting the billiard room, and Poppy following in pursuit. I'm Hunter at the front door. I'm Ethan frisking Ryan.

Ethan?

The synchronicity unfolds, culminating in Patrice's final moment, in a dark room fragrant with roses. Two hands grip mine, holding me captive. I can't see who they are; their forms waver chilly, restraining me in a dark corner behind the ill-suited man. The door opens. Light from the hallway casts Patrice's image across the room. Her dress falls to the floor, and a naked silhouette moves in slow, uncertain steps.

How can I see this? I was never here.

"*But I was,*" a voice said in my head.

Patrice?

She approaches apprehensively with a sudden look of recognition. The small man lunges a swift, brutal stab at her chest. I wince and close my eyes. *I don't want to see this.*

"Close your eyes and listen," the voice said.

The assailant's words come fast and fierce. Patrice's bloodcurdling cries are torture. Her assailant's angry words jab more brutal than his thrusts to her chest.

No, it's a woman, the murderer is a woman!

"Yes," the voice said beside me, wavering stronger and chillier with each thrust wielded by the assailant.

Angry words stop. I open my eyes to a silent, shivering figure standing over Patrice's body. Her eyes glisten in the dark. She backs away, into the adjoining bath still holding the knife in a firm grasp. Shaking uncontrollably, she places the blade on the sink, and frantically washes the blood from her hands and clothes. She flees down the back stairs bumping into a man at the bottom of the stairs.

Ryan!

She rushes away and continues into the basement.

"See her Allison."

The woman continues through a wine cellar and through a long stone corridor ending at a staircase which winds up into a small room. *A garden shed.* She slips through the shed's front door, and glances in the distance at the group gathered on the patio. In the dark, she rushes along the side of the yard, toward an open high, wooden door slipping into an adjoining side alley. Along the neighboring yard, she runs toward a blue BMW parked on the opposite side of the street.

Inside the car, she shakes uncontrollably. Holding her hands with her elbows pressed against her sides, she tries to tame nervous trembles with deep breaths. Catching her face in the rearview mirror, she rips a dark, short wig from her head and throws it on the back seat. Brunette hair escapes to her shoulder. Tears gush down her cheeks as she peers back and forth out the window, undressing and discarding clues of the man she'd assumed. She pulls a dark dress over her head, and her feminine figure appears. In the rearview mirror, she wipes her face, smearing a freckle of blood across her cheek, a tiny speckle, Patrice's blood. Swiftly, with shaky hands, she rubs the streak with hard swipes.

Her face, I know her face.

"Think Allison," the voice said.

I do. I remember.

"You need to understand more," two voices said in tandem, but distinctly inside my head.

I'm inside the house once more. Swift-moving synchronicity plays out in one long uninterrupted move from the moment I blacked out. Ethan and a large man wrap Patrice's body in a quilt and leave the room. Ryan enters, with a sweep and lift of my body into his arms. Penelope slides from the bed as Ryan approaches the backstairs. Quietly, she exits through the bedroom door. A kiss plays out more sensual than I remember. His handsome face is vivid and etched with worry. He lifts me over his shoulder in a whirl of small mishaps we're outside in the cold night.

"Allison, look."

With a firm grip, I'm back in the foyer, watching Penelope descend the stairs in a numb trance. No one sees her walk through the front door and toward her car.

Two hands grow tighter, icier, and more insistent. I'm no longer in front of the home but standing next to a rose garden. The cold grip on my left side releases. As she was the night of the party, Patrice stands before me in a black dress, her hair straight and shiny. But her feet are bare. She walks across the soil, leaving footprints behind. She stops and points down. Swiftly she's at my side again with an icy grasp. Now I realize they're holding my hand so I can see, see what they saw and know what they know.

The rose garden disappears. Ethan and the man I saw wrap Patrice's body in a quilt, exit the garden shed, pulling a large, black, antique trunk on the same white quilt toward a large trench. At the edge of the hole, they turn the chest on its side and the latch releases. A limp arm, foot, and blond strands slide into view. Through a cloud of tears, I understand. Patrice never left the premises. Stuffing her body inside and locking the latch, the two men push, and the trunk topples into the hole. Ethan gathers the quilt from the grass, throws it into the ditch, and buries a two-year mystery in an antique casket.

My hands dangle loose and free. The chill dissipates. Patrice and Poppy appear in front of me. I gaze at their visible figures sorrowfully. My mind fills with Poppy's unbearable pain. The agony of truth she couldn't reveal or live with, I now fully grasp.

A voice sounds near, yet distant. "Are those tears?"

Nikki wipes tears from my cheek. Lisa, Nikki, and the nurse's voices surround me. I can't see as I had before, but I sense their presence.

The nurse reassures Nikki. "She's okay. Sometimes patients cry when they're in a coma."

"She must be dreaming something sad to be crying," said Lisa.

I speak Nikki and Lisa's name, but they can't hear me. Again, a chill is beside me. Their voices fill my mind as they had before.

"Ryan knows about the rose garden," they said in unison.

"He's there tonight." They tug at my mind again. I see what they see.

35

A Brush With Death

AFTER CHECKING ALLISON'S status and learning her sister arrived at the hospital last night, I embarked on a dangerous course. The man who witnessed the Mercedes ram Allison's car assured me he'd corroborate her story. There's no better time to prove Emsworth's complicity. I send Jason a text, hoping he'll follow my instructions. I'm confident I can count on him.

Later in the day, when the Realtor prepares to close the viewing, I head to 1414 Kalorama Road. Getting inside the home isn't difficult, but I realize I could get my head blown off. Inside, a few stragglers are still admiring the main floor. Sneaking through the door, I zip straight to the basement, a place I've often wondered about, especially after the odd man barreled into my chest and hastened to the lower floor. Whatever lies below, he was in a rush to get there. If I'd been smart that night, I would have followed, but then again, I wouldn't have saved Allison.

Whoa! I hadn't expected such an elaborate wine cellar. Franklin invested considerable time and money down here. The area could be inside an Italian villa or British castle. But the further I roam about the well-designed cellar, an exclusive gentleman's lair comes to mind. This space is much more impressive than the billiard room above. Franklin must entertain his guest in this space. The realtor will indeed showcase the cellar on her tour. I start to worry and search for an area out of view. Ambling along stone walls stuffed with wine bottles, I stumble upon a long red-bricked tunnel lit with wall sconces. From the length, I'm sure it runs under and out to the backyard. The corridor's medieval design is thought-provoking, and I wonder what purpose it serves. Perhaps it's used as a fire escape or for home invasion. I laugh, given I'm the intruder.

Lined with granite steps that grows steeper with each rung, the corridor progresses on a subtle incline. The curving passage ends abruptly at a staircase leading to a closed steel door above. Apprehensively, and silently, I climb the stairs and stop at the only possible entry to the other side—a small, black button on the wall. I press softly, and the door slides open. Through a narrow hall, I arrive at a picturesque view. A lion head spewing water into a pond and an orange sunset appears through box windows. I remember the quaint, vine-covered, stone cottage when I interviewed Franklin. *I'm inside.* What I believed was a guesthouse, is just a garden shed. Sunset paints a wall of shelves holding pottery and garden chemicals. On the opposite wall, shovels, pitchforks, rakes, and various lawn tools hang from hooks.

In the far corner, a rectangular spot, three shades blonder than the surrounding wooden floor, reminds me of a dresser I moved across my bedroom, revealing planks brighter than trampled areas. It appears a longstanding object rested in that spot. I speculate, from the four-sided outline, it belonged to a box or chest. My curious mind is forever concocting some scenario, arriving at a sinister reason for its removal.

The view is perfect from the picture window. On the patio, the Realtor reclines in a chair, talking on her mobile and writing in a book, possibly an appointment calendar. She glances at her watch, rises from the chair with a quick survey of the backyard, heads inside, and starts closing every entrance to the yard. *Finally,* she's *locking up.* But rooms are still lit on the upper floors. With no better place to wait until she leaves, I take a seat at a small, white desk facing the window. For thirty minutes, I watch night descend. The home darkens, prompting me to act.

From the wall, I grab a shovel, unlocked the door, and step into the yard toward the dark, bone-chilling rose garden. Although Emsworth is in the hospital, there's an odd sensation of eyes watching from dark windows as the imposing edifice looms closer. As I move toward the garden, the frigid air I'd felt before grows icier. A breeze whirls about me, rustling the garden and swirling dirt midair. Rosebushes rattle as if someone moved through them. Cautious yet fearful, I follow whistling roses to the edge of the garden until a presence triggers my alarm. I step back, falling over a decorative boulder, but never taking my eyes from spectral footprints moving across the path. And just as they had two days before, prints stop in a concave spot. The breeze whirls, enclosing me in a frosty bubble. For lack of a better word, the manifestation is trying to tell me something. What I dismissed previously; I can't ignore any longer.

Rising from the ground and retrieving the shovel, I start digging at the concave footprint when a cold gust whip angrily behind me. Over my shoulder, I glimpse a face frighten whiter than a ghost. Franklin waves a gun from side to side, circling madly with the spinning gust.

"Go away ... Go away!" He screamed.

I drop the shovel and step from the garden, believing he's talking to me until he swings around in a mad circle as if he, himself, is orbited by an unseen force.

"Go away ... Leave me be!" He screamed again, turning wildly and firing two shots.

A bullet whizzes past my ear. I reflex and duck, but too slow to escape the second round.

He shot me!

I grab my shoulder. If I'd just stood still the bullet would have missed again. For a moment, shock holds me upright until a searing pain drops me to my knees. Franklin fires a third shot. I slump to the ground, grimacing with an exploding pain in my shoulder. *Shit! Did he hit an artery?* Blood spreads profusely across my shirt. *This is bad.* A vivid image springs to mind of survival camp as my brother applied a tourniquet to a camper's wounded leg. Swiftly and firmly, I apply pressure to the wound to prevent blood loss.

Franklin waves the gun as if swatting a swarm of bees. His face is expressive of someone besieged. Footsteps race into the yard in Franklin's direction. Two men I recognize as Ethan and the big-boned man I'd seen the night of the party. Ethan snatches the weapon from Franklin's hands, aiming the pistol in my direction.

"You should have listened when you had the chance," he said without an ounce of reservation in his body.

I'm not leaving here alive.

As I sit on my heels, the world starts to spin. I'm losing too much blood. The three men swim before my vision. I never believed I'd lose my life tonight, perhaps a few teeth and broken ribs but not death. I've made one fatal mistake, underestimating Ethan. I'd pegged him for many things, but never a killer.

Did I have it all wrong? Did Ethan kill Patrice?

"*Once a dog taste blood, they'll kill again,*" my brother had always said. And by the look on Ethan's face, I won't persuade him as easily as I had two years ago when I finessed my way through the front door. Even in my pain, I find the will to laugh. *How ironic.* The first time I met Ethan, Patrice's name was the pivotal leverage inside the exclusive party, and now she's the final key twisting Ethan's hand.

"Are you going to dump my body with Patrice in the grave, or something more sinister," I asked wanting to confirm my suspicions before I die. At least he can give a dying man that satisfaction. *Take a bullet like a man* rings in my ear, words of my brother who faced death bravely every day in Iraq. I never imagined facing a bullet head on. But as many soldiers and my brother had in their final moments, I show no fear, ready to accept my fate. And then my mother's face, wretched with the loss of two sons, triggers a button, bolstering me upright. The thought of her planting seedlings in the garden and mourning another dead son riles me. Every muscle strengthens. *She won't survive the death of another son; it'll kill her.* I scan three figures standing around me. Even if I lurch and tackle Ethan's ankles, he would shoot before I make it off my heels. And the other man would stop me in a heartbeat. I glimpse the shovel at arm's length and consider knocking the gun from Ethan's hand. I need to catch them unaware. Otherwise, I'll be dead the moment I move.

"How did you know she's here?" Ethan asked.

I chuckle and wince all at once turning my head toward the chilly garden. "Patrice... Can't you feel her? She led me here." Ethan doesn't utter a word and doesn't have to because I see the truth in his haunted expression. He's felt her too. And given Franklin's behavior, hell has been his domain the last two years, driving him to sell his haunted house.

Ethan raises his arm again. I brace for another bullet and flinch with Franklin's howl. He snatches the gun from Ethan's hand, firing around me, not at me as if aiming at a moving target. Rose petals splinter, flying in tiny pieces. A powerful gust sprays rose shards in Franklin's direction. The spectral garden grows icier.

Nearby, another gun fires and the side gate burst open. Two police officers enter a slow, steady progression ready to shoot in Franklin's direction.

"Mister, drop the weapon, and put your hands in the air!"

Outside the gate, between two officers, Jason appears through blurred vision. I'm relieved he received my message and carried out my plan to get the police to the house on suspicions of burglary. I signal thumbs-up. Even if it meant my arrest, I knew my plan would lead them to Patrice's body. Something flashes in the corner of my eye. For an instant, I see a woman's figure facing Franklin. Swiftly, he raises his hand, and the gun pops. Franklin drops to the ground. Chaos blurs around me as the strength I'd mustered to stay upright dissolves. Just as I roll to the ground, her pale bare feet appear next to the shovel.

36
Finally, Released

WAKE UP, ALLISON.

THE SCENT OF ROSES suffuses the air, spiraling tattered on dirt-speckled feet. Black and white, dark and pale buried beneath the soil, rich and bloodied with dead roses. It's time to wake, Allison! A gun pops. A force releases me from captivity. I spring upright ripping the I. V. from my arm, twisting my head much too fast, as the I. V. ping and drip on the metal bed frame. I grimace with the throb drumming my skull and wince with the stiffness seizing my neck. The room whorls in a dizzy haze, but urgency outweigh all physical discomfort.

I have to get to Ryan. He needs to know the truth.

The fragrant scent of roses lingers. The rose garden, I was there. I have to tell Ryan Franklin didn't kill Patrice. He's only guilty of covering up a crime and burying the body in his backyard. Ryan needs to know. Until the real murderer is revealed, Patrice won't rest, but will he believe me? Ryan saw and felt Patrice as I had. I move my arm too fast and wince at the cast bounding my right arm. I press the button beside the bed, and the steel rails lower. Awkwardly using my left arm, I slide toward the edge and just as my foot skims cold, hard linoleum, the nurse races into the room.

"No, no, lie back down, young lady," she said, rushing to the bed and lowering me to the pillow. "Welcome back," she said, adjusting the sheet over my body with a warm smile. "A lot of people will be happy you're awake. How do you feel?"

Before I can respond, the doctor enters. "Hello, Allison. I'm Doctor Bajwa." He approaches the bed with a smile wider than the nurse. "So, you've decided to return to us," he said with a warm chuckle, "and we're happy to have you back. How are you feeling?"

"I need to leave," exits hoarse from my cottony mouth. I swallow hard and force words up my dry throat. "I need to leave! I need to get a message to someone. It's urgent." A greater throb pierces my head. I close my eyes and lightly touch my forehead, grazing the bandage I'd seen outer body.

"You have quite a nasty bump on your head," the doctor said, signaling to the nurse. "Angela will give you something for the pain."

Angela. Angelic I think a suitable name for a nurse. She brings a glass of water with a straw and lifts my head gently, urging me to take a sip. I sip several long swigs soothing my parched throat. Angela lowers my head, but I spring up again. "I have to get information to someone right away. I can't stay here. He needs to know the truth. I have to leave now!"

"You're not going anywhere right now. You just woke from a coma. We need to make sure you're okay before we release you," the doctor said.

I try to lift my right arm, and then I remember the cast. "I feel fine; I'm fine," I said willful and set on speaking to Ryan.

"I need to make that determination first," the doctor said.

I glance back and forth at the nurse and doctor, realizing my outburst is to no avail. "I need to call someone; can I at least use the phone?"

"Once we've examined you, yes," the doctor said. "First, I need you to answer a few questions. Do you know why you're here?" Doctor Bajwa asked.

"Yes, I had a car accident."

"Good, good... Do you remember the car crash?"

He's trying to determine whether I've lost my memory. But I remember everything. I remember floating above the car and watching it land in the creek. I remember the black Mercedes hitting my car. But most of all, I remember how unreal I felt, how peaceful and light. In fact, I remember more than I did before the accident, even the off-campus party. Then I remember Ethan frisking Ryan and pointing the gun at him in Franklin's backyard. He knew who I was before he rescued me that day in the park. I'm sure now he pushed me. His slip was no accident, but intentional. But why didn't he kill me when he had the chance? All the time we spent together during my senior year; he was trying to find out if I remembered that night. He was working with Franklin the entire time.

"Allison?"

"Yes, I remember the car that chased me through the park and the crash into the creek. And I also remember what happened after the crash."

"After?" He asked with a lifted brow.

I pause with the out-of-body memory and hearing the doctor and nurse talking to Nikki and Lisa while I floated above the room. "I saw and heard everything while I was in the coma."

"Ah! That's not unusual. Many patients are aware of their surroundings when comatose. It's rather common," he said with a smile. Sitting on the edge of the bed, he takes my hand. "Your family will be happy to see you're awake. My staff will contact your sister promptly, but first, we need to run a few tests to make sure you're physically sound."

I want to tell him tests are unnecessary. My coma wasn't physical but spiritual. I'm sure he'd laugh or maybe not. They've probably heard otherworldly stories from recovering patients. Over the years, I've read stories about coma patient's afterlife, and out-of-body experiences as they wander hospital corridors aware of everything. I was a skeptic before the accident, but I'm not anymore. My own experience was much too real to refute. "What kind of tests?" I sigh impatiently wanting nothing more than to leave this bed.

"We need to run another EKG, CAT scan, and some blood tests, nothing scary," he said with a fearful expression, meant to be comical but it doesn't make me laugh.

"How long will it take?" My patience is wearing thin ready for the poking and prodding to end. "I need to get information to someone fast." Then it hits me. "Was a reporter named Ryan McThursten admitted to the hospital?"

The doctor throws the nurse a glance. She responds, "Mr. McThursten has been a celebrity around here the last five days. He sent the lovely flowers in the corner."

"Five days, how long have I been here?"

"You've been in a coma for seven days."

"Seven days!" I expected one or two days, not a week. What Poppy and Patrice showed me happened in one day.

Didn't it?

But I've been unconscious for a week. I turn my head sideways, and a big, red bouquet appears on a table near the window. They're real roses which explain the lingering, floral scent I'd believed was remnants of Patrice and Poppy. The nurse walks over to the table and brings me the attached note.

ALLISON, GET WELL SOON. WE HAVE MUCH TO DISCUSS. RYAN

"Can I see him?"

"Not right now, young lady. But he did ask me to notify him if you woke from the coma. I'm sure it will be okay for him to visit you. He's just two floors above, and he's recovering quite well from shoulder surgery."

I breathe a little calmer knowing he's only two floors away and soon I can tell him what I know, what I saw. This is so crazy. I'm starting to doubt my mind. But what happened was real, as real as this room, as real as this cast on my arm.

* * *

Later that morning, Nikki and Lisa arrived full of happiness and tears. Nik's wet eyes surprised me because I've never seen her cry except at Grandma Blu's funeral. That's the only and last time she's shed any tears that I've seen. Maybe it's the pregnancy. She and Lisa reveal I'd talked sporadically throughout the coma and had screamed Ryan's name several times scaring them all to death.

"What were you dreaming about?" Nikki asked.

I'd never spoken to Nikki about the off-campus party. She'll be upset I'd kept it secret so long. At the moment, I'm not ready for a barrage of questions. "It's hard to explain. We'll discuss it later." But I tell Nikki and Lisa about the out-of-body experience. "I heard every word you, Lisa, and the doctor said." Their expressions reveal plenty. They think it was a dream. I expound on the conversations I'd heard to erase their doubt. A glimmer of belief relaxes their dubious brows.

"Well, Grandma Blu always said, 'Child the world holds mysteries our eyes will never see,'" Nikki said with a grin.

"She did," I mumbled, recalling nights Nik and I huddled around the fireplace, listening to Grandma Blu's ghostly tales. I knew the stories were real experiences because they'd always take place in her childhood home. But mom said they were just silly stories.

"Did you call mom and dad?"

"Allie, you know I did. As soon as I heard about the accident, I rang them. But I couldn't reach mom. She's traveling with her show overseas. I finally spoke to her last night, but when the hospital called this morning, I convinced her to stay and take care of her business. She was so worried, as well as dad. He was scheduled to fly in tomorrow, but I told him not to come, you were out of the coma. They'd love to hear your voice."

"I'm glad mom didn't have to leave her work. She put so much effort into that show. I'll call them both later."

"Allie, I was scared shitless when I heard you were in an accident. When Nikki called me from New York, she was frantic! I jumped in the car and headed straight to the hospital. When I saw you bandaged up in a coma, I was horrified. Allie, what happened? How did your car end up in the creek?"

I can't tell Lisa with Nikki in the room. Nik will wonder why someone would run me off the road, and then I'll have to reveal everything. "I don't know. It all happened so fast."

"Well, it could have been worse. When the hospital called this morning, I've never been so happy in my life. Someone up there loves you," Lisa said, glancing up. "You do realize this is the second time you've hit your head and in the same spot," she said with a soft touch to the bandage.

"Yeah, strange..." I said, noticing her moist eyes. "Okay, enough of the pregnant tears." It hits instantly. My sister and best friend are both pregnant and hormonal. Ah! That's why the sappy blubbering or maybe they're just happy to see me alive.

Nikki grabs her stomach, and I notice the sick look on her face. "Are you still having morning sickness?" Then I realize my slip. Nikki has never told me about the pregnancy.

"How did you know?"

"I found your Pregnancy for Dummy books in the closet, besides all the ginger tea you were drinking was a dead give away Nikki. I was waiting for you to tell me when you were ready."

"With the car accident and the coma, I was afraid I'd never get the chance to tell you."

"Nik, I'm happy for you, and I hope you are too."

"I'm getting used to the idea, but not the morning sickness. Allie, I haven't been able to eat since your accident," Nik said glaring at me with a pained expression. "I think I'll grab toast and tea from the cafeteria. Something light always helps."

"Nik, go, I'm okay. I'll be here when you get back. I'm not going anywhere soon," I said with a sigh.

"I'll go with you. I could use a cup of tea as well," Lisa said, following her out of the room, finally, leaving me alone with my thoughts.

* * *

Ten minutes later, Lisa enters the room with a newspaper and a strange look on her face. She sits at the edge of the bed with the paper on her lap. "Allie, I have some good news," she said, raising the paper. "Ryan caught Patrice's murderer while you were in the coma." She stares expectantly. "Ryan's article made the front cover," she said, handing me the paper as if delivering flowers to console me. "I notice you didn't want to talk about this with Nikki, so that's why I waited to show you the paper."

I don't need a newspaper to tell me what happened. I was there. Without words, I take the paper from Lisa's hand. A large photo of Franklin Emsworth plasters the center of the page.

Patrice Jensen's Body Found: A Two-Year Mystery Unearthed Behind 1414 Kalorama Road: Franklin Emsworth Takes His Life

"I thought this would make you happy," Lisa said.

Lisa won't understand what I'm about to tell her, but I hope she'll keep an open mind. "There's more to the story... Franklin's not the murderer."

"Allie, Ryan found her body on Franklin's property. That's proof enough he's the murderer."

"Lisa, this might sound crazy, but I saw everything when I was in the coma. I know everything that happened the night of the party. Patrice showed me."

In one swift motion, Lisa's mouth and brow crumple. I expected the dubious expression, but nonetheless, it's irksome. She probably thinks drugs are affecting my brain. "What do you mean she showed you?"

"You probably think I was dreaming, but I wasn't. The entire time I was in the coma, Patrice and Poppy Murphy were with me. They showed me everything, Lisa." Disbelief spreads across her face, but I wipe it right off with my next comment. "I saw Ryan digging up Patrice's grave behind that house. I saw Franklin shoot him before he took his own life, and I also know who the real killer is, and it's not Franklin. Ryan needs to know," I said as swift as a lightning bolt. I try to lift my body upright, but my head begins to throb.

Lisa stands quietly staring at me as if I've lost my mind. "Allie that's unbelievable. Have you watched TV? Did the hospital staff tell you?"

"No, I've not spoken to anyone, watched TV, or read the paper. The nurse only told me Ryan is two flights above in the hospital, and that he's been a celebrity for a few days. I can only imagine it's because of what I saw in my coma. I know it sounds fantastical, and I wouldn't believe it either, but it happened. Lisa, there's no denying what I've experienced, it's true." I lift the paper and study Franklin's face. His last moments were more vivid than the newspaper print. Patrice's ghost, her body's discovery, and a looming indictment were too much for Franklin to bear. Watching Emsworth slink to such disgrace was disturbing. Did Patrice haunt Franklin to such extremes for reasons other than her murder? After all, he's not her killer.

"Lisa, after two years, Patrice's family needs to know who killed their daughter." I imagine the immeasurable pain the Jensen's will feel, knowing Patrice death was at the hand of someone who knew Patrice as a child, watched her grow up and become their daughter's best friend. I'm disturbed that a woman could be so heartless and brutally take another life. She had no idea her daughter was listening in horror. Mrs. Murphy's actions came at an insurmountable cost, the suicide of her child. "I need to tell Ryan. The Jensen need to know the truth."

"And they will," Ryan said from the door.

37

Allie and Ryan

THE NURSE WHEELS Ryan into the room. His face lights with a smile. Only moments ago, or so it feels, I saw him in Franklin's garden bravely facing a bullet and never showing an ounce of fear. But I haven't seen him in months, not since McClelland, and again, he leaves me speechless.

"Do you mind..." he said, addressing Lisa and the nurse, "...if I have a word with Allison in private?"

"She's all yours," Lisa said, rising from the bed. "Ryan, thanks for bringing Allison to the dorm that night and for finding that poor girl," she said with a mirthless smile.

The nurse pushes the wheelchair closer to the bed. "I couldn't keep this one away when he heard you were awake," she said with a wink at Ryan. Following Lisa to the door, she pauses. "I'll be back to fetch you soon. Hospital policy," she said, throwing me a smile and closing the door.

"Is she gone?" Ryan asked with a comical expression. "I didn't need a wheelchair. It's my arm, not my leg, but they kept spouting hospital policy. Allison, I'm glad to see you're okay. You had me worried."

"I'm glad to see you too," I said with an awkward smile. Lying here with messy hair, cracked lips, and a bandage on my forehead, I'm more self-conscious than the day Ryan entered my office. *Why didn't the nurse tell me he was coming?* At least I would have had the chance to fix my face and hair. Sitting upright, despite a dull headache, I gather my hair to one side, and run my fingers through matted strands."

He smiles. "Allison, you look great," he said, staring at me with warm, brown eyes I'd admired the first time I saw him.

"I hardly look great after seven days in a coma."

"You're just as enchanting as Sleeping Beauty."

Again, I smile. "Well, Sleeping Beauty is a fairytale, and I'm in the real world without an enchanted spell to keep my hair tidy."

He chuckles.

My eyes drift to his gorgeous lips.

"I'm just happy you're okay. I don't know what I'd do without my favorite editor."

Suddenly, the anger I'd felt toward his deception is gone. After seeing Ryan's bravery in the rose garden, and his efforts to secure me from Kalorama Road, I'm grateful and enamored by his actions, and at the moment, his lips. My core stirs with memories of our kiss. I hear those words he'd whispered two years ago as if he'd said them just now, "*...not here, not now, Allison,*" words thick with passion, and caring. My stomach flutters. *Is it possible to feel this much attraction?* I wince at the sling cradling his arm and recall the bullet striking his shoulder. "I hope that wasn't too painful," I said frowning at his arm.

"This little wound... Nah! We both have wounded wings," he said with a nod to my arm.

I laugh and touch the hard cast with no recollection of breaking my arm. "Yeah, it's a blessing I passed out before I could feel the pain... Ryan, I need to tell you something." I pause and look him dead in the eye. "You might think I'm crazy, but just hear me out." For a moment, I imagine my news deflating his victory. No, he found Patrice, a great journalistic effort that almost cost him his life. He stuck to his belief, unearthed the murderer's accomplices. That's a courageous feat. "Franklin's not the killer." I pause. There's no rebuttal.

"I'm listening."

I sigh and narrow my eyes. "Have you heard about coma patient's undergoing out-of-body or otherworldly experiences?"

"I've read some interesting stuff. Why do you ask?"

"I saw everything while I was in the coma. I experienced the off-campus party through Patrice and Penelope's eyes." I continue explaining every detail while Ryan listens unfazed. When I'm done, he just stares in silence.

"I believe you, Allison." From his robe, he removes an envelope. "This was hand-delivered yesterday. It's a letter from Penelope. She paid a specialty direct mail service to deliver the envelope the day before she took her life. Unfortunately, when it arrived at the Washington Post, I was in the hospital. My coworker directed them here. And as Penelope specified, they delivered it into my hands. Penelope addressed the letter to both of us, Allison."

38

Penelope's Letter

I CAN'T BEAR THE WEIGHT of Patrice any longer. I've tried to protect my parents but at the cost of my sanity. Allison and Ryan, I know that horrific night has haunted you as it has me. And I've wanted to tell you, but I couldn't. Ryan, I am the informant who supplied you with information about the escort service. Allison, I'm the one who sent the emails. I wanted you to remember. And when you didn't, I sent Patrice's manuscript, hoping her story would jar your memory. I needed someone else to expose the truth that I am too close to.

Ryan, I knew you would rage a relentless investigation as you've done as Hunter, the student reporter. I believed you would trail a path straight to Patrice's body regardless of the danger. But I'd hoped you would have found her at this point, before the intolerable burden of knowing got the worst of me. I need to tell you both the truth.

Now I fully understand what I hadn't recognized until I followed Patrice to Kalorama Road, to be true. Franklin Emsworth is the man who runs the escort business. A man, my family had close affiliations with, and who they befriended and respected for years. It was difficult discovering someone who treats me as a family member, and who I've called uncle is involved in such a deplorable business. As a child, both Patrice's family and mine spent many informal gatherings in Franklin's home. We both loved and respected him immensely.

After that horrible night, I'm confident Franklin didn't kill Patrice, nor does he know the killer's identity. He's only guilty of covering up Patrice's murder and disposing of her body. I assume his reasons were to protect himself and the escort service. Where he hid Patrice, I don't know, but I believe she's still someplace on his estate. I've not been back to 1414 Kalorama road since her death. I can't. I couldn't. Patrice's murder is too painful.

Allison, I know you saw me under the bed that night, and for two years I've waited for you to remember. I figured when you didn't go to the police, you were either too scared, or had forgotten. And I was right. When I approached you on campus a few days later, you didn't recognize me. I sat next to you and your friend in the student cafeteria. You looked straight at me, and I saw your anguish. I overheard your conversation with your roommate and realized you had no memory of what happened. You were so distraught with anger and uncertainty, believing someone might have taken advantage of you in that home. At that moment, I wanted to tell you nothing happened. Hunter saved you before those men returned to the room. I need to explain why I was there. I need the weight of this off your shoulder and mine. I want you to have a peace of mind I'll never have again.

Patrice was my best friend for years. After sophomore year, I noticed changes. She became distant and wouldn't tell me where she went most evenings, or who she was seeing. I finally figured out she was involved with the escort service. I had to stop her. I just didn't know how to do it without exposing her identity. So, I followed her one day, and that's when I overheard her invite you to the party. Allison, I couldn't warn you that day because she trailed you from the building. Ryan, I knew you would be interested, so instead, I brought the information straight to you at the school newspaper. I left a note on your desk and in your mailbox telling you the car Patrice would drive, and the time and place she'd pick up Allison. Allison, Ryan followed you and Patrice to Kalorama Road and posed as a guest with a password I supplied him.

I watched everything unfold from my car. I had no plan to go into Franklin's home; I just wanted Hunter to uncover the truth. Then I saw an opportunity, and I took it. I entered the backyard through a side entrance. I saw Patrice and followed her upstairs, figuring if I got her alone, I could talk some sense into her. But that never happened. I heard her horrific murder and her killer's voice.

I listened outside the door in denial and shock. I was so scared. I didn't know what to do. After the murderer fled, I entered the room, and on the floor, Patrice lay bloody and dying. All I could do was rock her in my arms. I knew who the killer was before she whispered her name in my ear. At that moment, a piece of my soul died with her. I knew my life would never be the same. When footsteps approached the room, I hid under the bed. Two men came into the room but did nothing. They just stood over her body and watched her die. Moments later, you stumbled into the room, Allison. You looked straight at me before you blacked out.

I watched as they wrapped my best friend in a blanket. I heard one of the men I believe his name is Ethan protect you from the other man who was bent on getting rid of you as well. Ethan told him you hadn't seen anything before you blacked-out. He convinced the other man to leave you, and he would handle you later. A few minutes after they took Patrice's body, Hunter entered and carried you from the room. Somehow, I made it to my car. I don't remember walking out of that house or driving. After the initial shock wore off, I was outside my parent's home. For several hours, I waited inside a dark house for their return. A place that always felt secure felt like hell.

When they finally arrived, mom pretended everything was normal, as if nothing ever happened. But I saw the strain in her eyes. She flitted about the house never stopping to talk, and she couldn't look me in the eye. I had planned to confront her. But when I saw my parents together, I couldn't. I pictured our shattered lives, dad's career in ruins, and mom behind bars. I was a coward. I should have gone to the police, but I couldn't. For days, I drove past the precinct, but I couldn't go in. I should have been braver.

Gradually, I slipped into a depression and couldn't leave my room or eat. I started hating the sight of my mother. I couldn't understand how she went about life with such ease after what she'd done. Every time I looked at her, I'd hear her murderous voice and Patrice's final cries. My dad drifted into his world, and I suspected he had inklings about mom. My parent's lives have splintered and will never be the same.

I've been a prisoner to what I saw. Patrice tortures me every day. I believe she followed me from Kalorama Road and has been haunting me since her death. She won't let me rest in peace. The scent of roses and her presence surrounds me, goading me to reveal her murder. I can't live this way any longer, but I need the two people who were in that room with me, whose lives were affected as much as mine, to know the truth.

Ryan, you are getting too close to dangerous people. You are on a perilous path. Allison, I believe Ryan hasn't come to you because he is protecting you from harm as he had that night. He is brave and honorable. After all this time I'm telling you because I want this all to end. With this information, I know you will do what I've failed to do.

Penelope

39

Poet's Corner

A Month Later

THE "FOR SALE SIGN" remains at 1414 Kalorama Road. The home, empty of life and ghost, appears eerier than ever. With a need to confirm Patrice is free, and to release a harrowing past, I drive toward the vacant home, a place that imprisoned my memory too long, study the façade, windows, and yard, searching for signs of Patrice. Though authorities exhumed her body from the garden, her spirit could still be on the premises, trapped eternally. However, the moment our connection snapped, and she released me from the coma, I sensed she'd gone for good. The strange aura vanished when Ryan drove a shovel through her footprint, confirming the anxiety attacks were Patrice's unearthly doings not intrinsic.

Ghostly doings...

The front door opens slowly. My breath catches and releases as the Realtor emerges from a dark interior through the stone portico, places the "Open House" sign on the lawn, and heads back inside. *Will the home ever sell*, I wonder? The estate may never find a buyer with the media blitz disclosing its history, but I'm sure someone will pay a premium for a house imbued with a wicked past.

"*Girl, it's freezing. Get in.*" Patrice's coaxing voice pierces my thoughts, the night I entered her car in front of the dorm. "*Loosen up!*

This is going to be fun!" Her playful tone as she led me from the garage, now seems surreal. The construct and insight of her last moments, her final night, sadden me. Were there warnings or inklings of impending demise? She must have felt some danger, but death's a mystery and not foreseeable. I sigh, regretting both our stolen innocence. Patrice and I were on different paths, but in some crazy way, I believe our journeys were meant to cross. For a brief moment, our lives intertwined, leaving me changed, more aware and existing in the moment, grasping life one step at a time. Now that Patrice is at peace, I can start fresh, on the right course. One final look and I drive on; leaving ghosts and my demons behind.

Entering Rock Creek Park's curvy roads, the crash site nears with vivid images of a chase that sent my car careening into the creek. Ryan revealed Ethan wasn't the driver, but the big-boned man we now know as Lance Emsworth, Franklin's second illegitimate son. Ethan admitted that for two years, he'd protected me from Emsworth as best he could. He regrets not saving Patrice, revealing his job was to safeguard the escorts.

My heart aches for Ethan; the man I'd met one beautiful autumn day in the park and spent my senior year with. I'd had my doubts about the rescue from a slippery fall. Now, I believe Ethan pushed me but couldn't go through with killing me. His secretive ways now validated. He couldn't tell me who he was, but a killer he's not, just a pawn entangled in Franklin Emsworth's web. If Ethan had reported the crime when he found Patrice, he wouldn't be behind bars, a convicted felon—an accessory after the fact to murder.

I continue past the crash site over Boulder Bridge toward Washington Memorial Parkway with thoughts of Mrs. Murphy. She didn't resist or deny murder charges when the police arrived at her home. She probably expected an arrest after Patrice's body surfaced on Emsworth's property. I've often wondered if Patrice haunted her as well. Newspapers present Mrs. Murphy's sullen face, depressed with weary eyes and dark shadows, indeed someone haunted, if not by Patrice, then her crime.

I imagine Patrice's unremitting torment caused Mrs. Murphy's willing acceptance of her new domicile, a six-by-eight feet prison cell, where she'll repent the rest of her life. The Jensen's, distraught as expected, can rest knowing the truth about their daughter and her killer. I can't imagine their pain, their loss, not only of their daughter but the loss of trusted friends.

An anonymous informant exposed renowned patrons of Emsworth's escort service. With Emsworth's death, I assume the unknown person felt no threat in revealing years of Franklin's abuses. However, I believe little will come of the allegations against patrons now that Franklin's gone, and the business has ceased.

Finally, I'm pursuing a career I should have started at Emsworth University. A week after release from the hospital, I submitted my resume to the Washington Post. Although I applied for an Assistant Editor position, they offered me a journalist position. I figure I can work toward my ultimate dream—editor of a prominent newspaper. Lisa agreed to keep me as a boarder until I find a place of my own. In a way, it's ideal for us both. We can help each other as we start new phases of our lives, and while Andrew works tirelessly on the restaurant.

Nikki's affair with Shane is now official, and I've given her the okay to move him into the duplex. I'm thrilled to see she's abandoned her fears. Mortified when I finally told her about the off-campus party, Nikki and I promised never to keep secrets from each other again. And she promised not to tell mom and dad. This will be our secret.

Merging with traffic onto the George Washington Memorial Parkway, I wonder what Ryan has planned. His request to meet at his favorite spot on the waterfront was mysterious. *"Ten o'clock sharp at 100 Hamilton and Vine,"* he'd said. Ryan will be happy to know I've sent his manuscript's final draft to Catrina. I hold no grudge against McClelland; the layoff was for the best, which I realize now, besides Ryan deserves the best publisher.

Ahead, Alexandria, Virginia's exit appears. I'm excited and a little nervous about my date with Ryan. Although we've talked almost every day since the hospital, we've never expressed our feelings toward each other. I'm beginning to worry he's not as attracted to me as I am to him. I wonder why he insisted on meeting at ten o'clock sharp. I turn onto Hamilton and continue to Vine Street, swerving onto a tree-lined lane bordering the Potomac River. Suddenly, the scenery strikes me as familiar. Then I notice the green door with a lion's head knob at 100 Hamilton and Vine.

Poet's Corner. CJ's coffee shop!

Oh, God! It's just as CJ described—a tree-shaded lane, sidewalk cafes littered with tables and chairs, the antique dealer, and small bookstore steps from Poet's Corner.

This can't be a coincidence.

So many times, I've imagined the coffee shop in my head. And here it stands, not intangible, but real, bustling with artsy patrons sipping coffee at outdoor tables. I park the car a few feet away and watch people come and go through the forest-green door. Is it CJ or Ryan on the other side? Perhaps they're both inside, oblivious of a mutual friend.

No impossible!

Something's wrong here. Why did CJ's text messages stop so soon after my accident? I was worried and found it odd he wouldn't respond to my last text. Eventually, I figured he'd grown bored with our discussions. Now, my instincts scream, *something's amiss!* My heart ticks a slow, uncertain beat as I stare from behind the wheel, wondering who I'll find inside. Ryan couldn't have known about CJ or this place unless ... *No, no*, I strike that thought. Raised in Alexandria, Ryan certainly knows about Poet's Corner. *Does he know CJ?* A man I hardly know anything about except he's a writer and owns a coffee shop. The night of my drunken texting CJ only revealed the color of his hair and the quill pen tattoo on his wrist.

Ryan's a writer and has dark hair.

But I've never seen a tattoo on his wrist. The day Ryan came to Mc-Clelland, his left wrist was swathe in bracelets that could have hidden a tattoo.

Okay, Allie, you're here, so get a grip. But my mind screams, this is not a coincidence! Did CJ lie about everything? Allie, how gullible can you be? But he hadn't lied about Poet's Corner. It's real, I confirm as I step from the car. "Okay, here goes," I whispered. Taking a deep breath, I open the café door, as I've imagined so many times. My pulse pounds through my ears with each step into the dimly lit space. I've stepped into a familiar fairytale.

The scenery I'd pictured in my mind, takes shape before my eyes. The loft appears just as CJ described, like someone's living room. Soft music ricochets off walls from overhead speakers. Small pendants dangle from the ceiling, casting spotlights on dark wooden floors. Art-covered walls, traversed by dark circular booths, surround glossy, dark-brown leather sofas, and colorful chairs scattered waywardly in the room's center. And there, lined with stuffed bookshelves, just as he described, sits our space. The table we'd pretend to be sitting as we texted each other, Ernest Hemingway's Corner.

Two wingback chairs in soft velvety rose and purple surround a small antique table, a place I've imagined us sitting together, eyes linked in face-to-face conversation. For two months, I've longed to see CJ's smiling eyes crinkle, and brows furrow with artistic expressions as he told his stories. I've wanted to see him, know if he's genuine. His words were so sincere, but I had my doubts. And now, here I am, in his shop.

In the back of the café, the coffee bar is as I've envisioned, with a black chalkboard highlighting the day's specials, a myriad of coffee concoctions named after famous poets. Bronze and chrome fixtures on countertops sparkle under silver pendants. Waveringly, I move toward the Barista but pause for thought at the sight of his raven hair. It's not him; he's too young, probably no more than nineteen. I search his wrist for a quill pen tattoo. No marks, nothing. Indeed, the owner wouldn't be behind the counter. But he'd told me he's always at the shop. What if he's here? What if he's watching me right now? Artfully, turning my head toward the room, I study patrons for clues.

"Good morning and what's your passion today fair lady?" The Barista asked with zeal.

"I'm meeting someone—"

"Are you Allison?" He asked before I can inquire about the owner.

"Yes."

"He's been waiting for you," he said, pointing toward the purple wingback chair.

"Is he the owner?" I asked to confirm my suspicions.

"Isn't he the person you're expecting?" The Barista asked with a curious smile.

For a moment, I'm uncertain, but I'm sure by his vexed expression, I look confused. "Yes," I said, finally, shaking my head, turning and crossing the room toward the purple wingback chair hiding the mystery figure.

"After the rush crowd has left, I take advantage of the quiet and write in my favorite spot near the window. I'm sitting in the velvet wingback chair you saw on my blog," CJ had revealed over text.

Is it CJ?

As I grow closer, dark hair floats above the arched wing. I ponder whether Ryan and CJ are the same. If so, Ryan will no doubt have an explanation. How can I mistrust him after his efforts to protect me? He must have a reasonable explanation. Penelope's letter said Ryan's a man of his word. We've been through so much, and I've grown to trust him the last month. *Just hear him out, Allie.*

Above the armrest, a black shoulder sling answers my first question, but not the crucial one, holding me in suspense. "Ryan?" He turns. Silently, I slide opposite him into the velvety rose wingback chair. Steamy coffee whiffs draw my eyes down. Two heart-shaped latte art sits atop twin coffee mugs, just like the coffee on CJ's blog.

"I'm glad you're here," he said with a heart-fluttering smile. Ryan's interrogating brown eyes examine my aloof demeanor.

Tension fills the space. Quietly, I reach across the table and grasp his left hand. His unblinking eyes never leave my face. I perceive he's been waiting for this moment of discovery. His fingers clasp my hand tightly. Time stands still, or so it seems. I twist his palm and the answer to my second question swirls across his wrist—a beautiful, purple quill pen tattoo.

"Should I call you, CJ?" I asked, staring at his altered expression.

"As I said, the tattoo will help you find me in a room of strangers," he replied tightening his hand on my receding grip.

"It was you the entire time! Why didn't you tell me?"

"Allison," he said, devouring me with caramel eyes I fell in love with the day at McClelland. "God, you're so damn beautiful. For months, I've wanted to tell you. Allison, I never meant to deceive you—"

"But you did."

"I admit I let it go too far. I wanted to tell you, but the right time never came. When you left New York for Washington, it got more complicated. I tried to tell you at the hospital, but I thought it best not to after what you'd been through. So, I devised our meeting here at Poet's Corner, in our spot, Ernest Hemingway's Corner, remember?"

"Yes, how can I forget?"

"Allison, for months, I've imagined sitting in this spot across from you and telling you how much I've wanted to kiss your perfect bee-stung lips since the first day I saw you on campus."

His sentiments melt anger and doubt with words I've waited to hear so long. We've both visualized this moment, but it's unexpected and much more romantic than I'd ever pictured.

"From the moment we took our first sip in your office, and after our second online coffee moment at 10:00 A.M., when you described your surroundings in the breakfast nook, I've wanted another face-to-face coffee moment with you," he said.

Coffee moments...

How soon I'd forgotten the long-distance sips shared over the Internet. It was Ryan. I'm embarrassed but delighted it was him and not CJ. How odd, I was attracted to Ryan even as he posed as CJ.

"Can we," he said, picking up his cup.

Right now, coffee is the last thing I want. I've waited too long to resume the kiss we started at 1414 Kalorama Road. This time, I don't care how brazen I appear. I rise from the chair, walk to his side of the table, sit on his lap, raise the cup to his lips, and whisper, "I believe we have some unfinished business."

"Yes ... we do."

Dear reader,

We hope you enjoyed reading *Kalorama Road*. Please take a moment to leave a review, even if it's a short one. Your opinion is important to us.

Discover more books by E. Denise Billups at https://www.nextchapter.pub/authors/e-denise-billups

Want to know when one of our books is free or discounted? Join the newsletter at http://eepurl.com/bqqB3H.

Best regards,
E. Denise Billups and the Next Chapter Team

Acknowledgements

WITH MANY THANKS to Ouida Billups and James Billups for years of support and lending an ear through this endeavor. Special thanks to Lawrence E. Crockett, Sandra Lerner, Julie Chan, Mirna Hamilton, Marsha Bullock, and Bibiana Krall for your feedback.

About The Author

An author with a rare mixture of Southern and Northern charm, E. Denise Billups was born in Monroeville Alabama and raised in New York City where she currently resides and works in finance and as a freelance columnist. A burgeoning author of fiction, she's published three suspense novels—Kalorama Road, Chasing Victoria, By Chance, and two supernatural short stories, The Playground, and Rebound. An avid reader of magical realism, mystery, and suspense novels, she was greatly influenced by authors of these genres. She's a fitness fanatic, trained in ballet, modern, and jazz dance, and uses the same discipline to facilitate creative writing.

Kalorama Road
ISBN: 978-4-86752-347-6

Published by
Next Chapter
1-60-20 Minami-Otsuka
170-0005 Toshima-Ku, Tokyo
+818035793528
27th July 2021